FROZEN VOICES

FROZEN VOICES

Dear Kathie,
I hope you enjoy
these stories about Hilliard,
Sadie, George, & Anna.
Happy Reading!

Lynne M Heinzmann
March 2022

A Historical Novel By
Lynne Heinzmann

Fairfield Book Prize

new
RIVERS
PRESS
MSUM

©2016 by Lynne M. Heinzmann
First Edition
Library of Congress Control Number: 2015953386
ISBN: 978-0-89823-350-6
eISBN: 978-0-89823-351-3

Cover design by Dan Edwards
Interior design by Trista Conzemius
Author photo by Eric D Wertheimer Studios

The publication of *Frozen Voices* is made possible by the generous support of Minnesota State University Moorhead, the McKnight Foundation, the Dawson Family Fund, and other contributors to New Rivers Press.

For copyright permission, please contact Frederick T. Courtright at 570-839-7477 or at permdude@eclipse.net

New Rivers Press is a nonprofit literary press associated with Minnesota State University Moorhead.

Alan Davis, Director and Senior Editor
Nayt Rundquist, Managing Editor
Thom Tammaro, Poetry Editor
Kevin Carollo, MVP poetry coordinator
Bayard Godsave, MVP prose coordinator
Thomas Anstadt, Co-Art Director
Trista Conzemius, Co-Art Director
Wayne Gudmundson, Consultant
Suzzanne Kelley, Consultant

Publishing Interns:
Laura Grimm, Anna Landsverk, Desi Miller, Mikaila Norman

Frozen Voices book team:
Kyle Courteau, Sarah Dyke, Meghan Feir, Christy Smith

 Printed in the United States of America on acid-free, archival-grade paper.

Frozen Voices is distributed nationally by Small Press Distribution.

  New Rivers Press
c/o MSUM
1104 7th Ave S.
Moorhead, MN 56563
www.newriverspress.com

This novel is dedicated to all those
whose lives were lost or inalterably changed
that February night, so long ago.

May their voices be heard.

Contents

PROLOGUE

February 1907

On February 11, 1907, 156 men, women, and children boarded the passenger steamship *Larchmont* in Providence, Rhode Island, for an overnight trip to New York City. By the following morning, 137 of them were dead—drowned, frozen, or scalded to death—and the ship sat in the muck at the bottom of the Block Island Sound. Only nineteen people survived the disaster, and two of those succumbed to pneumonia within a week.

At the time of the accident, Millard Franklin was a seventeen-year-old apprentice locksmith from Southern Massachusetts, trying to establish himself as a professional magician. Sadie Golub, a dressmaker from Boston, was eighteen and eager to begin a new, more independent life as a dressmaker in New York City. George McVay, from Providence, Rhode Island, was a twenty-six-year-old ship's captain, intent upon advancing his career so he could better support his young family. Anna Jensen, a wealthy forty-six-year-old wife and mother, also from Providence, was worried about her only child, Louise, and was anxious to provide the teenager with a fresh start in life back in the Old Country.

Millard, Sadie, George, and Anna were on board the *SS Larchmont* the night she sank. Here are their stories.

BOOK 1:
THE HOUDINI
RECEPTION,
SEPTEMBER 1906

Chapter 1: Famous in Boston
Millard Franklin

The enormous, gold-trimmed clock at Providence's Union Station read seven forty-five as I paced the platform, waiting for Uncle Henry. In one hand, I clutched two crisp train tickets. In the other, I held the crumpled telegram that had been delivered to my uncle at his locksmith shop earlier that morning:

FRIDAY, SEPTEMBER 14, 1906
MR. FRANKLIN [STOP] HARRY HOUDINI WANTS TO SEE YOUR MARINE PADLOCKS [STOP] BRING THEM TO PARKER HOUSE HOTEL, BOSTON, THIS MORNING [STOP] TWO TICKETS AT PROVIDENCE STATION FOR EIGHT AM TRAIN [STOP] WILL MEET YOU AT SOUTH STATION [STOP]
URIAH HOLMES—MANAGER, PARKER HOUSE HOTEL

For the past four years, whenever any magician, professional or amateur, performed within fifty miles of our home, I'd been in the audience, analyzing all of his routines. I'd seen Alexander read people's minds in Worcester; watched as Johnny and Nellie Olms made an old lady disappear in Springfield; and even saw tiny Annie Abbott single-handedly lift up four grown men at the Boston Music Hall last year. After every show, I'd gone backstage to ask the performers about their tricks, to see if they'd tell me just one of their secrets, because, more than anything else in the world, I wanted to be one of them: a professional magician. Which was why the prospect of personally meeting the Great One, Harry Houdini, now had me literally dancing from one foot to the other on the train platform.

Unfortunately, as my interest in magic had grown, Uncle Henry's dislike for the profession also had increased. He'd tolerated my "ridiculous hobby," as he called it, until my father's death last spring, but ever since then he'd made it very difficult for me to perform or even to see other magicians. Whenever my uncle found out that I had a show scheduled, he would insist I work at his lock shop during that time. If I mentioned that I wanted to attend a performance, he'd send me on useless errands until it was too late for me to make it to the show.

"Performers are the lowest sort of animal," he said. "Not the kind of people you should associate with and certainly not the type you should aspire to become." No matter what I said, I couldn't get him to see anything favorable about being a magician.

So I found it ironic that I was getting the opportunity to meet the Great Houdini courtesy of Uncle Henry. My uncle had invented a marine padlock that didn't rust or corrode. He had displayed his invention at a locksmiths' convention at the Parker House Hotel in Boston this past spring. Yesterday, when the hotel's manager overheard Houdini, a guest, complaining about his padlocks rusting, he remembered seeing Uncle Henry's marine padlock and mentioned it to the magician. And so—*abracadabra*—my uncle had been invited back to Boston to show his innovative locks to Houdini, and I was going along as his assistant. I'd tucked my interlocking rings and a length of chain into the black leather tool bag, just in case. Imagine the thrill of actually getting to perform for Harry Houdini! It would be simply amazing. I hadn't figured out how I was going to manage it, though. We were there to demonstrate a lock, not to show him any of my tricks—but I intended to try. When would I ever get this chance again?

As the smell of fresh-baked blueberry muffins from the push-carts filled the air, I looked up at the station clock again. After receiving the telegram at the shop, Uncle Henry had insisted upon returning to his home on Providence's East Side to change into his best suit, sending me ahead to the station to pick up the tickets. Now, my uncle, who had never been late for anything in his life, was in danger of missing this very important train. Important to me, not to him. He probably couldn't care less about meeting the one and only Harry Houdini.

If my uncle didn't get to the station in time, what should I do? Miss the train too and forfeit my chance to meet Houdini?

Or go to Boston by myself? I had the marine padlocks in the tool bag sitting on the platform by my feet. I could easily demonstrate them. Heck, I'd been the one who'd actually built them—based upon my uncle's design—so I knew them inside and out. If I went to the meeting without Uncle Henry, he'd be quite sore at me, but he'd probably get over it and I'd get to meet the man who invented the Chinese Water Torture Escape Trick. Really, not a very difficult decision. A minute later, when the Boston-bound train's whistle hooted a puff of steam announcing its impending departure, I grabbed the heavy bag and elbowed my way into the chattering crowd shuffling toward the doors of the train.

Just then, Uncle Henry hurried over to me, his black and gold walking stick clicking on the station's tile floor. "And where, may I ask, are you going?"

"Saving you a place in line." I handed him his ticket, my face hot with my lie. I was actually disappointed that my uncle had arrived in time to catch the train; I wanted to speak to Houdini alone, without Uncle Henry's interference, especially considering his bad attitude about magic...and Jews. I glanced over at my uncle, standing next to me in line, and caught him admiring his own reflection in the black lacquer of the train car.

We climbed on board and Uncle Henry let me sit near one of the big windows while he took the aisle seat next to me. I knew he hadn't done this because he knew I'd want to look out the window. No, he just wanted to be more visible to the other passengers so they could admire his appearance. The car was full of other businessmen, also reading today's *Providence Journal*, but Uncle Henry was by far the best dressed. I recognized the light gray suit he was now wearing as one he'd had custom-tailored in New York City a few months earlier. He'd probably been looking for just such an opportunity to show it off.

As the long train puffed out of the station, I sat up tall in my seat and peered through the heavy blue curtains. In the harbor below, I could see a passenger steamship cruising Narragansett Bay on its way to the open ocean. With its twin black smokestacks and double wooden side-paddles, I recognized it as the *Edgemont*, a vessel I'd seen often in the Port of Providence. I watched the ship slip away to the south as our train barreled northward, bringing me closer to personally meeting the best magician in the world. I could hardly believe my good fortune.

*   *   *

"South Station, Boston. End of the line. Everybody off."

I quickly gathered my hat, coat, and the loaded tool bag and hurried to follow Uncle Henry to the rear of the car. Descending the train's black metal steps, I inhaled the aromas of coffee and cinnamon from the vendors' stalls lining the station's tiled walls. My stomach growled loudly, reminding me I'd been too excited to eat any breakfast. Oh well. Eating would have to wait until later; I certainly didn't want to take the time now. We were on our way to meet Harry Houdini!

A middle-aged man in an ill-fitting red and black uniform strutted up to us, his stomach looking like it was about to explode out the front of his jacket. "Mr. Franklin," he said in a high, squeaky voice. "I'm Mr. Holmes, manager at the Parker House Hotel."

My uncle nodded. "Thank you for remembering me and my marine padlock, Mr. Holmes. I'm quite honored."

Holmes frowned. "I certainly hope it's as good as you said it was. It would be disastrous to disappoint such an important guest." He hustled us through the crowd to an elegant black coach emblazoned in red with the hotel's name. The driver, wearing a similar uniform, opened and closed the coach door for us and then climbed up to his perch behind the box. With one slap of his reins, his handsome bay-colored mare set off at a good clip in the weak morning sunlight.

I'd only been to Boston twice in my life, both times when I was much younger, so I couldn't help gaping at the big city's sights as they flew by the coach's large windows. I marveled at the massive white stone columns of the train station, the small lake full of graceful swan boats in the Boston Commons, the gilded dome of the capitol building, and all the citified people everywhere, rushing around in their high-buttoned collars and big-bustled skirts.

In less than ten minutes, we pulled up to an impressive eight-story stone building that had a large awning illuminated with twinkling electric lights. I'd never seen so many light bulbs in one place before, but the excess seemed appropriate for a place that would host the Great Houdini.

Another man wearing a red and black uniform opened the coach door for us. "Welcome to the Parker House Hotel."

Mr. Holmes hopped out of the coach and hurried through the gold and glass doors into the lobby. Uncle Henry clambered down and trotted after him. I started to drag the tool bag toward the carriage door myself but was glad when the tall porter reached in and easily picked it up for me, and then handed it to me after I'd climbed down to the sidewalk. I wished I had some change in my pocket for him.

Uncle Henry poked his head out the hotel door and hissed, "Millard, come on!"

Together we rushed through the lobby, with its ornately carved wood-paneled walls, oversized green leather furniture, and glittering golden chandeliers, and found Mr. Holmes waiting inside the golden cage of the open elevator. Once we were aboard, he barked, "Presidential Suite," to the operator, a skinny, frightened-looking boy about my age.

On the hotel's top floor, the boy opened the elevator's cage to reveal a long corridor with plush carpet and golden wall lights. As the three of us rushed down the hallway, I found myself wishing that I'd spent more time polishing my shoes before work that morning. As my older brother Thomas would say, the Parker House was a "swanky" place.

The manager rapped sharply on a door labeled "Presidential Suite," which was immediately opened by a huge man with bright red hair.

"Mr. Holmes," the giant said with a slight bow.

Gesturing toward my uncle and smiling obsequiously, the manager said, "I've brought Mr. Franklin, the locksmith."

"Come in." The giant opened the door wider.

"I'm needed downstairs," Mr. Holmes said, his nose elevated. He peered up at Uncle Henry. "Assist Mr. Houdini with whatever he requires," he said curtly and then hurried back down the hallway.

Uncle Henry and I followed the redheaded man into the suite's sitting room. "My name is Hewitt. I'm the Houdinis' assistant." He smiled and gestured to a grouping of striped velvet chairs. "Please wait here," he said and then disappeared through another door at the far end of the sitting room.

I was amazed that the suite was furnished even more lavishly than the hotel's lobby had been. Here, everything was made of walnut-stained wood, trimmed in gold, and upholstered in dark, rich, velvety fabrics. It was a place fit for royalty—magical royalty.

Uncle Henry took a chair on the other side of the room, pulling his newspaper from his overcoat pocket and snapping it open to a page in the center. Another newspaper sat folded on a table next to me, but I didn't bother to pick it up. I knew there was no way I'd be able to sit still long enough to read anything. In just a few minutes, I was going to meet the greatest magician who ever lived. Me—Millard Franklin. Imagine that!

Chapter 2: Working for a Living

Sadie Golub

I awoke with someone jostling my shoulder. "Sadie, wake up!" Bessie, my best friend and sister-in-law, stood next to my elbow, a look of concern creasing her young face.

I pushed my hair back from my forehead and realized that, once again, I'd fallen asleep at my sewing machine in the cramped apartment I shared with Bessie, Solomon, and their young son. Thin September sunlight slanted through the parlor's two small, drafty windows, painting yellow sunspots on the battered furniture that crowded the living room where I worked and slept. Lately, that room had become my whole world. I was working so hard—night and day—trying to get…somewhere. I wasn't sure where I wanted to end up, but I knew it wasn't here, in this cramped little apartment with my brother and his family. I loved them all, but I wanted something more, and I was determined to get it, whatever "it" might be. Through the open kitchen door, I heard Morris babbling as he ate his breakfast porridge and I smelled tonight's supper simmering on the stovetop. Cabbage stew…again.

"Mr. Miller is here for that suit," Bessie whispered urgently. "Is it finished?"

"Almost." With fumbling hands, I twisted my hair into a tight chignon and refastened it with the hair clip that had fallen out while I slept. My hair felt coarse and tangled and I realized I hadn't washed it in a few days. No time.

"Have some tea." Bessie handed me a steaming glass of Russian Caravan, sitting on a plate ringed with three sugar cubes. "And hurry. I'll go talk to Mr. Miller while you finish the trousers." She bustled off to the kitchen.

I popped a sugar cube in my mouth and took a sip of the aromatic tea, enjoying the sensation of the sugar dissolving on my tongue. Sugar cubes were the one luxury that Bessie, Solomon, and I allowed ourselves. I set aside my glass and rocked the sewing machine treadle with my feet. I had been up all night sewing the suit, I was exhausted, and my eyes felt full of sand, but I needed to finish the job. I snipped the threads, pulled the trousers from the machine, and checked to make certain they were perfect. "You come in now, Mr. Miller," I called out, wincing at my strong Yiddish accent.

My red-faced employer lumbered over, wearing a new camel-colored woolen overcoat that looked soft and comfortable. "So, Miss Golub, did you finish the work I gave you?" His balding head shone with perspiration even on this chilly fall morning.

"Yes, sir." I proudly held up the trousers and jacket for his inspection.

He examined the well-crafted seams, buttonholes, and other details. "I guess this will have to do." Mr. Miller never complimented my work. It was as if he was afraid that a kind word would cost him more in wages. But I knew I'd done a good job.

He pulled a lumpy white envelope from his overcoat pocket and handed it to me along with a large bundle wrapped in brown paper and tied with a piece of twine. "Here's your pay and some more work to do: six pairs of trousers to hem, a dress to design and sew, and another suit to make. The fabric and the measurements for the dress and suit are inside."

I opened the envelope to find four silver dollars, my weekly income. It wasn't much, but—as Bessie often reminded me—every little bit helped. I stifled a yawn and nodded toward the other bundle. "When you need them?" I hated the way I spoke: baby talk. In my head, I thought fluently in Yiddish, but I didn't know enough English to accurately translate my thoughts when I spoke. Not yet.

"The trousers by Monday, the dress and the suit by Thursday. Can you finish them on time?"

I saw Bessie peeking out from the kitchen, holding her son on her hip. Last night, I'd overheard her and my brother anxiously discussing their finances. His commercial painting business was finally showing a small profit, but barely enough to pay his employees. Counting Morris and me, he had four mouths to feed now, plus rent and all of his other monthly expenses. I felt I should do whatever I could to help. I nodded determinedly at

Mr. Miller. I wouldn't get much sleep next week either. So what? I was young; I didn't need sleep.

I'd started sewing for Mr. Miller just after I'd arrived from Russia, since it was something I already knew how to do and it didn't require me to speak English. Every Friday I turned my pay over to Solomon, as I should, since he was responsible for taking care of me. When I first arrived in Boston, he'd promised to let me keep some of the money I made, if we had any extra at the end of the week. But we never did. Something always came up. The baby was sick and needed medicine or my brother had to buy more paint for a job or one of our neighbors was out of work and needed a little help just until he found a new position. I loved my brother, Bessie, and Morris, and I was very grateful to them for taking me in, but I was beginning to fear that unless I made a change soon, I'd spend my whole life cooped up in their tiny apartment.

As Mr. Miller turned to leave, he patted my Singer 66 sewing machine, its shiny black body and gold filigree decorations looking out of place in the shabby apartment. "How do you like this machine?" It belonged to him, but he allowed me to use it in our home, since he had no room for me to work in his sewing shop.

I forced a smile. "Is the nicest machine I ever use."

"Don't forget, you may use it to sew some outfits for yourself and your family, in your spare time. I don't want my seamstresses walking around in threadbare clothes. What would people say?" He flashed an insincere smile.

I tried to sound appreciative as I thanked him and wrapped up the completed suit, remembering to enclose a sprig of evergreen to counteract any unpleasant odors the clothing might have picked up from our apartment building. Like the smell of our ubiquitous cabbage stew. Tying a piece of twine around the package, I handed it to Mr. Miller.

"I'll stop by Monday to collect those trousers. Three o'clock." He strode away and, a moment later, I heard the apartment door open and close.

I untied the new bundle of sewing work and carefully refolded the empty paper wrapper. I selected a pair of trousers, thinking after I finished hemming them, I'd go for a walk; the fresh air and exercise would do me good. I couldn't remember the last time I'd left the apartment. Tuesday? Or was it Monday? And here it was Friday already. Slipping the cuff under the needle of the sewing machine, I rapidly rocked the treadle with my feet.

I heard the kitchen door open and close. "Mr. Miller?" I asked loudly. Instead of my overweight boss, though, my trim brother, Solomon, rushed into the room, his dark hair flopping into his eyes. He smoothed it back with one paint-splattered hand.

"*Gute news!*" he said.

"No Yiddish. I told you—I not learn English if you talk Yiddish."

"Fine. Like I said, good news! The Houdinis are guests at the hotel today and they want you to sew for them." Solomon's company was currently repainting the interior of Boston's famously posh Parker House Hotel.

"Who are these Houdinis?"

"You know...Harry Houdini, the world-famous Jewish magician."

"Oh!"

"He and his wife are staying at the Parker House and Mrs. Houdini asked for a seamstress. But Miss Miller has the flu and left a message that if anyone needed a seamstress, the hotel should call you. She knows you from her father's sewing shop?"

"Yes, I see her there many times."

"She named you as her replacement. Mr. Holmes, the hotel manager, sent me to fetch you so that you could sew for the Houdinis."

Bessie bustled into the room. "We could really use the money." We were all doing our share to make ends meet. Even Bessie. Despite having the baby to care for, she took in wash from the other tenants in our apartment building.

Solomon nodded his agreement. "The hotel will pay well."

And maybe this could be a new beginning for me, I thought hopefully. A way for me to get out of their apartment.

"Now, stand up." Bessie grasped my hands and pulled me to my feet. "Let's see how you look."

We all looked at my worn, rumpled clothing and straggly hair and frowned. I certainly couldn't go to the Parker House looking like this.

Bessie headed for their bedroom, tugging me behind her. "I have an idea."

In their tiny bedroom, crowded with battered furniture, she yanked open a wardrobe and pulled out a stylish, off-white linen traveling suit trimmed with a small bustle. "You made it for me for my wedding, but we're the same size. Try it on." With her help, I was soon dressed in her suit, with my dark hair neatly tucked up under a small matching hat. Bessie and I did the best we could to shine up my scuffed black leather boots, the only pair of footwear I owned.

Back in the living room, Solomon inspected me and said, "You look just as good as the other women I've seen in the lobby, maybe even prettier."

I smiled my thanks. Then, with one hand clutching my wicker sewing basket and the other firmly clamped onto his elbow, we left the apartment for the short walk to the hotel.

*   *   *

As we rounded the corner from Tremont Street to School Street, I stopped in the middle of the sidewalk, forcing other pedestrians to step around us. Although I'd seen the Parker House from the outside before, this was the first time I'd actually get to go inside the elegant hotel and I wanted to savor the experience. Its white marble walls stretched from the sidewalk up to the sky. Shading my eyes with one gloved hand, I tilted back to view the fancy stone chimneys and pointy slate roofs eight stories up. And there were so many huge windows! I pitied the poor maids who had to wash all those. With a shake of my head, I stepped toward the entry covered by a gilded awning. A footman in a red and black woolen uniform with big gold buttons stepped forward and opened the door for us, waving toward the lobby with a white-gloved hand and a pleasant smile, but Solomon grabbed me by the elbow. "Not that way, `du silly meydl!` Over here." He led me around the corner onto Chapman Place, to the service entrance. Apparently, people like us didn't use the front door of a place like the Parker House Hotel. He guided me down a wide service hallway.

In the kitchen, the delicious aromas of chicken and basil filled the air as white-clad kitchen workers scurried about. While I waited for Solomon to find the hotel manager, I studied the terra cotta floor tiles and worried about working for Mrs. Houdini. I knew I could sew well enough, but what if she couldn't understand my heavy Yiddish accent? I was trying hard to improve my English; I really was. Every week, I spent three cents to buy a *Boston Globe* newspaper, laboriously read it front to back, and then practiced my newly learned English words in conversations with Solomon and Bessie. I was making progress, but I still had a long way to go.

I pulled off my white gloves, dropped them into my sewing basket, and used my palms to smooth out the wrinkles in Bessie's traveling suit just as my brother returned through the double swinging doors, followed by a scowling, middle-aged man, his chest thrust forward like a crowing rooster. I noticed that his uniform fit him too tightly across his fat stomach and wondered if I should offer to alter it for him.

"Is this the sewing girl?" he asked, jabbing his index finger in my direction.

I was surprised by his rudeness.

Solomon said, "Mr. Holmes, this is Miss Sadie Golub, my sister, and a very good seamstress."

"She'd better be. Follow me." The manager strode to the service elevator and pushed the call button. "Hurry!"

I didn't know if he was speaking to me or to the skinny elevator operator now opening the gilded metal doors, so I rushed into the wood-paneled cab and then shuddered when the boy closed the doors behind us. I'd never been in an elevator before. It was very small, Mr. Holmes was too close to me, and his breath reeked of onions. As the cab began to rise, my stomach lurched and I felt beads of sweat pop up on my forehead. I was afraid I might become ill. The elevator boy flashed me a sympathetic smile. When we arrived at the top floor, he quickly opened the doors, and I lurched out of the cab, gasping for fresh air.

"Follow me," Mr. Holmes said, seemingly oblivious to my discomfort. He hurried down a corridor, forcing me to trot to keep up with him. At the very end of the hallway, he knocked on a door.

It was opened by a very tall man wearing a well-fitted navy blue blazer, matching trousers, and shiny brown shoes. "Mr. Holmes," he said with a nod.

"I've brought you a seamstress, as requested," the manager said. He waved in my direction. "This is Miss...er..."

"Golub," I said and dropped into a polite curtsey.

"I am Hewitt, the Houdinis' assistant," the tall man said as he stepped aside. "Won't you please come in?"

"Once again, I am needed downstairs," Mr. Holmes said. He turned to me. "When you are done here, please find me so that I may see to your wages." He nodded to Hewitt and then strutted back toward the elevator. My initial impression of Mr. Holmes had not been a favorable one.

Hewitt gestured into the suite. "Miss Golub . . ."

I walked into a sitting room that was the most beautiful room I'd ever seen. Wood paneling covered the walls, velvety furniture perched on plush Oriental rugs, and fresh-cut flowers peeked from china vases all over the room. I wondered where they'd found such beautiful blooms in New England at this time of year. A dapper-looking older man in a light gray, pinstripe suit sat reading a newspaper in one corner, and a younger man who resembled him—his son?—stood in the middle of the room, holding a large leather bag.

"Please wait here," Hewitt said and then strode through another door.

I perched on the edge of the nearest armchair, set my sewing kit in my lap, and tried to slow my breathing. I wanted to appear calm and composed.

Hewitt returned. "Mrs. Houdini sends her apologies, Miss Golub. She has been temporarily detained but will be with you shortly. Do you mind waiting?"

I shook my head, appreciating the fact that someone important enough to stay in the Presidential Suite would bother to ask the indulgence of me, a mere seamstress. Clearly, these were people of good breeding.

Hewitt left the room once more.

I placed my sewing kit on the table, sat back in my chair, and glanced around at the framed paintings of Boston landmarks covering the walls. Everything was so elegant. And this was only the suite's sitting room. *Ploimdik!* I opened my wicker basket and withdrew a pair of Solomon's brown socks and began to darn one of them, hoping the routine act of guiding the needle in and out of the fabric would calm my jittery nerves.

The younger man standing near me dropped his big leather bag and it clanged loudly, making me startle and laugh.

He laughed, too, and then smiled.

"What is in bag?" I asked. "Dumbbells?" He looked like a weight-lifting street performer I'd seen on the Boston Commons recently: short, compact, and muscular.

He chuckled. "No, just some padlocks and chains."

I gasped. "Are you policemen, here to arrest someone?"

He chuckled again. "No, I'm a locksmith. Or rather, my uncle is." He nodded toward the older man across the room. "We're here to show a new type of lock to Mr. Houdini."

"Ah," I nodded.

"What about you?" he asked. "Why are you here?"

I pointed to my basket. "I seamstress. Here to sew for Mrs. Houdini." I was enjoying talking to this boy, a novelty for me, since I spent most of my days alone in our apartment. "You live in Boston, too?" I asked.

"No, I'm from a small town about fifty miles south of here. My uncle and I just arrived here on a train."

I wrinkled my nose. "I was on train once, when I come from New York City. Dirty."

He laughed. "Yes, it can be a dirty way to travel." He approached my chair and bowed slightly. "I'm Millard Franklin, locksmith from North Attleboro."

I bobbed my head. "Please to meet you. I am Sadie Golub, seamstress from Boston."

"Very pleased to meet you, Miss Golub. May I ask where you are from, originally?"

I quickly looked down at Solomon's sock and took an errant stitch. I could correct my poor sewing later; I just wished I could fix my terrible English as easily.

"I'm very sorry," he said. "I didn't mean to embarrass you."

Hewitt appeared in a doorway. "Miss Golub, would you please follow me?"

Rising, I returned my sewing to the wicker basket, and fastened the lid. "Nice to meet you, Mr. Franklin," I said with a small curtsey.

"And it was very nice meeting you too, Miss Golub."

We smiled at each other and then I hurried to follow Hewitt.

Chapter 3: Frayed Brocade

George McVay

Even though I was the captain of a steamship, for the past twenty minutes I'd been reduced to pacing my bedroom in my union suit and socks, waiting for our hired woman to iron my dress uniform. If she took much longer, she was going to make us late, and I hated to be late.

I leaned into the hallway. "Matilda, where are you?" I returned to pacing. As I walked past the mirror, I regarded my well-muscled arms and flat stomach. I wasn't very tall, but with my dark hair and intelligent-looking countenance, I would still cut a good figure at the reception today. Provided I had some clothes to wear.

I plucked the telegram off the bed and rechecked the message I'd received two hours ago:

> FRIDAY, SEPTEMBER 14, 1906
> TO ALL OFFICERS [STOP]
> SURPRISE PERFORMANCE BY HARRY HOUDINI TWO
> PM TODAY AT CHARLES RIVER IN CAMBRIDGE [STOP]
> FOUR PM RECEPTION AT PARKER HOUSE HOTEL 60
> SCHOOL STREET BOSTON [STOP] ALL OFF DUTY SHIP
> OFFICERS SHOULD ATTEND [STOP]
> F M DUNBAUGH

Thank God, I had the day off—a rarity. Although I didn't care to see the magic show—smoke and mirrors meant to befuddle the minds of the ignorant—I definitely wanted to attend the after-show reception, to see and be seen by the members of Boston's Brahmin elite who would be in attendance.

I heard the rustle of clothing behind me and turned to find Edith in our bedroom doorway, the late-morning sunlight from the hallway window highlighting her auburn hair, making it glow even redder than usual. She wore a fashionable light blue striped dress—borrowed from a neighbor—with her hair swept up in an attractive coif. Just having her on my arm at the reception this afternoon would warrant positive attention.

I sighed loudly. "Do you have any idea where Matilda is with my uniform?"

"No, dear." Edith walked into the room, her tiny shoes padding softly on the rag rug, her lavender eau de cologne pleasantly scenting the room. "But we still have plenty of time."

"Actually, we're scheduled to leave from Union Station in less than an hour. If any other complication arises, we will, in fact, miss the train." I sat down on the feather bed and then sprang back to pacing, darting another glance at my gold pocket watch, propped open on the dressing table.

Edith touched my elbow with her small, white-gloved hand. "George, you so rarely have any time off. Now that you're a captain, you are gone six days out of seven. Nights too. Why don't we skip the trip to Boston and take the children to Roger Williams Park instead? You know they love it there, running on those wide lawns and riding on the carousel. We could bundle them up and make a family day of it." She looked up at me with her huge emerald green eyes. "Ruth and Raymond would be thrilled to spend some time with their father."

I felt my jaw muscles clench. "Edith, sometimes I just don't understand you. I have the opportunity to go to this event and meet important men who could further my career. Charles Morse, the owner of the International Steamship Company, will probably be there, and I'm hoping I can talk him into giving me a job. Yet all you think about is what would make the children happy?"

Morse...I hoped he'd heard good things about me rather than the vicious lies that had circulated after the *Tremont* incident. Edith sat on the bed, frowning. "You already have a job. A good job, dear."

"Hardly! A captain of the International Line makes $2,500 a year. That's almost twice as much as I'm making now. Just think of what we could do with that much money."

She shook her head, clearly not interested.

I couldn't understand her apathy. Her family had always had everything—a fancy house, expensive clothing, servants, and foreign vacations. Not like the life I'd led as the son of a coastal fisherman, with our family just scraping by, barely affording to put food on the table. Marrying Edith and having her father give me a job aboard his ship had saved me from having to follow in my father's footsteps. But it wasn't enough. I still wanted the finer things for us and for our children. And I'd get them too. "If I worked for Morse, we could buy ourselves European clothes, instead of the homemade ones you sew." I held up a palm before she could object. "Please don't misunderstand me. You make sure we always look quite nice. But you have to work so hard to do it."

"I don't mind."

"Well, I do." I waved toward the outfit she was wearing. "Thank God Celia had a dress you could borrow today. Otherwise, what would you have worn to the reception?" I shook my head. "Don't you see? Once I get a better job, you'll have a whole wardrobe full of gowns, even nicer than that one. And we'll be able to buy a decent house on Blackstone Boulevard instead of living here. We'll even hire better servants, who complete their tasks on time." I directed this last comment loudly through the open bedroom door.

"Shh!" Edith waved her little hand at me.

As if on cue, Matilda appeared in the doorway, carrying my pressed and starched uniform on a hanger. She was very young— eighteen or nineteen, at most—but she was as much help as we could afford at my present salary. A dark-haired, blue-eyed Irish slip of a girl, Matilda could be described as pretty. Edith and our children thought the world of her, but I often found her to be slow and inefficient.

I snatched my uniform from her and gruffly thanked her, embarrassed about her seeing me in my union suit. I closed the bedroom door as she left.

"If I worked for Morse, we could afford to have a separate person to do our ironing and cooking and could let Matilda spend her time caring for Ruthie and Raymond, a task she obviously prefers."

Edith rose and came to stand beside me. "But we don't need another servant or expensive clothing or a larger house. I'm happy with the way we live right now."

"Well, I'm not!" I shrugged on my uniform. "Just look at this jacket." I pointed to a frayed piece of gold brocade. "It's a disgrace. An International captain wouldn't be caught dead in such a poorly made suit."

Edith retreated to her seat on the bed. "Do the International steamships run from Providence to New York?"

"No, their routes are from Boston to New York."

"We'd have to move again?"

"So?" I fastened the dozen brass buttons marching down the front of my jacket.

"We've made friends here."

I gestured to the second-hand furniture given to us by her parents. "Don't you want to live better than this, though?"

Edith looked around and shrugged. "I'm perfectly comfortable here."

"We'd be more comfortable in a bigger house," I mumbled as I opened the door and went in search of Matilda, hoping she could do something quickly to repair the frayed brocade.

*   *   *

Twenty minutes later, I was finally prepared to leave, finishing by combing my hair and mustache. "Are you ready?" I asked Edith.

She nodded and handed me my wool overcoat. We climbed the stairs to the third floor nursery.

"Dadda!" Raymond called out and toddled over to me from the dollhouse. I scooped him up, loving the weight and the warmth of him in my arms.

"Where are you going?" Ruthie asked, her little hands on her little hips.

I plunked down in the rocking chair and gathered her up on my lap too. Kissing the crown of her curly head—she was a redhead, just like her mother—I said, "To a dull adults' party in Boston."

She stroked the end of my mustache with one finger. "When will you come home?"

"You'll probably be abed by the time we get back."

"No, I won't. I'll wait for you to get home."

"Don't do that, Peaches." I kissed her again and then stood, placing both of them on the floor. "You need your beauty rest so that you'll grow up strong and pretty, just like your mother."

Edith kissed me on the cheek. Then she knelt and kissed Ruthie and Raymond. "You two be good. Mind Matilda."

"Will you please bring us a present from Boston?" Ruthie asked.

"I'm not sure we'll have time to buy anything," I said. "But we'll try."

"Present?" Raymond asked, honing in on one of his favorite words.

I chuckled and ruffled his hair. "We'll see, little man. Now, do as your mother says and behave."

"We will!" Ruthie said, both children already returning their attention to the dollhouse.

I watched them for a moment, considering the possibility of doing as Edith had suggested and spending the day at the park. That would be so much more pleasant and relaxing than hobnobbing with the elite at the Houdini reception. But when would I have another opportunity to meet Morse? I sighed. I had to take advantage of the moment. My career—and my responsibility to my family—demanded it of me.

Edith and I hurried downstairs and boarded the horse-drawn hack we'd hired to carry us to Providence's Union Station.

Chapter 4: Unwelcome News

Anna Jensen

The Back Bay Boarding House for Young Women, located on Fairfield Street, just off of Commonwealth Avenue in Boston, had its own private telephone. I knew this as fact because earlier this morning I'd had our butler telephone long distance to inform them I'd be arriving at eleven o'clock to pick up our daughter, Louise, who had been a boarder there for the past two years while attending music school. Yet, despite my advanced warning, Mrs. Beatty, the Irish housemother, had now kept me waiting in her office for a full twenty minutes.

I was no longer accustomed to waiting. When John and I had first arrived in this country, we'd had to wait for everything: wait at the immigration office for our papers, wait to rent an apartment, wait to apply for business permits, and even wait in line for food. All that waiting had been humiliating, making me feel like a second-class citizen. Now that we were wealthy business owners, I did not intend to wait for anything ever again.

I glared through a window at the bright fall foliage being tossed about by the wind and noticed a group of men hammering and sawing, constructing a building addition I knew to be largely paid for by a generous gift from John and me. I sniffed. If Mrs. Beatty planned to make a habit of keeping me waiting like this, the next time she requested such a donation from our family, she'd be sorely disappointed.

Next to the window sat a potted Boston fern in a deplorable condition. I pinched off three or four dried fronds. Honestly, hadn't this woman ever heard of fertilizer? It took so little to keep Boston ferns healthy. John and I had a greenhouse full of them in Providence that I'd personally tended for several years; it only took a few hours a week.

When Mrs. Beatty finally appeared—after four more minutes—I stayed by the fern as she shuffled to the desk, her leather boots scuffling across the threadbare carpet. Her baggy dress repulsed me. Even when we'd had little money, I'd made sure to wear clothing that fit me well. The woman could sew, couldn't she? Most Irishwomen could. She had no excuse for her ill-fitting frock; it showed a lack of self-respect.

She grunted as she sat. "What may I do for you, Mrs. Jensen?" she asked in her nasally voice.

What sort of game was this woman playing? She knew perfectly well why I was here. I leaned back against the windowsill, and frowned. "Mrs. Beatty, my husband and I came to this country from Sweden. You know this. *Ja?*"

She stared at me with a blank expression.

"Twenty-five years we've lived here, but still I admire the Swedes' way of saying things. Have you heard the saying, *säga inte av den gren du sitter på*—don't saw off the branch you're sitting on?"

Mrs. Beatty shook her head, dumbly.

I approached her desk and waved my hand in dismissal at the idiot woman, realizing that she wasn't worth upsetting myself over. "This morning, my butler, he tells you that I will come to collect Louise so that she may go with me to two social engagements here in the city. *Ja?* She'll be back by dinnertime." I saw my reflection in the glass-front bookcase behind Mrs. Beatty and noticed that my dark blue dress, trimmed in black, perfectly accentuated my still-slender figure.

"Ah, yes. Your daughter Louise." The housemother folded her hands, wearing a smug expression.

I lifted my chin and looked down at her. "*Ja*, my daughter. You will now tell her I'm here." I deliberately slid my gray kid-skinned glove down my wrist to reveal my gold and diamond wristwatch. Although I realized that *pengar* är *inte allt*—money isn't everything—I thought the high level of generosity we'd shown to this establishment should warrant me a bit more respect than what was currently being displayed. "To make our lunch reservations on time, we must go now."

But Mrs. Beatty remained seated, her pudgy fingers interlocked on her desk. "First, I would like to speak to you about Louise. Would you please take a seat?" She indicated one of the stained, upholstered chairs positioned in front of her desk.

"*Nej tack*. I will stand." I certainly had no intention of sitting in front of her like a schoolgirl about to be chastised.

Mrs. Beatty shrugged. "Suit yourself. But we might be here a while. You see, Louise has been caught sneaking into the boarding house after hours. Several times. Last week, I myself witnessed her returning to the house at one o'clock in the morning."

The nerve of her—an Irishwoman, no less—maligning my daughter! I scoffed. "You are wrong. Louise would not be out so late."

Mrs. Beatty pressed her thin lips together. "She's been keeping company with men—well, one man, mostly—and he's not the sort of person we permit to call on our young ladies."

Man? What man? Louise wouldn't dare dishonor our family like that. She was fully aware of how much John and I were counting on her to carry on the family name and business. "Rubbish!" I said.

"I assure you, it's not rubbish. She's violated curfew repeatedly, and her professors at the Music Conservatory inform me that she's missed many of her classes this fall." She drummed her stubby fingers on her cheap desk. "When your daughter moved in here two years ago, she had such impeccable references that we were happy to accept her into our little family. However, if this behavior persists, we might be forced to ask her to leave."

I'd had enough of this nonsense. Placing both of my palms on her desk, I leaned toward the rude little woman. "Mrs. Beatty, I have three things to say and you will listen closely. *Ja?*"

She nodded rapidly, her eyes darting to the door.

I held up one finger. "*Ett*: You are wrong about Louise and soon you will owe our family an apology." I raised another finger. "*Två*: Your threat of throwing Louise out of here I do not like. My husband and I have supported this institution for the past two years. Look out that window to see our generosity at work." I pointed to the construction crew. I held up a third finger. "And *tre*: You will have my daughter here in this office within the next five minutes or I will see to it that you lose your position."

I walked back to the window and ignored Mrs. Beatty as she scurried from the room, leaving the door open behind her. The smell of stale cabbage wafted in from the hallway. I made a mental note to question Louise about the food offered here. Maybe it was time for us to look for another—non-Irish—establishment in which to house our daughter.

Mrs. Beatty was being ridiculous. Wasn't she? There was no chance she was correct and that Louise had indeed been having assignations with some man. True, we'd had a few episodes with her and a manager from one of our greenhouses last spring, but John and I had nipped their little romance in the bud easily enough with some stern words and strictly enforced curfews. And, besides, that man had lived in Rhode Island, not up here in Boston. No, Mrs. Beatty *must* be wrong.

A few moments later, I heard Louise say, "Hello, *Mamma*." I turned to find her attractively attired in a pale green dress with dark green trim that perfectly complemented her golden hair. I'd certainly taught her how to dress well.

She dutifully kissed my cheek.

Without so much as a nod to Mrs. Beatty, who hovered near the doorway, I took Louise by the elbow and led her outside to the carriage I'd borrowed from my brother-in-law. Charles had offered me the use of one of his automobiles instead, but I still didn't trust Mr. Ford's contraptions enough to actually ride in one.

The autumn wind chased a few brown leaves around our ankles as Charles' coachman opened the door for us. When Louise mounted the carriage steps ahead of me, I noticed that she'd put on a little weight. Perhaps the food at Mrs. Beatty's boarding house was more palatable than it smelled. Or maybe... No. That wasn't possible; the ignominy it would cast upon our family would be unbearable. John and I had worked so hard to establish ourselves in New England society. Such an appalling mistake by Louise would undo all we'd strived to accomplish.

As we settled into our seats and placed the lap robe over our knees for the ride to the restaurant, I glared at my daughter. "If you've disgraced our family in any way, *min kära*, you will be sorry. I promise you that."

She quickly turned her face to the window and was silent for the duration of the ride.

Chapter 5: Meeting the Great One

Millard Franklin

I'd thoroughly enjoyed speaking with Sadie Golub in the Houdinis' sitting room. Usually I was very shy with girls, but for some reason I'd had no trouble talking to her. Maybe I was so excited about meeting the Great One. Or maybe I felt extra confident, dressed as I was in my best suit. Or maybe Sadie was just easy to talk to. For whatever reason, I was disappointed when Hewitt escorted her away.

I hefted the tool bag over to where my uncle sat, his nose still buried in the newspaper. "Did you see that girl, Uncle Henry? Wasn't she pretty?"

He sniffed. "Hardly the sort you'd want to associate with."

"What do you mean?"

He folded down his paper and frowned. "Didn't you hear her accent? A Russian Jew, I'd guess."

I shrugged.

"Dirty and uneducated."

I shook my head, disgusted with his old-world way of thinking. Didn't he know this was twentieth century America? "I thought Miss Golub was very pretty and intelligent."

He pursed his lips. "Obviously, you have a thing or two to learn."

Hewitt reappeared. "Mr. Franklin, please come with me."

My uncle sprang from his chair and snatched up his walking stick.

I picked up the tool bag, my heart suddenly pounding in my throat.

We followed the assistant into a very large room. Heavy striped drapes framed the floor-to-ceiling windows that afforded a breathtaking view of the Boston Common, one block away. But no one was looking out the windows. The two-dozen people in the room were all clustered around one man, who was seated in a blue armchair. I was too short to see his face over the milling crowd, but Hewitt soon elbowed us to the front of the room.

"Sir," he said, "this is Henry Franklin. He's the locksmith Mr. Holmes told you about, the one who invented that special marine padlock. He's just arrived from Providence."

There, seated in front of us in the center of the Parker House Hotel's Presidential Suite, was the one and only Harry Houdini, looking just as he appeared on all the posters, with his dark, wavy hair, light blue eyes, and well-muscled physique.

The Great One was right there...in person!

Houdini extended his small but powerful-looking hand to my uncle, a chunky gold and diamond ring glinting on his pinkie finger. "I am honored to meet you, Mr. Franklin. And I'm eager to see your locks that Mr. Holmes has been telling me so much about."

I wished that Hewitt would introduce me, too. I really wanted to shake Houdini's hand.

"The honor is all mine," my uncle said and then motioned for me to hurry up.

I crouched, placed the tool bag on the Persian carpet, and reached for its latch.

"No." Houdini raised his other hand, adorned with a simple gold wedding band. "I would rather see the locks in private." He winked at my uncle. "I must maintain my trade secrets, you know." He cast a sideways glance at his assistant and, in less than a minute, Hewitt magically cleared the suite of all other visitors. Only Houdini, Uncle Henry, the assistant, and I remained.

Houdini rose and gestured toward a large dining table near the tall windows. As we followed him, I was struck by how short the magician was, not more than five-two or -three. And I noticed that he moved with such grace—like a cat on the prowl.

Houdini seated himself in the high-back armchair at the head of the table and indicated a chair to his left for my uncle. He raised his eyebrows and nodded at my tool bag. After fumbling with the clasp, I handed him a marine padlock, my hands shaking slightly.

He carefully inspected the lock and turned the key many times, opening and closing the lock, his rings clinking against its metal casing. I wondered if Uncle Henry should offer some commentary about his design, but Houdini didn't ask any questions, so no one spoke. I stood behind my uncle's chair, waiting.

After a full five minutes, Houdini slid the padlock toward Uncle Henry. "This is made of brass to counteract the corrosive effect of seawater?"

"Exactly, sir."

"That feature would come in handy for me. The locks I've been using for my water-escape routines have a nasty habit of rusting. We had an incident a few months ago where I had great difficulty opening a lock while trapped in a tank of water on a stage in Brussels. It was most unpleasant."

I smiled at his understatement. I'd read an account of the "incident." Houdini had almost drowned.

"However," the magician continued, "I notice that you've also equipped this lock with a double ball locking mechanism."

"Yes, sir," Uncle Henry replied. "It makes it much more difficult to pry open."

"Which is exactly why I'm afraid it may not work for me. You see, I do most of my work with lock picks, not keys, so I require a padlock that is fairly easy to open."

"But this one is!" I exclaimed.

Both men turned to look at me. Houdini raised his eyebrows.

My uncle frowned. "Mr. Houdini, this is my assistant—and my nephew—Millard Franklin. I do apologize for his rude behavior."

The magician smiled at me. "Millard, you were saying?"

I knew my face was burning red, right up to the roots of my curly blond hair, but I finally had the Great One's attention. "I'm sorry to interrupt you, sir. But I do some magic myself and I've used one of these locks in my routine before and had no trouble picking it open."

"You do magic?" Houdini asked.

"Yes, sir. Just simple stuff."

"Show me," he said, pointing toward the padlock.

I looked at Uncle Henry, who raised both palms. Clearly, he felt I'd gotten myself into this predicament and would have to get myself out, without any assistance from him.

Me, performing for Harry Houdini? What if he laughed at my far inferior skills? I'd be devastated. But when would I ever get an opportunity like this again? To do a trick for the most famous magician who ever lived? I'd be insane not to at least try. If somehow, someway, I did manage to perform the trick, I'd have quite the story to tell all my friends! So why not try?

"I will need someone to help me," I said, my voice quavering. I looked toward my uncle again but he crossed his arms over his chest.

Houdini waved his assistant over to the table.

I knelt at the tool bag and withdrew several feet of chain. Reaching into my trouser pocket, I retrieved one of my home-made lock picks and hid it in the palm of my hand. Then I whispered instructions for Hewitt to wrap the chain around me four times—starting at my shoulders and spiraling down to my waist, pinning my arms to my sides—and then to secure the end of the chain to its beginning using my uncle's padlock. Hewitt easily did as I requested. If he noticed that I was shaking violently, he kept it to himself.

I paused to steady myself, afraid I wouldn't be able to manipulate the lock in my current state of agitation. When I looked up, Uncle Henry was still pointedly ignoring me, staring out one of the large windows, but Houdini nodded in my direction. My heart thumped loudly in my ears. I began to turn my back to him, as I normally would on stage, but then stopped myself. He wanted me to show him that these locks were easily opened, so I might as well let him see me try. The pick tapped against the lock casing several times before I managed to slip it into the keyhole. My fingers were sweaty. I paused again, and then with a deep breath, I slowly twisted the pick counter-clock-wise, waiting until I felt it engage with the locking mechanism. Then I pulled the pick toward the front of the lock and turned it another half-turn. I nearly cried out in relief when the lock popped open and fell with a clunk to the polished floor. The chain followed, uncoiling from my torso and clinking loudly as it puddled at my feet.

Houdini clapped.

I knew I was smiling like a fool, but I couldn't help myself. The Great One was applauding me!

"Well done, son," he said. "How long have you been performing magic?"

"Most of my life, sir."

"And you do shows for the public?"

I glanced toward my uncle. "Whenever I get the chance, sir."

"You've got talent. I might have need of a man like you."

"Need me, sir?"

"Yes, but first let's conclude this business." He held out a palm. "May I see the lock again?"

I hurriedly handed it to him.

Houdini withdrew a tiny lock pick—half the size of mine—from a concealed pocket of his trousers and used to quickly open the padlock. Five times, he locked and unlocked the mechanism, more quickly with each successive attempt. Nodding, he turned back to Uncle Henry. "Now that I know these locks can be picked"—Houdini shot me a smile—"I believe they would suit my purposes quite well."

My uncle nodded.

"How many of these do you have?"

Uncle Henry tipped his chin at me and I withdrew three more brass locks from the tool bag and laid them on the table.

"Just these, sir," my uncle said. "Plus some earlier prototypes back at the lock shop."

Using his lock pick, Houdini manipulated each of the other locks as easily as he had the first. "How much?" he asked.

"How much what, sir?"

"How much do you want for these locks?"

My uncle's eyes widened. "I don't know. I designed them for the Joy Steamship Line, a client of mine, and I haven't thought about—"

Houdini lifted a finger to Hewitt, who approached the table and gave the magician a leather wallet. Houdini withdrew five twenty-dollar bills. "Would this be sufficient?"

My uncle held the money, his mouth agape. "You're giving me one hundred dollars for four padlocks?"

Houdini laughed. "If that's acceptable to you. I would like to use them in my performance today."

"Today, sir?" I asked from behind my uncle's chair.

"This afternoon I'm to perform the Great Shackled Water Escape," Houdini said in a deep, booming voice. "I'll be bound with a full set of locks and chains and then dropped to the bottom of the Charles River, where I will free myself and swim to a waiting rowboat." He accompanied his words with a sweeping arm gesture.

"I haven't heard about this show," I said. If I had, I certainly would have planned to attend rather than just being in town by accident.

Mr. Houdini smiled. "I'm afraid it's all very last minute. We were supposed to be performing outdoors in Chicago this weekend, but they're predicting bad thunderstorms there for the next three days, so we changed our venue to Boston. I've hired extra people to hand out pamphlets up and down the Charles. For this type of show, I generally hope for a crowd of over five thousand."

"That's a lot of people, sir." I imagined how thrilling it would be to perform before such a large group.

"Let's hope we can find that many to attend. The mayor has personally promised me that he will invite as many local dignitaries as he can round up on such short notice." The magician paused. "Do we have a deal?" he asked pointing toward the money my uncle still held in his hand.

Uncle Henry recovered his customary poise. "Yes, sir. We have a deal."

"Good." Houdini stood. "I hope you both will stay and watch my Great Shackled Water Escape this afternoon. And then, afterward, the hotel is hosting a reception in my honor. I would be honored if you would attend and let me know what you thought of my show."

"Thank you very much!" I said.

My uncle glared at me.

"Splendid." Houdini summoned his assistant again, who handed us invitations to the hotel's reception.

A very pretty woman—tiny, with a delicate, pale face—entered the room, wearing a yellow dress and walking like a ballerina. We all stood as she approached and kissed Houdini on the cheek. "I'm sorry to interrupt you, dear, but a group of local politicians is waiting to meet you in the hotel lobby."

"What would I do without you to keep me on schedule?" he said, his features softening. He turned to my uncle and me. "May I present my wife, Mrs. Houdini?"

We each bowed as Houdini introduced us to her.

Then he asked us, "So, I will see you later?"

"It would be our pleasure," Uncle Henry replied stiffly.

"And don't forget, young man," Houdini said to me, "I still have that business matter that I wish to discuss with you."

My breath caught in my throat. "Yes, sir," I whispered.

"Will you be accompanying me to the lobby?" Houdini asked his wife.

"No, dear. I'm about to have a dress fitting."

"Ah, that's right. Then let me escort you back to your room." He held out an elbow to his wife and together they strode away.

As soon as the door closed behind them, my uncle scowled at me. "Why did you accept his invitation to the magic show?"

"We couldn't pass up the chance to see the Great Harry Houdini perform live!"

He frowned and shook his head. "I certainly hope no one sees us there."

I laughed. "I wish everyone I know could see me! Nobody's going to believe me when I tell them I saw Houdini perform live! And he said he wanted to talk to me about some sort of business afterward. What do you think that's about?"

Uncle Henry sniffed. "I'm sure I have no idea. He probably needs some locks cleaned or something trivial like that." He looked at the invitation. "The show's at two. I suppose we should go and find some place to eat lunch first." He pointed to the length of chain on the floor.

I packed up the tool bag thinking that this was—without a doubt—the best day of my life.

Chapter 6: Dressmaker

Sadie Golub

I stood in the center of the bedroom of the Parker House Presidential Suite, waiting for Mrs. Houdini, not sure if I should sit or remain standing since Hewitt had assured me that she'd join me in just a moment. This room was even more ornately decorated than the sitting room had been. Here, everything was either cream-colored, like the drapes, bedspread, and upholstery, or gilded, like the picture frames, lamps, and furniture. I noticed an unusual spicy scent that mixed with the floral aroma of expensive perfume. Even in Bessie's wedding suit, I felt common and out of place and wished I were back, safe, in our apartment.

A beautifully dressed woman floated into the room, wearing a pale yellow silk dress with smocking that had been expertly sewn. She certainly looked as if she belonged at the Parker House. I dropped into a low curtsey.

Mrs. Houdini, who was thin and small, with light brown hair and very delicate features, smiled pleasantly as she sank onto a settee. "You are the seamstress?"

"Yes, madam. Sadie Golub."

"Miss Golub, thank you for coming."

"Mr. Holmes say you have sewing for me to do."

"Where are you from, Miss Golub?" she asked, one eyebrow arched. "Do I detect a Russian accent?"

"I come from Raden." Once again, I was embarrassed that my accent was so obvious. I silently vowed to redouble my efforts to improve my speech.

"Then you are Jewish?" Mrs. Houdini asked.

"Yes, madam."

"Did you know that my husband is from Budapest, Hungary, and that he is also Jewish?"

"My brother told me this. He proud of Mr. Houdini being famous Jew."

She nodded. "Although it's been a trial at times." She walked gracefully to a large steamer trunk that was opened at the foot of the large four-poster bed and withdrew a beautiful, dark green silk gown. "The hotel is having a reception for my husband after his performance today. I had planned to wear this gown, but when I tried it on this morning, I found that I have lost some weight since it was made and it no longer fits me properly. Do you think you can alter it in time?"

I examined the construction of the dress. "Yes, I do this. You will please put it on now and I pin it?" I spoke my words slowly and was relieved that she seemed to understand me.

"Certainly," she said and left the room.

I opened my sewing kit and waited, imagining what it would feel like to be wealthy enough to stay in a place like the Parker House.

Returning, the magician's wife looked even more beautiful in the dark green dress, which accentuated her pale skin and light brown hair. She stood on a small footstool while I pinned the bodice of the dress, glad for the opportunity to do something familiar.

Mrs. Houdini said, "That linen traveling dress you are wearing is lovely. Where did you buy it?"

I looked down at Bessie's jacket and skirt. "I make it."

"Well, then, you should be calling yourself a dressmaker, not a seamstress."

I shook my head, not understanding the distinction between the English words.

"A seamstress is someone who is paid to sew clothing. A dressmaker is someone who designs the garments and then creates them. Before I met Mr. Houdini, I used to be a seamstress. But judging by that outfit you are wearing, Miss Golub, you are definitely a talented dressmaker."

I blushed at her compliment. "Thank you." I finished pinning the gown and stood up. "You take dress off now."

Mrs. Houdini glided out of the room and returned wearing the yellow silk gown again.

I took the green one from her and walked toward the door.

"Can't you sew it here?" she asked.

I stopped. "I thought I not bother you."

She smiled. "It's no bother. Actually, I'd love to watch you work, if you don't mind."

I returned to the footstool, turned the garment inside out, and began to stitch quickly. The alteration she required was actually quite simple, so I had no qualms about performing it in front of someone—even someone as important as Mrs. Houdini—as long as she didn't expect me to talk.

She settled herself comfortably on the blue settee. "How did you come to be a dressmaker?"

I frantically searched my brain for the correct English words. "My mother and her mother and her mother sewed for people in our village in Russia and they taught me." I stitched as I spoke, the routine of the action calming me somewhat. "When I come to Boston last year, I go to shop near our apartment and say to owner, 'I can sew. You hire me?' He gave me…test?"

"A trial?"

"Yes. He like my work. Now I sew for him."

She sipped water from a crystal glass and watched me intently.

After a few more minutes, I turned the gown right-side-out. "You try on?"

She changed her clothes once again and then studied herself in a gilded, full-length mirror. "You did an exceptional job, Miss Golub. I can't even tell where you took it in."

"Thank you," I said with pride. Maybe starting my own sewing business wasn't such a far-fetched idea, after all. I seemed to have done well enough for Mrs. Houdini. I gathered up my sewing supplies and re-stowed them in my kit.

She tapped a finger on her upper lip. "Miss Golub, would you be able to make me a traveling suit like the one you are wearing?"

I nodded slowly, trying to hide my excitement. This was exactly what I'd been hoping for. "I could do that."

"Then I would like to order four of them in different colors."

"Four!" I gasped.

"Yes. If it would be convenient, you could stop by this evening, after the reception, and collect my measurements. I will give you a deposit at that time, too. I'm sorry to have to ask you to return tonight, but unfortunately I must leave for my husband's show in a few minutes."

I remained on the footstool, my sewing kit in my lap, my mind racing. Could I sew four dresses for Mrs. Houdini? With all of the work I had to do for Mr. Miller? If I only slept for a few hours each night and I didn't go out for walks…

She apparently noticed my hesitation. "Unless you would rather not?"

"No! I mean, yes! I sew dresses for you." Somehow, I would have to figure out a way to get all of my work completed on time.

"Excellent." She smiled. "Then we'll have a fitting here this evening. Seven o'clock?"

"Yes, madam." Maybe this could be the start of my own business. I was afraid to let myself dream such big dreams.

"Excellent." Mrs. Houdini guided me to the door, her dress rustling as she walked. "It was very nice to meet you, Miss Golub. I'll see you this evening." She opened the door, but then paused. "Please, wait a minute." She walked back into the bedroom.

I clutched my sewing kit to my stomach. Had she changed her mind about the traveling suits already?

She returned within a minute and handed me an embossed cream-colored envelope. "It's an invitation to the reception at this hotel this afternoon. There will be other women attending who may want you to design clothing for them, too."

"Oh, I not go!"

Her eyes opened wide.

Oh dear! Now I'd insulted her. What should I do? "Thank you for inviting me," I said. "But my English is so bad."

"Your English is just fine, Miss Golub, but if you don't want to go…"

I took the invitation and curtsied. "I be there." My stomach felt as if I was inside the elevator again.

She smiled. "I would suggest you wear a gown that you've made yourself, as advertisement of your skill." She nodded to me and reentered the bedroom, closing the door behind her.

I hurried through the empty sitting room, disappointed to see that Millard Franklin was gone. He'd been handsome and nice, but it was probably just as well that he was no longer there. I doubted that Millard was Jewish so Solomon would never approve of him courting me. Speaking of Solomon...I walked down the eight flights of service stairs to the kitchen, in search of my brother.

Rounding a corner, I found him, his clothing splattered with olive green paint, a white canvas cap poised at a jaunty angle on his dark hair.

"Are you finished with Mrs. Houdini?" he asked.

I nodded. "But, I have problem."

"What is it?" His heavy, black eyebrows drew together.

I explained about my meeting with Mrs. Houdini and her subsequent invitation to the reception. I concluded by asking, "How I go to fancy party? What I wear?" I pointed to Bessie's suit. "This?"

He smiled and nodded toward a rack of clothing in a small room behind me. I knew immediately why. About six months ago, Mr. Miller had been hired to provide a new gown for the hotel's Guest Closet, a repository of clothing available for guests to borrow for formal occasions. It contained gowns and suits of many different styles and sizes. Mr. Miller had passed on the task of sewing a new dress to me. I had spent two weeks designing and sewing a hand-beaded pink gown, using myself as the model. I still remembered admiring the gown on me, wishing I had somewhere to wear such a beautiful dress.

I shook my head. "I not want to go." How would I possibly talk to anyone there? All the noise. All the high-class people. And then me—plain little Sadie Golub? I'd be such a *lib hobn a fish aroys hanoe vasser*—a fish out of water.

Solomon pulled the pink gown out of the closet and handed it to me. "There will be many men at that party. Maybe you will meet your future husband." He flashed me his stupid big-brother smile.

Future husband, no, but perhaps Millard Franklin would be there. He'd been very nice to talk to this morning. And besides...I wouldn't have to stay at the party very long. Just long enough to say hello to Millard and let Mrs. Houdini see me. It might be fun to dress up in the gown, too, like a princess at a royal ball. I'd probably never have such a chance again. Of course, if I was too uncomfortable, I could just leave.

I took the gown from Solomon. "I will go."

"Good girl!" He lightly patted my back and then pulled his cap lower on his brow. "Now, can you can find your way home? I need to paint."

I raised my chin an inch. "Of course. But first I ask Mr. Holmes for the money for sewing Mrs. Houdini's dress." I placed the pink gown in a garment bag and then followed my brother out of the room, already contemplating my hairstyle for the reception.

Chapter 7: The Hero of the *Tremont*

George McVay

As our train clacked northward from Providence, I stared at the bright fall foliage flashing by and considered my career with the Joy Steamship Line. After working for the Bangor/Boston Line for three years, I'd been with the Joy Line for four and had already managed to work my way up from steward to pilot and now, at only twenty-six years old, I was the youngest captain ever for a major East Coast steamship line. This final promotion, which had occurred two years ago, was due, in part to a misunderstanding, but I'd been astute enough to take full advantage of it.

*   *   *

Before daybreak on Sunday, February 7, 1904, I'd stood in the frosty pilothouse of the *SS Tremont* as a New York Harbor tugboat pushed us into our berth near the Manhattan Bridge. From my vantage point at the top of the steamship, I watched as our passengers, still sleepy from their overnight trip from Providence, shuffled down the gangplank, bundled in their winter coats, carrying parcels and bags. Much of the *Tremont*'s cargo, including two circus lions and a Great Dane, remained on board, to be removed when the dockworkers reported for their regular shift on Monday morning; the owners of the Joy Line were far too frugal to pay overtime for the cargo to be unloaded on a Sunday.

That afternoon, when Captain Olweiler had left the ship, he'd placed me, his first pilot, in charge. At the age of twenty-three, I was responsible for an entire steamship for the first time in my life. I paced the hurricane deck in my officer's uniform, debating what I should do with my first command.

I really wished that Edith could see me. We'd been married for two years and were expecting our first child in a few months. My sole goal in life had become to provide Edith with a life as comfortable as the one she'd enjoyed with her family in Maine, which was why I planned to quickly work my way up to captain.

"You there." I pointed to a crewmember lounging against a covered lifeboat, smoking a hand-rolled cigarette. "What are you supposed to be doing?"

The man stood and saluted my uniform. "Nothing, sir. I mean, I'm off duty at present."

"Oh. Carry on then." Red-faced, I hurried away and quickly descended the ship's ladder to the galley, where the ship's cook saluted me in his stained apron.

"Hello, Mr. McVay," he said. "Did Captain Olweiler put you in charge while he's out on the town?"

I returned Cookie's salute. "Yes, and I wanted to speak to you about something."

"What was that, sir?" He went back to scraping the ship's grill with a metal spatula.

"What do you usually serve for breakfast Monday morning?"

"I just put out some rolls and coffee." He slid a glob of grease into a large tin can.

My stomach, always queasy aboard ship, contracted at the sight of the congealed fat; I was glad I'd eaten at a dockside restaurant hours earlier. "Tomorrow morning I want you to cook up a big spread for everyone. With this cold weather, I think a good hot breakfast would really hit the spot." And—more importantly—it might help increase my popularity with the men.

The cook put down the spatula and wiped his hands on his grimy apron. "Unfortunately, I won't be here, sir. The captain gave me shore leave, and I won't be back on board until we sail tomorrow night."

"Who will be doing the cooking?"

"Herbert Jones, sir, but he's not much of a cook."

"Surely he could prepare a bit of breakfast for the crew." I heard the irritation in my voice.

"I don't know, sir." Cookie frowned. "He's rarely done anything more than boil water for coffee. This stove can be tricky, if you're not used to it."

Now I really was getting mad. "I would think that even Jones could handle making oatmeal, toast, and eggs."

"Aye, aye, sir. I'll let him know." Cookie saluted me again, still looking skeptical.

I climbed back up the ship's ladder to the deck, feeling frustrated. How could I make the crew respect me more? If I was going to become a captain, I *had* to find a way.

*   *   *

In the pre-dawn hours of Monday, February 8, 1904, I awoke to the terrible smell of fire. I shoved on my uniform over my pajamas, jammed my bare feet into shoes, and rushed into a corridor already filling with acrid gray smoke that made my eyes water and my throat burn. Practically crawling on my hands and knees toward the pilothouse, I spied a steward hurrying aft.

"You, there. Williams. What's going on?"

The man stopped, his eyes wide. "A fire, sir!"

"That's obvious. Where?"

"It started in the galley, sir, but it's spreading. And we can't find the captain."

The fire had started in the galley? I groaned. "The captain went ashore. I'm in charge. Take me to the fire."

Crouched over, we hurried to mid-ship, the smoke growing thicker and blacker with every step. Approaching the stairs, I heard the screams of frightened animals coming from the cargo hold.

Three men rushed past, knocking Williams and me back into the corridor wall.

"Sorry, Mr. McVay!" one man said, touching the brim of his hat with a blackened hand. His face and uniform were likewise coated with sooty grime. "But you don't want to be going down there, sir."

"Why not?" I asked. "What's the status of the fire? Is it almost out?"

"Out? No, sir. The whole lower deck is on fire now. There ain't nothing we can do. Mr. Orlav just sent me to radio the Port Authority for some fireboats."

"Fireboats? Is it really that bad?" Panic and heavy smoke threw me into a coughing fit.

"Yes, sir. I've got to go make that call." The man touched his hat again and hurried down the corridor.

Five more soot-covered men charged up the stairs, including the quartermaster.

"Mr. Orlav, a status report please," I said, trying my best to sound captainly.

He was bent over, coughing. When he caught his breath, he said, "If you're in charge, Mr. McVay, you'd better issue an abandon ship order, sir."

"Abandon ship? Surely it's not that bad."

"Go see for yourself, if you want to, sir. But you can take my word for it. This ship's a goner."

"What about the cargo?" I no longer heard the cries of the circus animals.

"All burnt up, sir. Those bags of grain we were carrying went up in a flash a few minutes ago and lit up everything else in the hold, too."

The smoke roiled up from below, and I saw the light of flames approaching the bottom of the stairs. The deck beneath our feet groaned.

Orlav grabbed my arm. "Mr. McVay, it's time to get everybody off this ship. Now." He led me down the corridor, following the other men to the stairs and then up to the hurricane deck. At the quartermaster's suggestion, we pounded on each cabin door as we passed. By the time we all stood on the quay, two New York City Harbor fireboats had arrived and were pouring water on the ship, now fully engulfed in flames.

An hour later, the fire was extinguished, Assistant Cook Herbert Jones was found dead, and the *Tremont* and all its cargo— including the three dead circus animals—were at the bottom of the harbor. Thus ended my first ship's command.

The next morning, I boarded a northbound steamer, where I hid in my cabin for the entire trip back to Rhode Island. When I disembarked in Providence that afternoon, I saw Mr. Dunbaugh, one of the owners of the Joy

Steamship Line, waiting at the pier. I expected him to fire me on the spot.

Instead, he thumped my back. "Here's our man of the hour! First Pilot George McVay."

Flashbulbs popped as newspaper reporters snapped photographs of the dapper-looking owner shaking my still-sooty hand.

"Excuse me, sir?" I said.

Mr. Dunbaugh handed me a folded copy of *The New York Times*. "You're a hero, Mr. McVay. Or, should I say, Captain McVay?" He chuckled. "I'm sure you'll be getting another promotion very soon." He thumped me on the back again. "And why not? You deserve it!"

I whipped open the *Times* and scanned the headlines. A reporter had declared me to be the hero of the *Tremont*, supposedly risking my life by repeatedly returning to the burning ship to lead passengers safely ashore. But that didn't make any sense! The ship had been docked at the time of the fire. No passengers were aboard. Jones had died and the whole thing was my fault; if I hadn't insisted upon a hot breakfast, the whole incident never would have happened.

But I was smart enough to say nothing. Instead, I smiled for the photographers and repeatedly shook my boss's hand.

Just as Mr. Dunbaugh had predicted, a few months later, right after the birth of our daughter Ruth, I was promoted to captain of a steamship, the *Larchmont*. I was proud of this accomplishment and viewed it as a stepping stone to reach my desired post: captain of a larger, more luxurious steamship for one of the more prestigious lines. If I accomplished this ultimate goal, I felt sure that people like my father-in-law, a steamboat captain himself, would be proud of me and I'd be able to provide Edith and our family with a good life.

In the months and years following the fire, I was able to gain a healthier perspective on the incident. I realized that it hadn't been my fault after all. As the officer in charge of the *Tremont*, I'd been well within my rights to request a special meal for the crew. The fire had been caused solely by Jones, an inept fool incapable of making a simple meal. And, as the reporter had written, I *had* knocked on doors on my way out of the ship, which may indeed have saved the lives of a few crew members. All things considered, the newspaper article hadn't been such a gross exaggeration after all; I truly was a hero.

*   *   *

As our train approached Boston's South Station, I studied Edith's regal profile as she sat beside me, reading a book. I knew that thus far I had adequately provided for her and our children, but I planned to do even better in the future. If I maximized my opportunities—such as the reception we were about to attend—I, George McVay, was going to go places. People just better stay out of my way.

Chapter 8: More Unwelcome News

Anna Jensen

I didn't speak to Louise during our brief ride to Evelyn's, my favorite Boston eatery. Even though they didn't serve any Swedish dishes, I still appreciated the way the place always smelled of fresh-baked bread and the wait staff treated me with the deference I deserved. (Mrs. Beatty could learn a thing or two from the personnel at Evelyn's.)

Nor did I say anything to Louise while we gave the maître de our coats and were seated at our usual table. A quartet of white-clad musicians played Bach nearby, while our young waiter gawked at Louise, who really was quite beautiful.

But as soon as he collected our menus and left the table, I was very direct with my daughter. "Mrs. Beatty, she says you've come back to the boarding house late, unchaperoned, many times. *Ja?*"

Louise studied her silver teaspoon.

"Do you hear me, *min kära?*" I pressed my fingers to my temples, trying to stave off a migraine.

Louise tapped the spoon against her butter knife.

"Harriette Louise Jensen, you put down that silverware and answer me. *Den som talar val ljuger val.*"

Louise replaced her spoon on the table. "Honestly, *Mamma*. You and your silly Swedish sayings. 'The one who speaks well, sleeps well?' What does that even mean?"

"It means you should tell me the truth. You have been out past curfew. *Ja?*"

"There's really no reason for you to be upset." Her smile displayed a dimple in each cheek.

"Does Mrs. Beatty tell the truth?"

The musicians now played a monotonous Beethoven sonata.

"I've been out past curfew, that part is true. But I haven't been unescorted; I've been with someone." She wound her hair around her finger, refusing to look at me.

"Who?" My stomach gurgled and churned, reminding me of the nine months of morning sickness I'd endured before her arrival eighteen years ago.

"He's actually someone you know."

My queasy feeling intensified.

Louise flicked her hair back over her shoulder. "If you must know, I've been spending time with Mr. DeThestrup."

"Our greenhouse manager?"

She nodded.

I worked to keep my expression neutral. Hans DeThestrup was the laborer from the south side of Providence whom Louise had been mooning over this past spring. When John and I had discovered they were keeping company, we'd investigated him, had found him to be entirely unacceptable for our daughter, and then forbade her to see him socially. She'd made our lives unbearable for several weeks in April and May, slamming doors and pouting, but we'd thought she'd ended the relationship, as we'd requested. Apparently, we'd been wrong. "You know your father and I do not approve of that boy."

"He's not a boy, *Mamma*. He's a man. And I truly care for him."

That wasn't defiance I saw in her expression. It was something more...like sincerity. This relationship had progressed much further than I'd feared. "You must learn to care for someone else, someone more *lämplig*—more appropriate."

Louise leaned forward in her chair, placed her elbows on the table, and crossed her arms. "And why isn't Hans 'appropriate' for me, *Mamma?* Because he's not wealthy? *Pappa* wasn't rich when you met him and yet you loved him."

"That was different, *min kära*. Your *pappa* had plans for our future."

"Hans has plans, too," Louise said. She sounded so sure of him.

"Really? What?"

She sat up straight. "He's saving to buy his own home. And then, in a few years, he plans to buy a greenhouse and start his own company."

I tried hard not to sound condescending. "You plan to live in a tiny house with this man? This man who *might* own a small business someday? *Ja?* He might never be able to buy you nice things or take you to nice places."

"That's not important to me."

"Because you have those things now. *Ja?* Remember, *man saknar inte kon förrän båset* är *tomt*—you don't miss the cow until the stall is empty."

Louise frowned, small wrinkles appearing at the corners of her mouth, and then smiled at the handsome waiter as he delivered our salads.

After he left the table, I reached across and took her hand. "Your father and I, we have worked hard so that you may live *ett got liv*—a good life. Your clothes come from Paris and you went to the best boarding schools in New England. You have many advantages. *Ja?* Use those advantages to find a good man, one who will see you as you are: a wonderful young woman."

"Hans does see me that way." Louise tugged on her gold necklace, pulling it from inside her dress collar to reveal a gold ring suspended on it. "I know that because we were married in July."

"*Ursäkta mig?*" I gasped.

"We were planning on telling you and *Pappa* after I graduate in December."

The string quartet paused between pieces. A woman on the other side of the restaurant tittered at her dining companion. One of the waiters coughed as he cleared a table. A horse and cart clattered by outside on the cobblestone street. But at our table, the air had stopped moving; it had solidified into something noxious and unbreathable.

Louise had been married for two months? To Hans DeThestrup? I stared at the gold wedding band swinging on the gold chain, back and forth in front of my eyes like a hypnotist's watch. My stomach felt as if it was on fire, threatening to burn through my skin and clothing. I took another sip of water but it did little to alleviate my pain. "How? Where?" I whispered.

"A small ceremony at the Providence City Hall just before I returned to school. Ralph and Edwina were our witnesses. The whole process was really quite simple: a justice of the peace, our best friends, a Bible, and in fifteen minutes I was Hans's wife."

Fifteen minutes to ruin all that John and I had planned for her entire future.

The waiter cleared our untouched salads and delivered our entrees.

I pushed my meal away, the smell of the fish upsetting my already agitated stomach. "You are our only child. *Pappa* and I have *stora planer*—big plans for you."

"Now those 'big plans' will have to include Hans." She spoke as if I had no choice but to accept her decision. Me, her mother, who'd been deciding things for her since the day she was born.

"No," I said firmly.

Louise laid her fork on the edge of her plate, her eyes boring into me. "What do you mean 'no'?"

I leaned forward and whispered, "You and Hans were married in July but you've been at school ever since. You've never lived together as man and wife. *Ja?*" I rapped my knuckles on the tablecloth. "We will have your marriage dismissed—annulled."

"No, *Mamma*." She bunched up her linen napkin and placed it on the table.

"*Pappa* and I, we will pay off some official in the records department—"

"No, you don't understand." Louise slid her chair back. "We can't have the marriage annulled."

"Yes, *min kära*." I waved away her objection with one hand. "It will be quite simple."

Louise's silk gown rustled as she stood. "*Mamma*, I'm pregnant. Hans and I are expecting a baby in April."

Chapter 9: The Great Shackled Water Escape

Millard Franklin

Uncle Henry and I wove our way through the crowd gathering near the Charles River. The afternoon sun shone brightly from the pale blue sky, but the air remained chilly. At half past one, the banks of the river already teemed with bundled spectators anxious to witness Houdini's two o'clock show. I hoped that Uncle Henry and I could still find a good vantage point from which to see the great magician. I wanted to study his every move.

When we finally arrived at the river's edge, I was amazed at the wide mix of people gathered there. Young boys in tattered clothing stood next to gentlemen in top hats, girls in puffy petticoats, and ladies carrying lacy parasols to keep the sun off their pale faces. There were laborers and businessmen, flower girls and store clerks, all waiting for the magic show to begin. On the stage that still smelled of freshly cut wood, two dozen well-dressed men and women were seated comfortably in upholstered chairs. I especially noticed two very pretty women, one older and one younger, dressed in expensive-looking gowns, sitting in the front row, frowning and staring straight ahead as if they didn't want to be there. How could anyone not want to have a front-row seat to see the Great One?

Ten minutes before show time, Houdini's giant assistant Hewitt arrived in one of the hotel's box carriages. Hopping out, he stood at the base of the stage, scanning the audience while buttoning the brass buttons of his blue blazer against the chilling breeze that blew off the river. When he saw Uncle Henry and me, he pushed through the crowd toward us. "Hello, Mr. Franklin and Mr. Franklin," he said, nodding. "Mr. Houdini asked me to invite you to sit on the platform with the other dignitaries."

"Up on the stage?" my uncle asked incredulously.

"Yes, sir. As thanks for providing him with dependable locks for the show this afternoon."

Uncle Henry lifted his chin high. In a louder voice than was necessary, he said, "If Mr. Houdini wants us to sit on the stage…"

Hewitt looked at me and winked.

I smiled. "Thank you, Mr. Hewitt."

"It's just plain Hewitt. And you're welcome." He waved his arm in a theatrical gesture that reminded me of his boss. "This way, if you please."

We followed him and took our seats in the second row on the stage just as another shiny black hotel carriage arrived, pulled by a pair of massive black stallions.

"Enjoy the show," Hewitt said and hurried away.

Houdini stepped from the carriage and strode onto the stage as the audience erupted in thunderous applause. The magician was flanked on one side by Boston's Mayor, John F. Fitzgerald, looking natty in a pinstripe suit, and on the other side by Mrs. Houdini, now dressed beautifully in a fur-lined cape and os-trich-feathered hat. Houdini himself wore a plush black robe adorned with gold stars and reminded me of a boxer entering the ring for a championship bout.

What a life he must have, wearing fancy costumes and cre-ating magical illusions to amaze thousands of fans! I knew I would be forever grateful to Houdini for inviting us to this show so I could witness first-hand what it was like to be a top-notch magician, just as I knew that one day I, Millard Henry Franklin, would be the one up on stage thrilling a huge crowd.

Mayor Fitzgerald stepped to the front of the stage. With his short stature, red-brown hair, and impish expression, I thought he looked like a leprechaun. Honey Fitz, as he was called in the newspapers, raised his hands and the crowd fell silent. "Ladies and gentlemen of Boston," he began in a loud, clear voice. "Yes-terday I received a telegram from Mr. Jonathan Whimbley, an entertainment agent. In this telegram, Mr. Whimbley proposed the most outrageous piece of showmanship I've ever heard de-scribed. It seems he represents a man who wanted to come to our fair city today to be locked in chains and then thrown into the Charles River!"

The spectators laughed.

"My first thought was that Mr. Whimbley was perpetrating some elaborate joke. After all, no one willingly jumps into a Boston river in September, and certainly no one who is wrapped in chains."

Again, the crowd chuckled.

"Mr. Whimbley's telegram claimed that the gentleman he represents is the *finest* magician and escape artist in the world, and that this man has successfully executed similar feats in other cities, such as New York and London. Of course, I became even more skeptical. Who was this man and what gave him the right to call himself the world's premiere magician? But then the last line of the telegram identified the performer by name. Once I read it, I contacted Mr. Whimbley immediately and agreed to this show. After all, don't we want this great man to say that he's accomplished this amazing feat in New York, London, *and Boston*, the finest city in the world?" The crowd erupted into its wildest round of cheering so far.

Honey Fitz continued, "And this man is not performing only once during his visit to our fair city. Not at all. In addition to his great escape planned at this venue today, he will also appear in two shows at Symphony Hall tomorrow, one at two o'clock and another at eight, where he will perform even more of his amazing feats. Tickets are still available for these shows at the concession stand you see to my left." He waved one arm toward a table where several men were already doing a brisk business selling tickets. "And so, ladies and gentlemen of Boston, it gives me great pleasure to present to you, the finest magician who ever lived: The Great Houdini!"

The crowd exploded into thunderous applause as the two men shook hands and the magician replaced the mayor at the podium. Houdini flourished his black cape and stood smiling at the cheering crowd. A full minute elapsed before the audience settled down enough for him to be heard.

"Thank you for that enthusiastic welcome to beautiful Boston, Massachusetts," Houdini said, enunciating each word loudly and clearly.

The spectators cheered.

"I am a magician, not a speechmaker and, as the saying goes, 'actions speak louder than words,' so, without any further ado…" He untied his velvet robe, took it off, and tossed it to Hewitt at the side of the platform. The magician, who was now wearing pale blue bathing trunks embroidered with a large yellow "Y," assumed a "muscle man" pose on the stage. Some people in the crowd booed good-naturedly.

Houdini pretended to be confused. "What's wrong? You don't like my bathing trunks? I thought everyone here would be big fans of Yale University." He referred to the archrival school of Boston's Harvard University.

The crowd laughed and booed louder.

"Oh, then maybe you would prefer these." Mr. Houdini ripped off his light blue trunks to reveal a pair of maroon trunks emblazoned with a huge golden "H."

The crowd went crazy, cheering for their home school and for the magician who wore its colors.

Uncle Henry leaned over to me. "He certainly knows how to rile up the crowd, doesn't he?" Though he'd never admit it, I could tell that my uncle was enjoying himself, too.

I joined with the throng of smiling faces. "He *is* quite the showman." I planned to imitate some of Houdini's phrases and gestures in my own magic shows.

The magician motioned for another man to come up on stage.

When he could be heard again, Mr. Houdini said, "Since my Great Shackled Water Escape wouldn't be much of a feat of magic if I simply unlocked the devices with a key, I've asked Boston's chief of police, Chief Patrick McHenry, to carefully examine me to ensure that I don't have such a key concealed anywhere on my person. Chief McHenry, if you would be so kind."

The policeman carefully searched the magician, peering between his fingers and toes, looking into his mouth, and even thoroughly examining his hair. Finally, he declared, "Mr. Houdini does not have a key or lock pick hidden anywhere on his person."

The magician said, "Thank you, Chief McHenry. And now, please oversee your officers as they bind me with the chain and shackles."

The chief waved to two other police officers, who carried a long length of iron chain, handcuffs, and two of my uncle's marine padlocks to the stage. Directed by their chief, the men carefully wound the chains around Houdini eight times, from his shoulders to his knees. When they were finished, he resembled a chain-shrouded mummy, his arms pinned to his sides.

Seemingly unconcerned by his predicament, the magician smiled. "Of course, I must have a good luck kiss from a beautiful lady."

Mrs. Houdini, her hat's feather bobbing in the wind, gave her husband a long kiss as the audience shouted their delight. Such a public display of affection struck me as being quite out of character for the magician's wife.

The magician said, "All right, gentlemen. Whenever you're ready."

The two police officers grunted as they lifted Houdini, carried him to the edge of the platform, and dropped him toward the murky Charles River. When Houdini splashed into the icy water, the crowd let out a collective gasp and a shiver ran down my spine. As he sank out of sight, dragged down by the weight of the metal chain, I tapped my uncle's elbow. "Get out your watch. I want to see how long he holds his breath." He pulled out his gold pocket watch and flipped open its lid.

Hewitt and three other men in two white wooden rowboats rowed to the middle of the river and floated there.

I focused my attention on the spot in the river where the great magician had disappeared, darting quick glances from there to my uncle's watch. Thirty seconds…sixty seconds…ninety seconds…Something was wrong! He should have surfaced by now. Others in the crowd apparently agreed and called anxiously for the men in the boats to jump in and save Houdini.

Hewitt stood in his rowboat and held up a hand while staring at his own pocket watch. Obviously, Houdini had instructed his assistant to rescue him only after a certain amount of time had elapsed. But how much time? He'd already been in the frigid water for two full minutes. Surely he should have surfaced by now.

My teeth were chattering, partially from the cold and partially from fear. How awful it would be to witness the death of such a fantastic magician!

The other man in Hewitt's rowboat stood and removed his coat. The men in the second boat followed suit, while staring intently at the magician's assistant. At two minutes and fifteen seconds, Hewitt raised his arm high above his head... Just as Houdini's head violently broke the water's surface. He had a triumphant smile on his face, the opened padlocks in his hands, and water streaming from his wavy hair.

The applause and cheers from the crowd—including me—were deafening.

Houdini dropped the shackles into Hewitt's rowboat and then hoisted himself into it, as well. He donned his black robe and waved to the raucous spectators as the men rowed back to shore. Mrs. Houdini gave him a warm hug and then the two of them were whisked away in the carriage, the magician waving through the window to the still-clapping crowd.

I sagged against my uncle's shoulder, exhausted, as if I had been the one performing the death-defying stunt.

*　　　*　　　*

By the time Uncle Henry and I had threaded our way through the crowd and walked back to the Parker House Hotel, the reception for Houdini was in full swing, with a long line of carriages at the curb dropping off guests. I'd never seen so many fancy outfits and glittering diamonds in my life.

As soon as we stepped inside the gold and glass entrance doors, Mr. Holmes rushed up to my uncle. A guest had locked himself out of his room and the hotel's regular locksmith was unavailable. The manager was beside himself. Uncle Henry said he owed this favor to Mr. Holmes and so retrieved our tool kit from behind the hotel's reception desk.

"You find out what Houdini wanted to talk to you about so that we may leave as soon as I'm done," my uncle instructed me and then followed the manager to the elevator.

I looked around the lobby to find that, in the past few hours, the space had been completely transformed. The green and gilt plush furniture I'd seen earlier had been replaced with long, linen-covered tables laden with a variety of gourmet foods: whole salmons smothered in fruit, steaks shaved thin, and chickens roasted until they were shiny and golden. White-clad servers stood at attention behind the buffets and the room was filled with the aromas of sage and butter. A dozen musicians in black dinner jackets played stringed instruments in one corner of the room. Gold bunting was draped from the crystal chandeliers, creating the illusion of floating clouds. Ornate pots of many shapes and sizes filled with unusual plants lined the perimeter of the room, making me feel as if I'd been transported to an exotic island somewhere. Although perhaps a bit grandiose for most occasions, all of this seemed appropriate for the great Harry Houdini.

I stepped behind a large potted palm to the right of the entrance doors to observe the party guests and noticed they had divided themselves into distinct groups. Near the hotel's reception desk, some politicians and their spouses chatted and nibbled on hors d'oeuvres. Mayor Fitzgerald stood with his arm around his beautiful wife. They were talking to the Massachusetts governor, Curtis Guild, and his wife, Charlotte, whom I recognized from the newspapers.

A cluster of flamboyantly dressed couples laughed loudly in the middle of the room. The women wore elaborate gowns and expensive-looking jewelry; some of the men sported capes and carried walking sticks. Performers or artists, I guessed, although I didn't recognize any of them.

My attention was next drawn to a group gathered at the foot of the grand staircase. Judging by the men's uniforms, I'd say they were ships' officers. Their female companions were pretty, although not as eye-catching as those with the politicians and artists. I particularly noticed one very attractive red-haired woman on the arm of a young man in a blue captain's uniform. They were currently chatting with Mr. and Mrs. Houdini. I too wanted to talk to Houdini, about his dip in the Charles and the "business opportunity" he'd mentioned earlier, but figured I shouldn't interrupt him while he was mingling with his guests. Maybe a little later…

A flash of pink caught my eye and I turned to witness the arrival of Sadie Golub, the petite seamstress I'd met in the Houdinis' sitting room that morning. She paused just inside the hotel entry, wearing a sparkling gown and chewing on one of the fingers of her white gloves.

Good! Someone I could talk to until Houdini was available.

I walked up to Sadie and tapped her elbow.

She jumped and dropped her purse.

"I'm sorry, Miss Golub," I stammered. I was so embarrassed. "I didn't mean to frighten you. We met before, in the Presidential Suite." I picked up her purse and handed it back to her.

She laughed nervously. "You Millard Franklin, the locksmith, yes?"

I nodded, surprised that she remembered my name. Up close, I saw just how pretty she was, with her nearly black hair and even darker eyes. And her skin…It looked so smooth; I wanted to reach out and touch her face. Suddenly, I couldn't think of anything intelligent to say.

Sadie twisted her purse in her hands and studied the marble floor.

Say anything! I told myself. "Did Mrs. Houdini invite you to this party?" I blurted out.

She nodded. "She said it be a great op-oppor…"

"Opportunity?"

"Yes, that is word." She shook her head, her cheeks turning pink. "I sorry. My English not good."

"Your English is fine, but where are you from…if you don't mind me asking…again?" I was afraid of embarrassing her, as I had earlier.

But she didn't seem to mind this time. "My family from Russia, a small village called Raden, near Kishinev. I lived there with parents, brother, and two sisters."

"How long have you been here, in the United States?"

A white-clad waiter approached and offered us a tray of clear, bubbling drinks. I nodded and we each took a glass. After a few sips, I decided that it must be champagne, a drink I'd never tasted before. I felt like such a man, dressed in my best suit, attending a party, chatting with a pretty girl, and drinking champagne. At the same time, everything seemed so foreign, like a scene from a book. Actually, this whole day felt like something I'd read about somewhere. So many things were happening to me, things I'd never forget. Glancing at Sadie as she stood stiffly next to me, sipping her champagne, I wondered if today was special for her, too. She didn't seem like the sort of person who would attend parties like this very often, either.

She answered my question. "I live in Boston now a year and a half."

"Why did you leave Russia?" I hoped she didn't think I was being too nosy.

Sadie grimaced. "Life there was hard. We are Jewish, so we not own property, not have businesses, and not have rights. Then, the government started—how do you say—*pogroms*?"

"Raids?" I guessed.

"Yes, raids. Soldiers came to our village and beat Jewish men and arrest them."

"That's terrible!" She'd been through so much already, but yet she seemed so young. I wondered how young.

"My father said, 'My children not live like this.' He gave all our money to my brother Solomon and say, 'You go to America, get job, and send money so your sisters can go there, too.' So Solomon left."

Another waiter appeared with a tray of ruffle-edged crackers topped with some sort of orange meat. We each took one. It tasted salty and fishy and I didn't like it. As I chewed, I nodded at Sadie, encouraging her to continue her story. All the music and the other voices in the room faded into the background as I focused on Sadie and what she was saying.

"For three years, Solomon work here in Boston and send money to Russia. Then last year, my sister Katerina and I come to America, too."

"How did you get here?"

"We took trains from Russia to France and boat to England. Then we took big ship, *Carmania*, across the ocean. In New York, Katerina married Hillel, who came to America with Solomon. After wedding, I come to Boston on train to live with Solomon and Bessie and their baby."

"What about your other sister?" I asked. "Will she be coming to America as well?"

"Solomon and I send money to Russia so Esther can come, next year maybe."

"And your parents? Will they come with Esther?"

She shook her head. "My father say they too old to travel. He say he is happy that children have better lives." She looked out the hotel's glass doors, her eyes suddenly filling with tears.

I felt badly for making her cry and I wanted to distract her, so I asked the first question that popped into my head. "How old are you?"

Her eyes flew open wide. Then she squinted, suspiciously. "I am eighteen. How old are you?"

"Seventeen. Do you mind that I'm younger than you?"

"Why? We are just talking, no?" She looked up at me with her dark eyes and soft lips. She was standing so close to me that I could smell her flower-scented soap. I touched her sleeve with a finger. "That dress is beautiful. Did you make it?"

"Yes, but is not mine." She laughed at my baffled expression. "This morning, I sew gown Mrs. Houdini is wearing, and so she invite me to party. I had no fancy dress to wear so I borrow this one I make for hotel Guest Closet last year."

"Guest Closet?"

"Hotel has room of clothes guests borrow for special occasions. Fancy dresses for ladies, nice suits for men." She pointed to her gown. "This came from there."

"Well, it looks beautiful, and so do you."

Her face pinked again. "Thank you." She sipped her champagne as I swallowed the last of mine. As we deposited the empty glasses on a tray, I noticed her hand shook slightly.

She smiled up at me. Her eyes surveyed my features and then focused on my lips for a long, warm moment.

I wondered if she was starting to have feelings for me, because I already liked her...very much. She was unlike anyone I'd ever met before. So pretty and so smart.

Houdini's redheaded assistant, Hewitt, appeared in front of us, smiling. "Good afternoon."

"Good afternoon," I said, taking a step away from Sadie.

"Mr. and Mrs. Houdini would like to have a word with you both. Would you please follow me?" He strode toward the room's grand staircase as Sadie and I followed him.

Maybe now I'd find out what Houdini had meant when he'd mentioned a "business opportunity." I had to force myself to walk slowly and not rush across the room.

Chapter 10: Shared Confidences

Sadie Golub

As Millard and I followed Hewitt through the crowd, I concentrated on not tripping over the hem of my borrowed gown. Talking to Millard had been easy but the thought of trying to converse with Mr. and Mrs. Houdini unnerved me. When we reached them, they were talking to a young sea captain and his beautiful wife. An attractive older woman and a pretty girl stood close by. The rest of their group was made up of three gray-haired gentlemen wearing nautical uniforms and their female companions.

"Ah, Mr. Franklin," Mr. Houdini said to Millard, smiling. "Where's your uncle?"

"He was called away, sir. Mr. Holmes had a locksmithing emergency."

Turning to the others in the group, Mr. Houdini said, "Everyone, I would like you to meet a fellow magician, Mr. Millard Franklin."

Millard bowed slightly.

A magician? What did he mean? Millard had introduced himself to me as a locksmith.

"Actually," Mr. Houdini continued, "Mr. Franklin was kind enough to show me one of his escape routines this morning and—I must admit—it was well done."

Millard looked as if he would explode with pride as he bowed even deeper.

"But you're just a boy," the young captain said to him, frowning. "Where do you perform?"

"Mostly at children's birthday parties and such," Millard admitted with a wry grin. "I'm a locksmith, by trade and only do magic as a hobby."

"But I hope we'll be able to change that," Mr. Houdini said with a wink.

Millard's eyes flew open and I heard his breath catch in his throat.

What was Mr. Houdini talking about?

Mrs. Houdini stepped forward, her green silk gown glowing in the light of the chandeliers. "Everyone, I'd also like you to meet Miss Sadie Golub, who altered this gown for me this morning. As you can see, she does first-quality work." She smiled at me. "And Miss Golub is a talented dressmaker, too. She's agreed to create four outfits of traveling clothes for me, and I believe she designed and made the gorgeous gown she is currently wearing."

I sank into a low curtsey, hoping to avoid speaking.

Mrs. Houdini said, "Miss Golub and Mr. Franklin, please allow me to introduce you to some of our other guests." She gestured toward the matronly woman. "This is Mrs. John Jensen and her daughter, Miss Louise Jensen, from Providence." I admired the mother's navy blue gown and the daughter's moss green one, both expertly made. These were obviously women of means. I wondered if they might be in need of the services of a seamstress.

Indicating the young captain and his companion, Mrs. Houdini said, "This is Captain and Mrs. George McVay. They are also from Providence. The captain commands a steamship that carries passengers back and forth to New York City." Mrs. McVay's gown was attractive but not as well-fitted as Mrs. Jensen's.

Each time we were introduced to a new couple, Millard shook the man's hand and I curtsied.

"And this is Captain and Mrs. George Stevens from Maine, Mrs. McVay's parents." Mrs. Houdini smiled at a stately looking older couple, both with gray-white hair. "Mr. Stevens has been a steamboat captain on the Bangor-to-Boston Line for decades and has been sharing wonderful stories of some of his adventures with us." Looking beyond the Stevenses, Mrs. Houdini said, "I'm afraid I haven't met these other charming guests, yet."

Mr. Stevens quickly introduced his first and second pilots and their wives. Handshakes, curtsies, and pleasantries were shared by all.

Millard said, "Captain McVay, this morning I saw the steamship *Edgemont* in the Narragansett Bay. Is your ship similar in size?"

I was impressed that Millard was willing to enter into conversation with these distinguished guests. Even if I'd known fluent English, I'm not sure I'd have the *chutzpah* to speak in such a group.

The young captain smiled coldly, his white teeth in stark contrast to his dark mustache. "The *Larchmont* is comparable to the *Edgemont*, very similar in fact. Do you have an interest in steamships, Mr. Franklin?"

"I enjoy watching them and have often thought that traveling by steamship would be grand."

Captain McVay smiled again. "The next time you're at the Port of Providence, stop by the Joy Steamship dock. I'll give you a tour of my ship. We sail at six-thirty every evening, except Sundays."

"Thank you, sir," Millard said. "I'd enjoy that."

"I'll look forward to your visit." He didn't sound very sincere and I wondered if Millard noticed.

Bowing to Mrs. Jensen, the captain said, much more warmly, "And I would be delighted to give a tour of the *Larchmont* to you and your daughter as well, if you ever find yourself in port." Now he sounded like a *macher*—a schemer.

Mrs. Jensen said, "Thank you, Captain," and then turned to me. "Miss Golub, I admire someone who is willing to work hard to get ahead in life. You strike me as such a person. So many young folks these days seem intent on becoming acquainted with the 'right' people and then expect to be offered unearned opportunities." At this last comment, she cast a sideways glance at Captain McVay. Returning her attention to me, she said, "From what I can see of your sewing ability, it's superior. My sister-in-law lives on Tremont Street and is currently searching for a good dressmaker. How could she get in touch with you?"

Two private sewing clients? What a day! I opened my purse and withdrew a slip of paper I'd prepared earlier. "My name and address. Your sister can send note and I come to her house. Yes?"

Mrs. Jensen carefully tucked the paper into her small purse with a nod.

Houdini chuckled. "Gentlemen, may I suggest we leave the ladies to talk about sewing while we go in search of more beverages?" He strode away, quickly followed by the other men in the group.

Millard tagged along with them while glancing back at me.

Without him by my side, I was even more afraid to speak. I suddenly wanted to go home.

The young Miss Jensen stepped forward and beamed a beautiful smile to the group of women. "I'm famished. Would anyone like refreshments from the buffet table?"

"That would be very nice, dear," her mother said. A few of the other women murmured their assent as well.

Looking at me, Miss Jensen asked, "Would you be so kind as to assist me?"

Surprised that someone of her station would talk to me, I nodded and followed her toward the long white tables laden with rich, buttery food.

Halfway across the crowded room, she turned to me and held out her hand. "Hello, I'm Harriette Louise DeThestrup, but please call me Louise. All my friends do."

I shook her hand, confused. "Your surname is…?"

"DeThestrup."

"But Mrs. Houdini, she say…"

"*Mamma* introduced me using my maiden name. You see, she didn't know about my marriage until today. I suppose it will take her some time to get used to the idea."

I was becoming even more confused. "How your mother not know you married?"

"My husband and I were secretly wed at the Providence courthouse last month on my birthday before I came back to school here in Boston. Only our best friends, Edwina and Ralph, knew anything about it. They were our witnesses."

I nodded but still didn't understand at all. In my experience, weddings were big, joyous affairs that lasted for several days and were attended by entire villages. Why would anyone marry in secret with only two friends in attendance?

Louise tugged lightly on my sleeve. "Come, I'm starving." She handed me two china plates, each decorated with a golden *P.* "For the ladies." Taking two plates also, she preceded me down the buffet table. Since I was unacquainted with most of the foods, I copied Louise, collecting a serving of whatever she requested. At the end of the buffet line, Louise summoned two boys in white jackets and handed them our plates. "Please deliver this food to those ladies." She indicated her mother and the others in the group by the stairs. The boys strode off as Louise turned to me. "Now, some food for us." We repeated our food-gathering process, filling only one plate each this time, and then perched on a settee near the fountain. Guests and conversations swirled all around us.

I noticed Louise's plate. "You eat much food," I said and then clapped a gloved hand over my mouth.

Louise laughed, her blue eyes sparkling. "Don't worry. It's true; I do eat a lot." She leaned toward me and whispered, "I'm eating for two."

I frowned and shook my head, not understanding what she meant.

"I'm pregnant. I'm going to have a baby in April." Louise smiled. "Hans and I are so happy."

I didn't know what to say. In Russia, a woman would never speak to someone outside her family about being pregnant. Instead, she'd disguise her condition for as long as possible. When she could no longer hide her growing belly, she'd stay home, not daring to be seen in public in such a condition. But Louise was confiding this most intimate secret to me, a stranger, in the crowded lobby of a hotel. Why?

My expression must have shown what I was thinking because Louise said, "I'm sorry. I probably shouldn't be telling you this. But *Mamma* and I had a terrible discussion at the restaurant this afternoon. She doesn't understand about me and Hans, our marriage, or the baby. Then we went to Houdini's show and came straight here to this reception because *Mamma* promised Uncle Charles we'd come. So, here I am talking to you about my troubles! I hope you don't mind."

I shook my head, astonished that she'd consider me a suitable confidante. We sat in silence for a few moments, nibbling our food. "You have any brothers or sisters?" I asked.

"No. Just a best friend, Edwina, the one who was at my wedding. I've known her my entire life. Her family lives two houses away from mine."

"I had Russian friend, Yuliya. She had no brothers and no sisters, so we were like sisters."

"That's how it is with Edwina and me too. She has two brothers but no sisters, and I am an only child, so we've been together constantly."

"Is Edwina married too?" I asked. "Or does she go to a school like you do?"

"No. Mostly, she just goes to parties. She says she's shopping for a husband."

I took a small bite of some sort of fruit but didn't enjoy its slippery texture. Louise ate with much more gusto and soon emptied her plate. "Finished?" she asked. I nodded and she took our dishes and handed them to another white-coated boy with an easy thank-you smile. Although I felt awkward and out of place at this reception, Louise seemed completely at ease.

She reseated herself on the settee and took my hand. "You are a very easy person to talk to, Sadie. You don't mind if I call you Sadie, do you?"

"No."

"And, of course, you'll call me Louise. I feel like I can tell you anything. But after today we will probably never see each other again. Isn't that sad? You live here in Boston but, when I finish music school next month, Hans and I will probably find a house in Providence, near his place of business."

"Where he work?"

"He's the manager of one of my father's greenhouses. That's how we met, actually. *Pappa* was giving me a tour last year and he introduced me to some of his workers. Hans and I knew immediately that we were meant to be together. Of course, my parents didn't agree. They wanted me to be associated with someone with more social status. Almost like a business merger."

"Your mother and father not like Hans?"

"They strictly forbade me to even see him. But we discovered ways to be together. And now we're married, so my parents can't do anything." Louise chewed her lower lip. She was so pretty, with her pale skin and wavy blonde hair. To me, she looked like the ideal "American girl."

I was suddenly acutely aware of my much darker complexion and was grateful to be wearing long white gloves, hiding my hands and arms. "You love Hans?" I asked.

"Oh, yes!" She sighed. "He is so handsome, kind, and intelligent. And he's thrilled about being a father, too. He wants to call the baby Hans Vigo DeThestrup II." She laughed. "I don't know what he'll do if it's a girl."

As she spoke about her baby and her husband, Louise smiled with her whole face. Here was a woman in love who was willing to oppose her parents to be with her husband. What a strong person! I had a feeling that someday Louise Jensen DeThestrup would be a great lady.

A dark-haired man in a well-tailored tuxedo approached us. "Louise! It's been ages."

She stood and allowed him to kiss her cheek. "Reggie, how have you been?"

"Bored to tears! Father has me 'learning the business' and it's really no fun at all." Gazing at me, he asked, "Who is this lovely creature?"

"Reggie, this is Miss Sadie Golub, a Boston dressmaker. Sadie, this is Mr. Reginald Harrington of the Cambridge Harringtons."

He drew me to my feet and kissed my gloved hand, allowing his lips to linger uncomfortably long. "A dressmaker, huh? How nice. Does that mean we wouldn't have to deal with any of that 'proper society' nonsense?"

I was flattered by his attention but confused by his words and so gave him a lopsided smile while trying to withdraw my hand from his uncomfortably tight grasp.

Louise said, "Mr. Harrington, I'll have you know that Miss Golub is a friend of mine and I expect you to show her the same respect you'd show me." Although she smiled sweetly, I could hear anger in her voice.

Mr. Harrington released my hand and raised his palms. "I certainly meant no affront."

"Of course you didn't. Now, if you'll please excuse us . . ." Louise placed her arm around my waist and drew me away from Mr. Harrington. "I apologize if he offended you," she whispered.

"Is all right."

"And to think that my mother tried to match me up with that buffoon." She rolled her eyes.

We each collected a crystal cup of red punch from a serving table and stood near the musicians. Louise suddenly grinned brightly. "I just had a wonderful idea! I'll be getting bigger pretty soon." She held out a hand in front of her belly. "So, I'll need some new clothes. Do you think you could sew some for me?"

Three private sewing jobs in one day? *Oy!* I nodded rapidly. My own sewing business was starting to seem like a real possibility now.

"Marvelous. Why don't you come by my boarding house tomorrow morning to measure me?"

"Ten o'clock?"

"That would be fine. And it will give us more time to talk."

"Talk?" I didn't imagine we had much to talk about.

Louise smiled. "I saw the way you were looking at Mr. Franklin earlier. We could certainly talk about him. Is he courting you?"

"I not know," I mumbled, embarrassed.

She laughed. "Oh? So this is a new romantic development?"

"We just meet today."

"But he's handsome. Don't you think?"

I shrugged. "I not know if my brother will let me see him."

She frowned. "What does your brother have to do with Mr. Franklin and you?"

"He will pick my husband."

Louise's eyes flew open wide. "Excuse me?"

"In Russia, Papa pick my husband. Here, Solomon pick."

"Oh, my goodness!" She plopped her crystal cup on a waiter's tray with such force, she nearly knocked it from his hands. "You mean you have no say in who will become your husband?"

I was afraid that I'd ruined her good impression of me. "My brother will pick good man. He wants me to have good life."

"But what if you don't love the man Solomon selects?"

"A wife learns to love husband."

"Learns to love...?" She shook her head. "I certainly would never agree to anyone selecting my husband for me."

I placed my punch glass on the corner of a buffet table and tried to deflect her attention. "The music is nice. Yes?"

Louise would not be dissuaded. "Do you think Solomon would allow you to be courted by Mr. Franklin?"

"He has good job, but is not Jewish. I think is okay for husband not to be Jewish, but I not think Solomon agrees."

"Your brother probably wouldn't approve of Hans, either. He's a greenhouse manager. He doesn't make much money and still lives with his family. But I love Hans and he loves me and that's all that matters." She hopped to her feet. "Listen to me prattle on and on! I must be boring you. We should rejoin *Mamma* and the rest of the group." We crossed the crowded room again, arm-in-arm.

Back at the foot of the grand staircase, I smiled and nodded to Mrs. Jensen and the other women, disappointed that Millard and the other men had not returned to the group.

"Mrs. McVay, how many children do you have?" Mrs. Houdini asked the young captain's wife.

"We have two. Ruthie is two and a half and Raymond is one. Do you and Mr. Houdini have any children?"

Mrs. Houdini clutched the small cameo of a girl, pinned at her throat. "No. We haven't yet been blessed, but we continue to be hopeful."

The whirring of the elevator reminded me of my sewing machine and of the work waiting for me at home. I glanced over my shoulder at the gleaming entrance doors.

Louise smiled. "Miss Golub just mentioned to me that she must leave for an appointment."

I nodded, playing along with her charade.

"I'm sure I speak for everyone else here when I say that it was a pleasure meeting you." Louise extended her hand to me and then leaned in and whispered, "Thank you for listening to me!"

I whispered back, "Good luck to you and Hans and the baby," and squeezed her hand.

"Oh, yes!" Louise said. "I almost forgot." She withdrew a calling card from her satin clutch purse and handed it to me. "I'll see you tomorrow at ten o'clock?" I nodded as she explained to the group, "Miss Golub has agreed to make me some clothing, too."

Mrs. Houdini smiled. "But I'll see you first, at our fitting this evening?"

All this sewing work! Was I going to be able to handle all of it? I didn't want to disappoint Mrs. Houdini or Mrs. Jensen or Louise. And then I had my work for Mr. Miller, too.

I curtsied to the women and then forced myself to walk slowly toward the door. Once I was in the service corridor, though, I hurried to the Guest Closet where I changed back into my street clothes and hung the beaded pink gown on a hanger.

I smiled to myself, thinking how glad I was that I had gone to the reception. Three private sewing customers. I'd finally be able to make some money of my own! And I'd very much enjoyed talking to Millard Franklin again. My only regret about the day was that I'd probably never see him again. He really was quite handsome. And kind.

I placed my cool palms against my warm cheeks.

Chapter 11: See and Be Seen

George McVay

By the time our train finally pulled into Boston's South Station that afternoon, Edith and I were too late to see Houdini's magic show, so we went directly to the reception at the Parker House Hotel. I was eager to mingle with the guests there, to see and be seen by some of the wealthiest and most influential men in New England.

An hour after our arrival at the hotel, however, I found myself checking my pocket watch for the fourth time and trying to mask my annoyance. So far, all I'd accomplished was to spend a great deal of time listening to the idle chatter of Edith's parents and other people of little consequence, none of whom could help me achieve my primary objective for the afternoon: meeting Charles Morse, the owner of the International Steamship Company. On several occasions, I'd seen Morse milling about the lobby—easily recognizable with his bushy white beard and mustache—but, so far, I'd been unable to speak with him. And then, to make matters worse, Houdini had just led a group of us men to the hotel bar, on the opposite side of the room from where Morse stood. I feared that the day was going to be a total loss, professionally speaking.

"Sometimes a man must make his own luck," I muttered, clicking my watch case shut. I murmured my excuses to the men and strode back to Edith and the other women. Bowing to them, I boldly addressed Mrs. John Jensen, a handsome woman in her forties, who'd been introduced to me by Mrs. Houdini. "Madam, I was wondering if I could impose upon you to present me to your brother-in-law, Mr. Charles Morse?"

Edith frowned at me as Mrs. Jensen's blonde eyebrows shot up. "Why do you want to meet Charles, Mr. McVay?"

"I believe him to be a man worthy of my admiration."

She seemed to study me intently and then slowly said, "*Ja*. I could introduce you, I suppose."

"Thank you." I pointedly ignored Edith's disapproving look, no doubt a reprimand for my social clumsiness. Too bad. I certainly wasn't about to let this opportunity pass me by. I bowed to her and the other ladies again and followed Mrs. Jensen across the room.

As we approached a large cluster of people in the middle of the lobby, Charles Morse looked up, smiled, and kissed his sister-in-law on both cheeks. "Anna! I'm glad you're here. Perhaps you can convince this chowderhead to sell me the Boston Pilgrims." He wore a very expensive business suit, probably made on Savile Row and worth more than I made in a month.

Mrs. Jensen smiled warmly at him. "*Hej*, Charles. I don't know any Pilgrims from Boston, but your friend probably has a good reason not to sell them to you, *min kära*."

"Brava!" said a slightly portly middle-aged man. "Spoken like a true lady! Please allow me to introduce myself as the chowderhead in question. I'm Charles Taylor, and this is my wife, Georgiana."

"Very nice to meet you, Mr. Taylor," Mrs. Jensen replied. "I am Mr. Morse's sister-in-law, Mrs. John Jensen." She extended her gloved hand for a kiss from him and nodded at his wife.

Bored with their idle chitchat, I loudly cleared my throat.

Mrs. Jensen frowned at me. "Charles, I'd like to introduce you to *Kaptan* George McVay. He commands a steamship for the Joy Line and is quite anxious to make your acquaintance."

Morse shook my hand. "And why did you want to meet me, Captain McVay?"

I was careful to look him directly in the eye, even though he was several inches taller than I was. "For one thing, sir, I wanted to compliment you on your fine steamships."

"Thank you. To which vessels are you referring?"

"The *Kennebec* is one that comes to mind, sir. A smart-looking ship. She must be well over a thousand tons."

"One thousand six hundred tons gross or one thousand one hundred net."

I whistled softly. "That's a good size for a ship on the Maine coastal route; large enough to handle some weather but small enough to still respond well to helm."

Morse nodded.

"And then your *Priscilla* and *Puritan* are simply elegant. The *Priscilla* pulled up alongside my *Larchmont* a few months ago and I was astonished at how large she was."

"Four hundred twenty-five feet, stem to stern," Morse supplied.

"And yet she still has such graceful lines."

"We think so."

Mrs. Jensen said, "*Kaptan* McVay, you sound like a man trying to talk himself into a job." The corners of her mouth pinched downward.

I chuckled. "To be honest, Mr. Morse, I *was* wondering if you might have any positions available for a man with my experience."

"And what sort of experience do you have?" he asked.

"I've been the captain of the *Larchmont* for nearly two years now."

Morse nodded. "That's impressive for someone so young. Are you looking to switch companies?"

I shrugged in deliberate nonchalance. "I'm a young man with a wife and two small children, Mr. Morse. I'm always trying to improve my situation in life."

Anna Jensen asked him pointedly, "*Min kära*, don't you generally promote from within your company?"

I wished the woman would quit her blasted interference and go away.

"True enough," Morse said. "But I do admire ambitious people. McVay, if a captainship opens up, I might consider you."

"Thank you, sir. I'd appreciate that." From my breast pocket, I withdrew a white calling card with plain black printing—simple but dignified—and handed it to Morse.

He glanced at the card and then tucked it inside his jacket.

I pulled out another one and offered it to Mrs. Jensen. "If there's ever anything I can do for you, like that tour of my steamship, please don't hesitate to contact me."

She dropped the card into her small purse without looking at it. I could tell she did not approve of my aggressive behavior. She'd probably had everything handed to her on a silver platter her whole life and had no patience for someone like me who'd been forced to go it on his own.

Morse said, "Captain McVay, let me introduce you to some people."

I nodded to Mrs. Jensen, glad to be leaving her company. As we stepped into the nearby circle of partygoers, I recognized Mrs. Isabella Stewart Gardner standing in its center. I'd seen her photograph in the newspaper a few years ago when she'd opened a new art museum in her Boston home. Mrs. Gardner looked up and smiled as Morse introduced me and then she presented her other companions, who turned out to be three relatively famous art personalities from around the world: American John Singer Sargent, Swede Anders Zorn, and Japanese art historian Okakura Kakuzo. Each man was accompanied by a beautiful woman, none of whom was named. Charles Taylor, previously referred to by Morse as "the chowderhead," was further introduced as the editor of *The Boston Globe* newspaper and owner of the Boston Pilgrims baseball team.

Mrs. Taylor, a corpulent woman of about sixty, smiled at us. "We were just discussing Mrs. Gardner's museum, Fenway Court. Have you ever been there, Captain McVay?"

"I've not yet had that pleasure."

Mrs. Gardner said, "I've just opened a special exhibit of some of Mr. Sargent's portraits. They truly are exquisite."

Mr. Sargent, a large man with a heavy brown beard and mustache, bowed at the waist. His suit looked even more expensive than Morse's and that bothered me. Why should a man who splatters paint on canvases all day be dressed better than me, a hard-working career man?

"Of course," Mrs. Gardner added, "since I am the subject of two of his portraits, I might have a somewhat biased opinion."

Everyone laughed.

Mrs. Gardner said, "If I might make a suggestion, Mr. Sargent…"

"Of course," the artist said.

"I think you should ask that woman to sit for a portrait." She pointed at someone behind me.

Somehow, I knew she was referring to Edith.

"Honestly," Mrs. Gardner said. "Just look at her; she has a milk-and-honey complexion, such gorgeous auburn hair, and an adorable little figure. I would think she'd be a dream to paint. Unless, of course, you're afraid that such a beautiful woman wouldn't be enough of a challenge. I suppose after struggling to make an old bat like me look good—twice, no less—painting that beautiful woman might seem like child's play."

We all laughed again.

"I wonder who she is," Sargent said.

I forced myself to smile. "If you are referring to the woman in the blue and white striped gown, I have the pleasure of identifying her as my wife, Edith."

"Then I must congratulate you, Mr. McVay," Sargent said. "She truly is a beautiful woman." He held out a small white card, elegantly embossed in gold. "If she'd be interested in sitting for a portrait, please have her contact me."

As if I'd ever allow a man like him to ogle my wife for hours on end! But I politely took the calling card from his hand. "Thank you for your compliments, Mr. Sargent. It's always gratifying for a husband to hear that others share his opinion of his wife's beauty."

Mr. Sargent bowed slightly.

Hoping to turn the conversation away from my wife, I asked the Swedish artist, "Mr. Zorn, do you have any pieces exhibited at Fenway Court?"

Mrs. Gardner said, "Mr. Zorn is supposed to be working on several pieces for me so that I may have an exhibition of his work next year. However, he keeps painting portraits for other people—presidents and kings, mostly—and hasn't graced me with a single one of his pieces so far."

"As I've said before," the artist responded with a very strong Swedish accent, "I will have plenty of paintings ready for your show, Madam. And a few sculptures, too." He then launched into painfully detailed descriptions of the various pieces he was currently working on.

I found all of this talk about art to be extremely dull, so I stood next to Zorn, watching his mouth move while unobtrusively tearing Sargent's calling card in half behind my back. I'd achieved my goal of meeting Charles Morse. Now, I just needed to put in sufficient time at this party so that I could leave gracefully. I was still hoping to find an open shop somewhere nearby so that Edith and I could buy gifts for the children.

Chapter 12: Personal Histories

Anna Jensen

I excused myself from the group of people surrounding Charles and wove my way back through the crowd to Louise and the other women, anxious to leave the reception, return home, and talk to John about our daughter. What were we going to do with her? I still couldn't believe she was married to—and pregnant by—Hans DeThestrup. I had never liked that man, not from the moment I'd first met him. And then the things that John and I had found out about him, his reputation and history, had only confirmed my opinion that he was entirely unworthy of Louise.

Captain McVay's beautiful wife smiled at me when I rejoined their circle. She reminded me of Louise: someone who'd been well brought-up—good manners, well educated, well groomed—and yet had married poorly. Even though I'd just met her husband, I found myself utterly despising the man; he was such a gauche social climber, not willing to put in the hard work necessary to obtain a higher position in society.

I returned her smile. "Mrs. McVay, how did you and your husband meet? I was wondering."

"As you know," she said, "my father is a steamboat captain on the Bangor-to-Boston Line and has been for nearly thirty years. About nine years ago, a woman was speaking to my mother after church and happened to mention that her teenage son, George, was seeking employment. Dad had been looking for a new bow watchman and so hired George on a trial basis. Eight months later, my father invited him to join our family for Sunday supper as a reward for the good work he was doing.

"That day, I'd pretended to have a headache so I didn't have to go to church, so I was home alone when I heard Florence, our maid, answer a knock at the door.

"'I'm Geroge McVay,' a squeaky voice said. 'Captain Stevens invited me to join him and his family for supper.' I peeked out the screened door to see a rail-thin boy in a too-big brown suit standing on our porch. I thought he was adorable."

As she was telling her story, Mrs. McVay's face was positively radiant. Here was a woman who clearly loved her husband. I wondered what she could possibly see in him.

She continued her story. "When I told George that my family had not returned from church yet, he started to leave, but I stopped him. Something told me that he was special, someone I should get to know. So we sat on my porch, drank iced tea, and talked for nearly an hour until my family came home. We talked about everything. He asked me what books I liked to read. I inquired about his work aboard my father's steamship. He was curious about what 'the Captain' was like at home. I asked about his family. The time passed so quickly! I found him to be intelligent, funny, and well-read and I thoroughly enjoyed the time we spent together. George joined us for Sunday supper that day, too. By the time he left our home that evening, I had decided I was going to marry him. I was only fifteen and he was only seventeen, but I knew I was in love with him and that no one else would ever suit me better. And it turned out he felt the same way about me, too."

Mrs. McVay finished her story with a look of complete contentment on her face, which oddly made me feel better about Louise. If Mrs. McVay could care so much about her husband, even though they came from such different families and circumstances, maybe Louise might be able to find happiness with Hans.

Mrs. McVay asked, "Mrs. Jensen, how did you meet your husband?"

She, Mrs. Houdini, and all the other women in the group turned toward me, vague smiles upon their faces. Louise looked embarrassed, as if she didn't want me airing our family history in such a public place. I resolved to be brief.

"John and I met in Sweden," I said. "He was the oldest son of a wealthy landowner and I was the youngest daughter of one of their tenant farmers. His family had deemed me *ovardig*—unworthy to be his wife." I looked toward Louise.

She frowned.

"John was supposed to wed the daughter of a neighboring landowner. But he and I were in love, so one night we convinced a local minister to marry us. We wrote two notes: John gave up his claim to his family's fortune and I told my parents I was sorry for abandoning them. Then, with only a small inheritance from John's grandfather, we set out for the New World."

"How brave of you," Mrs. McVay said. "What did you do once you arrived here?"

"We settled in Rhode Island, since its climate was similar to Sweden's. We both knew about farming and raising plants, so we used John's money to purchase three greenhouses and a home on the East Side of Providence. It took us a few years, but eventually our business became quite successful."

"That's wonderful," Mrs. Houdini said. "I always love hearing stories about people succeeding through their own hard work."

The conversation drifted to other subjects.

I smiled and nodded as the women spoke but I wasn't actually listening to them anymore. Instead, I was remembering what life had truly been like for John and me when we'd first arrived in the United States. How, at first, we'd just pretended to be *rika företagsägare*—wealthy business owners.

For the first five years, we didn't invite guests into our home so no one could see the empty rooms or witness our hungry nights without suppers. Every penny we made we reinvested into our business or spent on clothing and carriages, creating the appearance of wealth before the reality actually arrived. Finally, halfway through our sixth year in this country, our business began to flourish. At last, we were able to furnish our home, hire servants, and return to Europe to visit our families and show them how successful we'd become.

At around the same time, we rejoiced at the news that I was expecting our first child. Six weeks later, cramps and bleeding signified the end to that dream. Over the next two years, I became pregnant three more times. Each pregnancy ended in bitter disappointment. Finally, when I discovered I was expecting once again, I took to my bed for eight full months. Every day, I ate my meals, vomited copiously, and then ate again, determined to become a mother. On July 11, 1888, at eight o'clock at night,

Harriette Louise Jensen was born, the only child that John and I would ever have. We declared her to be *en gåva från Gud*—a gift from God.

Louise—that's what we called our daughter from her very first day on Earth—was a bright and happy child, always friendly and willing to help others. John and I were extremely proud of her. She did what was expected of her and never gave us a reason to worry. Which was what made this present situation so impossible for me to understand. Why had she suddenly defied our wishes on this, the biggest decision in her life?

I looked at Louise's beautiful face now and sighed. Maybe I should have told her how terrible life had been for John and me after we left Sweden together. Day after day, night after night, we'd clung to each other, hoping just to survive. I remembered one afternoon during our third year in America when I'd looked out our front window and sobbed when I saw a neighbor walk by with her little brown and black dachshund. John had wrapped his arms around me and asked why I was crying, something I rarely did. I pointed to the street. "I want a puppy," I said, knowing that we couldn't afford to feed ourselves, let alone a pet. Three years later, when our greenhouse business finally flourished, John bought me not one but two dachshund puppies.

What would Louise say if I told her that story now? For eighteen years, she'd been instantly granted her every desire. Looking back, I wondered if that had been a mistake. As *Farfar* Jennings used to say, *idel solsken gör* öken—constant sunshine makes a desert.

And what would happen to Louise now that she was married to Hans? Would John and I have to help support them so they could live the life Louise was used to? Or would Hans insist on them surviving on his paltry income? They wouldn't be as poor as John and I had been when we'd first arrived in America, but nearly so. What would poverty do to Louise's spirit? Would their marriage survive? What about their child?

Maybe she'd be fine, and the baby, too. John and I had eventually flourished despite the odds stacked against us. And, after all, *der äpplet faller inte långt från trädet*—the apple does not fall far from the tree. I closed my eyes and sent up a prayer to God, begging him to help Louise in any way He could.

Chapter 13: A Business Proposition

Millard Franklin

When Houdini invited the men to join him at the bar for a drink, I felt I had to accompany them or be the only man left talking to a group of women. Also, I was still hoping to get a moment to speak to him alone. So I nodded to Sadie and followed the men across the room. At the mahogany and brass bar at the far end of the lobby, they collected their drinks: dark amber liquor in small, short glasses.

Mr. Stevens, another steamboat captain, lifted his glass. "Cheers!"

The men downed their drinks and then smacked their glasses on the bar and received refills from the bartender. I stood to one side, empty-handed, feeling more awkward by the moment. Ten minutes ago, when I'd been talking to Sadie alone, I'd felt like a man. Now I felt like a little boy. Until I noticed that Houdini wasn't drinking either.

He smiled at me. "Mr. Franklin, I would like to know if you have a professional opinion about how I was able to undo the locks during my Great Shackled Water Escape this afternoon."

I stopped breathing.

"Yes, we'd love to hear your ideas, *Mister* Franklin," one of the other men said with a smirk.

Houdini patted my back and announced to the group, "Let's make a contest of it. Each of you tells me how you think I freed myself, and then once everyone has offered his opinion, I'll let you know if anyone has guessed correctly."

They all agreed to the game.

"I think you had a key hidden in the water under the bridge," Captain Stevens said.

"I think you just paid the police to say the locks were unaltered," his first pilot said.

"Or maybe," a third man said, "the chain was cut so that you just had to unhook one of the links to free yourself."

When it came my turn, I felt the group's attention focus on me. I swallowed hard. "Well sir, I noticed that right before you went into the water, Mrs. Houdini gave you a kiss." When I said "kiss," my voice cracked and squeaked. I felt my cheeks burn red.

The other men snickered. Houdini smiled kindly and signaled for me to continue.

I cleared my throat. "When she kissed you, she could have passed you a lock pick that you held in your mouth until you were underwater."

Houdini nodded several times. "Interesting," he said.

The game continued with the rest of the men giving their opinions.

When everyone finished, Houdini smiled. "A good magician never reveals his secrets, so I'm not going to tell you exactly how I managed my escape."

Everyone groaned.

"But," he continued, "what I can tell you is that Mr. Franklin guessed closest to the truth and so he has won the contest."

The other men slapped me on the back, congratulated me, and prompted the bartender to bring me a soda water to celebrate my victory.

I downed my drink wondering how close I'd come to guessing Houdini's method of escape.

A few minutes later, he bowed and said, "If you gentlemen would excuse us for a few moments, I have a matter of some importance that I must discuss privately with Mr. Franklin." He walked toward the elevator, motioning for me to follow him. Hewitt trailed behind us, a silent but very large shadow.

In the elevator, the operator closed the metal doors behind us. Houdini sighed and undid his bowtie as the cab began its slow, clanking ascent. "Mr. Franklin, I hope you don't mind me taking you away from the reception for a few minutes."

"No, sir." Instead, I was flattered and curious.

We arrived at the eighth floor and walked into the plush Presidential Suite. Houdini handed his coat and tie to Hewitt and turned to me. "Mr. Franklin, would you join me in a glass of freshly squeezed orange juice? I have some at this time every day. I find that it helps me maintain my stamina."

"Thank you, sir." It would be something else that I could add to my list of new experiences for the day.

The magician held up two fingers to Hewitt and we sat in the blue and gold armchairs arranged near one of the tall windows. Late afternoon sunshine slanted across the shiny wood floor as Hewitt served the juice. I took a sip and found I liked its sweet, tangy flavor. Houdini downed his in one gulp and set his empty glass on the dark, wooden coffee table. "Mr. Franklin, I have a business proposition for you."

I held my breath, afraid that I didn't know enough about business to understand his proposition.

"For the past several years, I have been performing through-out the United States and Europe, doing shows for various enter-tainment companies. It recently occurred to me that if I was the one organizing the shows, I would have more control over their quality and would make quite a bit more money."

I sipped my juice and nodded.

"So, this spring I'm launching a new vaudeville production of my own, called the Great Magical Spectacular. Each show will begin with some young magicians performing basic routines and then will progress to more experienced performers doing more complicated tricks. The show will culminate with me doing one of my marquee stunts, a different one in each major city."

I wondered why he was telling me his plans.

"Would you like to join my show as one of the junior performers?"

I sprang from my chair, splashing orange juice onto the knee of my suit. "What?"

Houdini laughed. "Should I take that as a 'yes'?"

"Yes! Absolutely!" I pulled my handkerchief from my pocket and swiped at the stain on my trousers.

The great man held up his hands. "Maybe you should sit down and think about this for a moment first. I didn't get the impression that your uncle is a big fan of magic."

I sat on the edge of my chair and shook my head. "Mr. Houdini, I don't care what my uncle thinks. Magic is the only thing I've ever wanted to do. There is no way I would pass up this opportunity to work with you. The things that I'll learn will be amazing."

"But aren't you an apprentice at your uncle's lock shop? If you joined my show, we'd be on the road for months on end. You wouldn't be able to work for your uncle anymore." A frown creased the magician's forehead.

"Yes, sir. But this is the chance of a lifetime. He'd have to understand that."

"If you're sure…"

I nodded emphatically.

"Very well." He leaned forward and thumped me on the back. "Then plan on attending a meeting here at this hotel in March. Hewitt will contact you with an exact date and time. All the show's performers will be there so that we may plan the show. After all, our first performance is already scheduled for June 1 at the Boston's Orpheum Theatre."

"I'll be here," I said.

Houdini held out his small but powerful hand and we sealed our agreement with a handshake.

He sighed. "And now, I'm afraid I must return to the reception downstairs. By now, someone has probably noticed that the guest of honor is missing. And, if not, I'm sure my wife is wondering what's become of me. Will you rejoin the party, too?"

I shook my head. "It's getting late, sir. I think I'll find my uncle and suggest that we start on our way home."

Houdini nodded. "That's probably a wise decision. So, I'll see you again in March?"

"Yes, sir."

"Very well. Make sure you leave your address with Hewitt so he knows how to contact you."

"Yes, sir. And thank you for this opportunity. You won't regret it."

"I'm sure I won't."

We rode the elevator back down to the lobby while Hewitt helped Houdini re-dress into his party attire. When the doors opened, he smiled at me and then stepped into the crowd, immediately greeting several partygoers by name.

I exited the elevator and scanned the lobby, looking for a sparkly pink dress. I was quite disappointed when I didn't find one.

Hewitt, towering next to me, pulled a few sheets of paper and a fountain pen from his inner jacket pocket. "Your address, Mr. Franklin?"

I dictated the information to him.

He jotted it down in surprisingly prim handwriting and then paused. "And is there any message you'd like me to give anyone else?"

"Excuse me?"

"Did you perhaps want me to share your address with a certain young lady?"

"Sadie...er...Miss Golub? You know how to get in touch with her?"

He nodded, a mischievous grin playing across his lips. "It just so happens that Miss Golub has been contracted to do some sewing for Mrs. Houdini and is scheduled to stop by her suite later this evening to take some measurements. If you give me a note for the young lady, I'll make sure that she receives it."

"You'd do that for me?"

"Just call me Cupid's helper." He handed me a pen and paper.

I plopped down on a nearby chair and composed a brief note. Blowing on the ink, I folded it in half and handed it to Hewitt. "Thank you."

He tucked the note and the pen back into his blue blazer. "See you in the spring."

Chapter 14: Three Envelopes

Sadie Golub

Mrs. Houdini gracefully stepped down from the upholstered footstool in her hotel bedroom, her slippers making no sound on the thick carpet. I jotted her numbers on a piece of paper and then tucked it and my measuring tape into my sewing kit.

She smiled. "Thank you for coming back tonight, Miss Golub. And those fabric samples you brought are lovely, just what I wanted."

I'd begged Bessie for a few pennies from her household account and then had bought some small pieces of appropriate fabric.

Mrs. Houdini said, "I look forward to receiving my first traveling suit in a few weeks." She nodded toward their giant assistant. "Hewitt will give you an advance for the fabric and shipping expenses and will furnish you with our next address." She brushed a lock of hair from her forehead, causing her large diamond ring to sparkle in the lamplight. "I'm afraid I don't have the foggiest idea where we'll be in a few weeks."

"Thank you, Mrs. Houdini." I picked up my coat and my sewing kit and followed Hewitt through the suite's sitting room into the hotel hallway.

He pressed the call button for the elevator. Opening his jacket, he withdrew three envelopes that he handed to me, one at a time. "Here is an advance so you may purchase the fabric and mail the suits, with a little extra money to pay for your carriage ride home tonight. And here is the Houdinis' itinerary for the next two months, so you'll know where to mail the outfits." He paused and smiled a naughty little-boy smile, which looked adorably odd on such a large man. Holding out the final envelope in his huge hand, he said, "And here is a note to you from a certain locksmith-magician who is eager to continue your acquaintance."

"Millard Franklin?" My cheeks grew hot.

The assistant nodded and handed me the note just as a loud chime announced the elevator's arrival.

"But how…?"

Hewitt smiled. "As I told him, you two may just call me Cupid's helper." He bowed goodbye as I stepped into the elevator cab and the operator closed the doors.

I didn't become queasy at all during my descent to the lobby, my attention fully focused upon the white envelopes that were now tucked into my sewing kit. On the ground floor, I hurried down the service corridor, walked out onto Chapman Place, and ran smack into my brother. "Oof!" Bouncing off his chest, I landed on the cold concrete sidewalk.

Solomon's eyes widened in shock. Then he laughed and extended a hand toward me. "*Gutn ovnt*, Sadie." He helped me to my feet and then led us to the edge of the sidewalk under a gas streetlight. "Why are you just leaving now? The party ended a long time ago," he said with narrowed eyes.

"Mrs. Houdini ask me to sew more," I said, fidgeting with the handle of my basket.

Solomon's face lit up. "That's good news! More money. What does she want you to do?"

"Make four traveling dresses like Bessie's."

He frowned. "How do you pay for the cloth and how do you deliver the dresses? The Houdinis are leaving the hotel soon."

I opened my sewing basket and pulled out the envelopes. "This one has money for fabric and mailing. This one has addresses."

Solomon nodded and then jerked his chin toward the third envelope, which clearly had my name written on it in a man's handwriting. "What's that one?"

I hurriedly tried to slip the three envelopes back into my basket but my brother was quicker, snatching Millard's note from my hands. I reached to grab it back, but he held it up high, out of my reach, reminiscent of an annoying game he'd played with me when we were children.

I squinted at him. "You not acting like a growed-up!"

He laughed. "It's 'grown-up' not 'growed-up.'" He turned over the envelope and studied the handwriting. "Who's this from?"

I bit the inside of my cheek. "A man I met at party."

Solomon pulled the letter from the envelope and read it.

As my older brother and guardian, he had a right to read my correspondence, but I still resented his intrusion into my privacy.

He looked down at me. "Are you going to write to him?"

"I not know," I spat. "I not read letter yet!"

He handed it to me.

September 14, 1906

Dear Sadie,

    I enjoyed meeting you and speaking with you today. Since we live too far apart to see each other very often, I hope we may correspond and get to know each other through letters. Please write to me at the address below.

Sincerely yours,
Millard Franklin
101 Park Lane
North Attleboro, Massachusetts

Millard had written to me! My face lit up with a huge smile that I immediately squelched when I realized that my brother was staring at me. I shoved the note to the bottom of my sewing basket and fastened the lid.

"So, who is this Millard Franklin?" he asked, frowning.

I shrugged. "A man from party."

"Is he a Jew?"

I rolled my eyes. "I not ask him."

"How old is he? Does he have a job?"

I fixed Solomon with an irritated stare. "I talk to him for five minutes. I not know his life story."

He crossed his arms over his chest and stared at me as a large coach-and-four clattered by on the dark cobblestone street. Solomon shook his head. "I don't want you to write to this fellow. With a name like Franklin, I'm sure he's not Jewish. *Tate* and *Mame* would certainly not approve of him."

I huffed, my stomach suddenly burning with irritation. "This is America. My men not have to be Jewish."

"Your men? So how many 'men' have been courting you? I introduced you to my friend Elijah a few weeks ago, but you did not talk to him."

"He has face like dog."

Solomon frowned. "So Millard Franklin is a pretty boy?"

"He is not ugly like—"

My brother held up a hand. "Just stop. Millard Franklin is not Jewish, so he cannot court you. End of story."

What an old-fashioned, pig-headed idiot my brother could be! But talking to him further would gain me nothing, so I held my tongue.

Solomon misinterpreted my silence as acquiescence and bobbed his head once as an end to the conversation. "We are painting the lobby tonight, so I have to go. Do I need to take you home, first? You should not walk around Boston alone at night."

"Is only eight o'clock," I said. "And Mrs. Houdini gave me money for a cab."

With a final frown in my direction, he strode to the service entrance and disappeared.

I glared at the door. Millard liked me and I liked him, but Solomon said I should not write to Millard because he wasn't a Jew? Millard didn't care that I wasn't whatever religion he was, so why should I care? And what difference did religion make, here in the New World anyway?

Still standing under the streetlamp, I withdrew Millard's note and read it through two more times. I hugged it to my chest and closed my eyes. A man liked me and wanted to get to know me better. Even if nothing ever became of our acquaintance, just that realization made me feel appreciated and validated. I tucked Millard's note back into my sewing kit and walked slowly in the direction of our apartment, deciding to save my cab fare as the first money that truly belonged to me.

Chapter 15: The Next Show

George McVay

Edith and I were seated in one of the hotel's carriages, the horse's hoof clops echoing off the buildings as we traveled toward South Station.

She leaned back against the seat and smiled tiredly. "Did you enjoy yourself at the party, dear?"

"I suppose." I yawned, glad I didn't have to be back on board the *Larchmont* until noon tomorrow.

"And did you manage to speak to everyone you wanted to?"

I nodded. "I believe Mr. Morse might contact me to offer me a captainship."

She frowned, the skin between her eyebrows wrinkling. "I wouldn't be so sure about that. I don't think his sister-in-law thought much of you. She seemed quite disapproving of your intentions."

"So, what of it?" I asked with irritation. "Is it a crime for me to want to better my lot in life?"

"No, but sometimes you can be so painfully obvious, dear, almost embarrassingly so." She patted my forearm. "I wish you'd at least try to be a bit more subtle."

"Subtlety never got anyone anywhere. Besides, I think I still made a favorable impression on Morse, despite Mrs. Jensen's comments." I watched a stagecoach pass us at a trot, pulled by a pair of poorly matched horses. As an afterthought, I asked, "What about you? Did you have a good time?"

She shrugged. "I was disappointed that we weren't able to see Mr. Houdini's show. I would have liked to tell the children about it."

I instantly felt guilty and selfish. I'd been so caught up in what I wanted to accomplish today that I'd never considered what Edith might want. I took her hand and squeezed it gently. "I didn't know you wanted to see the show. Why didn't you say something?"

She smiled and patted the back of my hand. "You didn't ask me. Besides, I know you don't really care for magic shows."

I tried to think of a way to compensate her. "Houdini mentioned to me that he would be returning for another show this spring, in June. Let's bring the children up to Boston to see that one. They'll be a little older by then and will enjoy the train trip and the performance even more."

"That would be nice," Edith said, although I could tell by her tone that she didn't truly believe we'd go.

But, I'd see to it that we did make it to that show in June. By then, I planned to be working for Morse's International Steamship Line so we'd be living up here in Boston. With Edith's charm and my intelligence, we'd easily fit right in with the upper-crust crowd. And with my increased income, I'd see to it that Edith had a nice dress to wear to that show—her own, not one borrowed from a neighbor.

Our lives were going to improve soon; I'd see to it.

Chapter 16: A Family Meeting
Anna Jensen

After the Houdini reception, I decided not to return Louise to the Back Bay Boarding House for Young Women but instead opted to bring her to our home in Providence. Even in this modern American society, a boarding house was certainly no place for a married, pregnant woman. Louise said she agreed with my resolution, but I suspected she was just hoping to see more of her new husband, who lived on the seedy South Side of Providence, only a few miles away—but a world apart—from our family's home on the much more civilized East Side.

Arriving at Boston's South Station, Louise and I found we had an entire private railcar to ourselves and were to be waited on by our own steward and maid, courtesy of my brother-in-law, Charles, who also owned the railroad line.

But the car's opulence did not appeal to me that night. The pâté tasted like sawdust, the plush cushions felt like sandpaper against my skin, and the attentive staff annoyed me. I just wanted to be home, where I could talk to John and decide what we should do about our daughter. As a child, whenever I'd become frustrated, *Farfar* Jennings would say, "*Svårigheter finns till för att övervinnas*"—adversity exists in order to be overcome. During the entire ride home from Boston, I hoped and prayed John and I would be able to overcome this adversity.

In Providence's Union Station, I took Louise's elbow and led her through the cavernous yellow and red brick building to where Amos awaited us at the curb with our own box carriage.

He tipped his silk top hat. "Mr. Jensen said to tell you that he's waiting up for you, Madam." He clicked our door closed and climbed up onto the box of the carriage, where he snapped the reins, propelling us over the Providence River Bridge and up the steep hill of Waterman Street. I stared out the window as we passed the stately red brick buildings of the Rhode Island School of Design and Brown University and then turned onto Butler Avenue and finally onto Blackstone Boulevard. When we stopped, our three-story Tudor-style house loomed large in the night, its red brick and white stucco panels glowing orange in the gas lamplight.

Two men greeted us at our front door: Moses, our grizzled butler, and John, my silvering husband. As Moses collected our coats, John cheek-kissed Louise and me, his paisley velvet smoking jacket shining in the lamplight. Returning his kiss, I caught a whiff of his bay rum aftershave, which made me smile, despite everything.

John said, "Louise, what a surprise. I didn't know you were coming home with your mother."

"She insisted." Louise shrugged.

I was amazed at how casual our daughter was behaving. She and Hans had virtually destroyed the life John and I had spent eighteen years carefully crafting for her, but there she stood, calmly shrugging her shoulders.

"John, *min kära*, we must talk," I said, frowning. I led the three of us through the grand entry hall into our parlor, which smelled of wood smoke and lemon furniture polish.

I'd always loved our parlor; it had been the first room John and I had decorated. We'd begun with the wood floors. Working late into the night, John and I had stripped, sanded, and refinished the narrow oak planks in this room and then throughout the house until they gleamed in hues of gold and red. Even now, I still felt a small burst of pride when I noticed what a good job we'd done on them. Our first decorative purchase for the house had been the parlor's large Persian carpet, with its delicate floral patterns of tan, white, and peach, handmade and authentic. After waiting so long for furnishings, I wouldn't put up with cheap imitations. The furniture had come next, nothing but the finest antiques from a reputable dealer on Thayer Street. The couches, settees, chairs, tables, and ottomans were all made of blonde hardwoods with thick upholstery in shades of cream and tan. Then came the accessories: the paintings on the walls were Impressionistic, the sculptures scattered here and there were Art Nouveau, the drapes were made of heavy flax-colored crepe, and the lamps were by Tiffany and Company, of course—

nothing but the best. Even with the excessive amount of money we'd spent on furnishings, our parlor felt more comfortable than pretentious and I was quite pleased with its overall effect. At the moment, however, it was destined to become the setting for a very uncomfortable discussion between John, Louise, and me.

Closing the room's heavy wooden double doors, John asked, "Would either of you ladies like an aperitif?" Even after more than a quarter century in this country, I could still detect the Scandinavian lilt in his voice—similar to my own. Unlike me, however, John had deliberately banished all Swedish words and phrases from his vocabulary.

"*Ja*," I replied. "I think a drink—or two—would definitely be in order." I sank down onto the sofa.

He poured two small glasses of sherry and a *nubbe* of vodka and settled into an armchair drawn up to the blazing fireplace. Louise joined me on the facing sofa. Although it was only September, the weather had already turned rather chilly in the evenings, so I appreciated the fire's warmth. Slipping off my shoes, I stretched my cold, aching feet toward the flames.

After a few minutes of sipping our drinks in silence, John looked from Louise to me. "All right then, suppose one of you tells me what's going on."

While Louise pulled pins from her hair, releasing her golden locks to cascade down her back, I briefly recounted the day's events and revelations. When I finished, John plunked down his vodka, stood, and faced Louise, his hands on his hips. His eyes looked pinched around the edges. "Is there anything you'd like to add?"

Louise raised her chin. "Hans and I love each other very much. You and *Mamma* were being unreasonable by not allowing us to see each other, so we took matters into our own hands."

"And now you're married and are expecting a child in April?"

"We're both very excited about the baby."

"Excited?" he barked. "I certainly don't understand why you'd be excited. How in the world do you expect to care for a child when you're just a child yourself?" He clenched his hands at his sides. "Hans DeThestrup barely earns enough to support himself, and certainly not enough to pay for you and a baby, too!"

Louise flicked her hair over her shoulder. I couldn't help but admire the way she unflinchingly faced our anger and disappointment. "I don't know why you both object to Hans so much," she said. "Just because he isn't a wealthy man yet doesn't mean he won't be a good husband and a good father. *Mamma*, aren't you always saying, 'happiness can't be bought for money'?"

I nodded. "But I also say, *kärleken* är *blind*—love is blind."

John flung himself into his chair, downed his vodka, and smacked the empty glass on the claw-footed coffee table, denting its polished surface. He, like most men I knew, could manage business matters very well, but became angry and irrational when confronted with emotional or personal issues. I could see that he'd be of little assistance in this matter; it was up to me to make our daughter see reason.

"Louise," I said, "imagine your friends wearing *haute couture* while you wear five-year-old frocks. Or them vacationing on the Continent while you have nothing more than weekends in Newport—if that. Or them in their fine homes here on the East Side, knowing that you cannot invite them to visit you because you live in a dumpy *stuga* on the South Side. Is that the life you want?"

She shrugged and sipped her drink. One of the fire logs popped loudly.

I took her hand in mine. "*Pappa* and I, we want what's best for you. You know this. *Ja?*"

She stood abruptly, the beaded bodice of her green gown sparkling in the firelight. "You *think* you know what's best for me and that's why you've been advising me to stay away from Hans. But I'm eighteen now, old enough to make my own decisions. I love Hans and he loves me. We *are* married and we *are* going to have a baby, whether you like it or not." Her features softened, her lips trembled. "Isn't there any way you can find it in your hearts to be happy for us and to support us?"

I realized that in order to save Louise, I'd have to cause her considerable pain. One glance at John, though—who was staring out the window into the night—confirmed that I was on my own in this. I sighed. "We object to Hans, not only because of his bank account. We also found out that he's not *en hedersman*."

The color drained from Louise's face. "Not an honorable man? What do you mean?" She sank onto the sofa and placed her half-full sherry glass on the table beside her father's empty tumbler.

"Hans bragged to a co-worker about keeping company with you," I said.

She gasped.

I nodded. "Then he wagered that he'd marry you, *min kära*, and lay claim to your inheritance from us before the end of the year." I hated telling her these things, but I knew it had to be done, for her own good.

"He wouldn't say such things!" She leapt to her feet again, her hands in fists by her sides.

She looked so much like John: her facial expression, her balled-up hands—her whole demeanor. It reminded me of how much I loved her and lived for the sole purpose of making her happy, which made this scene even more painful to me.

"I don't have to listen to this slander of my husband!" she said and stomped toward the door to the hallway.

I blocked her exit and pointed back toward the sofa.

Louise glared at me and strode over to the bronze dancer on the mantel.

"There is no reason we can't discuss this like civilized people," I said, tugging the maroon velvet bell-pull. A moment later, the door slid open and one of our maids appeared.

"Helga!" Louise cried and ran over to hug the short, stout woman who'd been with our family since before Louise was born. "You never look a day older."

"Thank you for saying so, miss." Taking a step back from Louise, the maid looked at me. "May I get something for you, Madam?"

I nodded and ordered a tea tray and some sandwiches and then excused her with a wave. "Let's return to our discussion. *Ja?*" I wanted to remedy this situation as soon as possible.

Louise sat next to me and crossed her arms. "I have no intention of listening to you tell lies about Hans."

"They're not lies," I said.

"How do you know?"

I sighed. "Because we hired a *privatdetektiv.*"

"A private detective?" Her lower lip quivered again.

I cupped her shoulder with my palm. "Mr. Jones, he found out that you weren't the only girl Hans was keeping company with last spring; he was seeing others, too, some of a very low class."

"That's a lie!" A tear ran down her cheek and splashed on her gown.

I handed her the lace handkerchief I'd had tucked in my dress sleeve and then retrieved some papers from the desk and dropped them on the coffee table. "Here is the detective's report. Mr. Jones, he was very thorough."

She dabbed her eyes and glared at the papers as if willing them to burst into flames.

I put my arm around her shoulders. "*Min kära,* I hate telling you these things. I know you truly care for Hans. If I thought there was any chance he'd be a *hygglig make*—a decent husband—I'd try to help you, instead."

"You're wrong about him. I know you are," Louise said with a sniffle. Helga reappeared with a tray of refreshments that she laid out and then left the room.

Louise pointed a shaky finger at the documents. "What else did this detective supposedly discover?"

I fixed myself some tea while deciding how much I needed to tell her. Tapping the teaspoon against the cup, I asked, "You know Bernadette Williams. *Ja?*"

She nodded. "She's the sister of one of the other greenhouse workers. I heard that she got in trouble—with child."

"Hans DeThestrup, he is the father of that baby."

"No! That can't be true!"

"Hans was spending much time with Miss Williams before her…difficulty. *Pappa* caught them once together in the storage room. Her collar buttons were undone."

Louise's head snapped toward John, who simply nodded without diverting his gaze from the view through the window.

Red splotches appeared on Louise's cheeks. "Hans has never been anything but a perfect gentleman to me."

This conversation was accomplishing nothing since Louise was obviously too in love with Hans to view the situation clearly. It was time to end it so that John and I could speak privately to come up with a course of action. Turning to Louise I said, "A woman in your condition, she needs plenty of rest. You should retire now. *Ja?*"

She did, in fact, look exhausted as she frowned. "I know you want me to leave the room so that you and *Pappa* can talk things over without me and decide what should be done. Of course, you two are free to talk all you want, but don't forget that it's my life you're discussing. In the end, the decision of what's to be done will be mine."

John rose and kissed the top of her head. "Good night, dear."

She narrowed her eyes and frowned at both of us before leaving the room.

Feeling close to exhaustion myself, I leaned my head back against the sofa and closed my eyes. "What do we do now?"

"I know what I'd like to do," John growled. "Wring DeThestrup's scrawny little neck. The nerve of that man! Marrying Louise behind our backs and then showing up every day for work at the greenhouse for the past two months as if nothing had happened. I never did trust that man and the idea of having him as a son-in-law is nothing short of repulsive to me."

"But what can we do? Louise is eighteen years old, now—an adult. Their marriage is legal. *Ja?*"

"Yes, probably." He snatched up his empty glass and reached for mine. "You want another one?" I nodded and he returned with refills.

I said, "You should talk to Hans, *man mot man*, to see if he really loves our Louise."

"I'll go speak to him tomorrow at his home." He tossed back his second glass of vodka. "I must admit, though, I don't have much hope for the scoundrel. It wouldn't surprise me a bit to find out he married her just to get to our money."

I swirled my sherry. "She thinks he's *kärleken i hennes liv*—the love of her life."

"She's wrong."

"*Ja.* You know that and I know that, but not Louise. And what about their baby? Do we want Louise's child—our grandchild—having him for a father?"

"Not a comforting thought." He rose, kissed the top of my head, and squeezed my shoulder. "I'm going up to bed."

"*Huvadkudden* är *bästa rådgivaren*—the pillow is the best advisor?" I asked.

He chuckled. "Sometimes. Are you coming?"

I patted his hand. "In a few minutes, *min kära.* I want to sit here and finish my drink first."

After John left, I sat and watched the fire's embers die away. The sweet sherry soured on my tongue. I placed my half-empty glass on the table and whispered a prayer. "God, You know how much we love our daughter and we want to protect her. Please help us do the right thing for her now. Amen."

I fervently hoped that God did not consider Hans DeThestrup to be "the right thing" for Louise.

BOOK 2:
NEW YEAR'S EVE/
NEW YEAR'S DAY 1907

Chapter 1: In the Locksmith Shop

Millard Franklin

On December 31, 1906, at ten in the morning, I looked up from my cluttered workbench at the Providence Locksmith Shop. Through the glass panel of his office door, I could see Uncle Henry sitting at his desk, mulling over his accounting books. Glancing at the front room with its huge plate glass windows overlooking snow-covered Main Street, I was glad to see there weren't any customers in the shop. I pushed aside the padlock I'd been working on and quietly opened the cabinet next to my bench, turning up my gas lamp to combat the day's gloom. Inside hung a new pair of iron manacles I'd received in the mail yesterday. The accompanying hand-written note read, "Thought you might enjoy playing around with these. Sincerely, H. H."

As I lifted the manacles from the hook and laid them on my wooden workbench, I could feel my heart beating faster. Reaching into my trouser pocket, I pulled out one of my homemade metal lock picks. I grasped the manacles' locking mechanism firmly in one hand, inserted the pick, and began to finagle it, twisting it first to the left and then to the right. If I were going to be a professional escape artist, I needed to be able to open this sort of device easily. What would Houdini say if he saw me struggling over it? Would he take back his job offer? I glanced over my shoulder at the poster of the great magician tacked up next to my desk.

"What are you doing?" my uncle asked from a foot away, causing me to jump. "And what are those?" He wore his gold wire spectacles at the very tip of his nose, magnifying his brown eyes and making them appear enormous and bug-like.

I quickly covered my lock pick with one hand. "Just some manacles. I was trying to figure out how they work."

"I see the manacles, boy, but what was that other thing? That key or whatever?" He was standing so close to me, I could smell the woodsy aroma of his pipe tobacco clinging to his tweed jacket.

"Nothing, sir." I secreted the pick in my trouser pocket and then showed him my empty hands.

He frowned. "You're not being paid to play with toys, Millard. You're supposed to be repairing that padlock for the railroad company. Did you finish it, yet?"

I pushed away the manacles and pulled the lock to the front of my workbench. "No, sir."

Uncle Henry shook his head. "Ever since we saw that Houdini show in Boston a few months ago, you've been so preoccupied with handcuffs and manacles and such." He pointed to my poster. "Do you still intend to become an escape artist like him one day?"

I shrugged, not daring to tell him how desperately I wanted that very thing. I still hadn't spoken to him or my mother about Houdini's job proposal; I knew I was behaving cowardly but I didn't want to see the disappointment in their eyes.

Shaking his head again, my uncle said, "You'd do well to forget such nonsense. You have a good job here and, until recently, you were doing well at it. Just forget all about this magic folderol and refocus your energies on learning a useful trade."

I nodded and mumbled, "Yes, sir."

*   *   *

I went home early that afternoon, telling Uncle Henry I wasn't feeling well. Truth was, I'd signed up to do a magic act at our church's New Year's Eve Variety Show that night and I wanted to get in a few more practice sessions before the curtain went up. Out in our family's barn, I was uncharacteristically nervous. Partially because I was scheduled to be the last act in the church show—the grand finale—and I was determined to "bring the house down," as they say. And partially because Sadie Golub had written to say that she was coming to see me perform. She and her sister-in-law, Bessie, were scheduled to take a train from Boston to Taunton, and then transfer to a trolley for their trip to North Attleboro, arriving at around six for the seven o'clock show. This would be the first time we'd see each other since our initial meeting at the Houdini reception. And she was scheduled to meet my whole family at the church. With those stresses added to my worries about the show, I found I couldn't concentrate on practicing my trick. After fumbling it three times, I gave up and paced our yard, muttering to myself and kicking snowballs into the side of the barn.

My mother found me drumming my fingers on the thick wood slab of our scarred kitchen table when she came in to do laundry mid-afternoon. She tied a white apron around her waist and then ruffled my hair. "Milly, you look like you're about to jump out of your own skin."

I ducked away from her hand and smoothed my hair back into place, frowning. "Mom, remember, when Sadie gets here…"

"…I'm not allowed to call you 'Milly.' I know. Would you like me to address you as 'Millard' or 'Mr. Franklin'?" She grinned as she lit the stove and pulled out our huge copper kettle.

"'Millard' will be just fine." I filled the kettle outside at the yard pump and then hefted it back into the kitchen for her.

Mom placed it on the stove. "You really like this girl, don't you?"

My face felt hot. "Yes, she's really smart and nice. And she's pretty, too. Wait 'til you see her."

"We're all looking forward to meeting your Miss Golub."

"And you don't care that she's a Jew?"

Mom frowned. "I don't see why her religion should matter."

I shrugged. "It's just that Uncle Henry said . . ."

"Oh, Uncle Henry does have his opinions, doesn't he?" She smiled. "As long as your Miss Golub is a nice girl, I don't know why it should make any difference where she worships. Do you?"

I just hoped the people at our church would be as open-minded as Mom. "But don't forget—she's from Russia and has only been in this country for a year and a half. Her English is good but not perfect."

Mom frowned. "I think we know how to make a guest feel welcome."

"Yeah, but it doesn't matter," Thomas said as he entered the kitchen and poured himself a cup of coffee from the pot simmering on the side burner. "Once this girl sees me, she won't remember that you're even alive, *Milly*."

Mom rapped him on the top of his head with a wooden spoon.

"Hey, that hurt!" He laughed, rubbing his scalp.

"None of that, you smart aleck. I expect you to be on your best behavior when Millard's friends are here."

"I can't help that girls find me irresistible. I'm just naturally charming."

"I'm sure that Christine wouldn't appreciate you using your 'natural charm' on other women," she said. "You remember Christine, don't you? Your betrothed?"

He drizzled some honey into his coffee and then plopped down on the bench next to me, looking dejected. "Yes, I remember her. But she's boring."

He received another sharp rap with the spoon.

Thomas rubbed his head again. "Jeez, Mom! I was just joking. You know I love Chris. We're getting married in May, for Pete's sake!"

"As far as I'm concerned, that girl is a saint for putting up with you." She dragged the washing vat to the center of the room and poured the heated water into it.

This time, it was Thomas's turn to fill the copper kettle from the yard pump and replace it on the stove.

Unable to sit still any longer, I popped up off the bench and grabbed my woolen cap and coat. "I think I'll go over to the church to see if they need help setting up the stage or tables or whatever."

"That's a good idea," Mom said. "And you're meeting your young ladies at the trolley station at six?"

"Yes."

"You're just trying to keep Sadie from seeing me," Thomas said and then ducked out of the kitchen before Mom could smack him with the spoon a third time.

Chapter 2: New Year's Eve Magic

Sadie Golub

I sighed as Bessie and I settled into our leather seat on the train from Boston to Taunton. We were on our way to see Millard perform at his church's New Year's Eve festival in North Attleboro, me as an invited spectator and her as my chaperone. This would be the first time I'd see Millard in person since we met at the Parker House Hotel in September and I was quite nervous. Over the past twelve weeks, we'd written a dozen letters back and forth to each other, but that didn't help quiet the butterflies fluttering around in my stomach. I stared out one of the train's windows and saw a steamship paddling in Boston Harbor and wondered if it might belong to Captain McVay, the steamboat captain we'd met at the hotel the same day.

For the past three months, Bessie had conspired with me to keep Millard's letters secret from Solomon, because, unlike my narrow-minded brother, she was in favor of me writing to Millard, Jewish or not. "When Mr. Franklin inherits his uncle's lock shop, he'll be able to provide well for a wife and children," she'd said with a conspiratorial grin. But in his most recent letters, I'd noticed Millard's growing preoccupation with magic. I was afraid Bessie would soon notice it too and would withdraw her approval of my relationship with him.

On the chilly train, breath clouds formed in front of our faces. Many of the other passengers had brought blankets to tuck around their legs. I shivered and pulled my white woolen cape more tightly around my shoulders. Under it, I wore a new yellow traveling dress with matching hat and gloves. I hoped Millard would think it attractive on me. Bessie, who never seemed affected by the weather, sat next to me, looking warm and comfortable in a new, pale blue outfit I'd completed just yesterday. She was chatting easily with an elderly woman seated across from her. I wished I felt that at ease. Instead, I retrieved a man's suit vest from my bag, pulled off my gloves, and began to sew on some brass buttons.

I did some financial calculations in my head. Once I finished with these buttons, Mr. Murphy would pay me eight dollars for his suit. Added to the five dollars I'd made for Mrs. George's bustled skirt earlier this week, that equaled an additional thirteen dollars. That would carry my savings fund to over eighty dollars—a fortune, by my standards.

Every week, I continued to give Solomon money to help pay for my living expenses and to send back to our family in Russia. He was probably aware that I was saving some money for myself, but I doubted that he had any idea that I'd accumulated such a large sum. Had he known, he might have insisted that I turn it all over to him. "There's no reason for a single woman to have that much money," he'd say. So I hid my savings in a cigar box under the couch where I slept. I hadn't decided exactly what I wanted to do with the money yet, but I was hoping to discuss the matter with Millard after the magic show today. If there was time and if we could get away from Bessie. Millard had already offered me some sound business advice in his letters, so I trusted his judgement.

*   *   *

Ninety minutes later, Bessie and I sat beside Millard's mother in the front row of the white-clapboard North Attleboro Congregational Church Hall. Millard's funny older brother, Thomas, pretended to flirt with me while Thomas's girlfriend, Christine, laughed and poked him in the ribs. His mother was very friendly to Bessie and me, too, and introduced us to all of their neighbors and friends. By the time they lit the footlights on the stage for the variety show, I was feeling very comfortable at the church. No one seemed to care that we were Jewish, which I found quite surprising.

I thoroughly enjoyed all of the other acts of the show, from the one-legged ventriloquist with his one-legged dummy to the dour-faced woman demonstrating how she called her pigs home for supper. Millard's escape trick was scheduled to be the last performance that evening. A hush fell over the church hall as the blue velvet curtains closed in preparation for his appearance. After a brief pause, the curtains reopened to reveal Millard standing center stage next to a tall wooden barrel banded with two metal rings, its lid propped against its side. Millard's brother, Chester, stood next to him, fidgeting in his brown Sunday-best suit, but Millard wore a confident smile with his black shirt, tie, and trousers. He appeared completely at ease performing in front of his entire church community.

"Ladies and gentleman," Millard began in a loud, clear voice. "In September, I was fortunate enough to travel to Boston to witness a performance by the greatest magician in the world, Mr. Harry Houdini. That day, Mr. Houdini was chained and shackled and then thrown into the Charles River. He'd been searched for keys by none other than Boston's chief of police, so it was a mystery how, two minutes later, Mr. Houdini was able to free himself and to swim to an awaiting rowboat."

Millard paused for effect and a murmur of anticipation skittered through the audience. I felt a lift of pride at knowing such an accomplished performer. I supposed he might even be considered to be my suitor. The thought shocked me but made me smile. I'd never had a suitor before.

Continuing, he said, "After the show, Mr. Houdini was kind enough to speak to me and to encourage me to become an escape artist too. Although, I'm not ready to do anything as fancy as being chained and thrown into a river . . ." The audience laughed. ". . . In a few moments, I will be wrapped with chains and padlocked with four different locks. Then, my assistant," he gestured toward Chester, "will enclose me in this barrel. After two minutes, I hope to emerge unshackled."

Another murmur ran through the crowd.

"Of course, that wouldn't be much of a feat if the padlocks were somehow rigged to spring open or if I had a key hidden in my pockets or in the barrel, so I would like to ask an audience member to come up on stage and check to see that none of these is the case. May I have a volunteer?"

A dozen people raised their hands.

"How about Reverend Foster?" Millard asked.

Everyone loudly agreed and the portly pastor made his way up to the stage. He carefully checked each of Millard's locks and the entire length of chain and declared that all were sound and in normal functioning order. He then searched Millard and the wooden barrel for a key and reported that he found none. A louder ripple of excited chatter rolled through the church hall.

Chester shook his brother's hand and said very solemnly, "Good luck." Millard climbed inside the barrel. Chester wound the length of chain around him and fastened it with the locks. With a last nod to the audience, Millard crouched down inside the barrel and Chester placed the lid on top.

I held my breath.

Next to the barrel, Chester made a big show of pulling out a gold pocket watch, which looked huge in his small hands. Audience members whispered excitedly. I saw Thomas accept a coin from his friend and wondered if they were wagering on the outcome of Millard's performance. After two minutes, Chester knocked twice on the side of the barrel and then pulled off its lid with a grunt. Slowly, Millard appeared, rising up out of the barrel, the opened padlocks and chain in his hands and a huge smile on his face. The crowd roared. I think I yelled loudest of all. I was so proud of him, my maybe suitor.

When the hubbub over Millard's performance died down, Reverend Foster retook the stage to declare the show over and the New Year's Eve dinner ready to begin. Everyone streamed to the rear of the hall, following their noses to the buffet tables groaning under the weight of platters of delicious-smelling roast turkey, baked potatoes, baking soda biscuits, cranberry salad, and pumpkin pie.

Bessie and I sat at a table with Millard and his family, everyone talking excitedly about his performance. Halfway through the meal, Reverend Foster approached us. "I had to come over to congratulate the star of this year's show." He shook Millard's hand. "I have a suggestion for you, though. You should call yourself the 'Boy Houdini.'"

"That's a great idea, Milly…er…Millard," his mother said. "I'm certainly not as good as Mr. Houdini," Millard replied.

The minister patted him on the back. "One day you will be, you mark my words."

A woman sitting at the next table leaned over. "The Boy Houdini? I have a cousin who runs carnivals in New York and New Jersey. I'll write to him and tell him about you. Maybe he could arrange some engagements for you down there."

I noticed that Mrs. Franklin was quick to caution her, "But only on weekends or holidays."

As I nibbled on my dinner, the exciting conversation continued to swirl around us, all focused on Millard, the Boy Houdini. I was so happy and proud of him, and I realized I was most certainly in love with him, too.

*   *   *

All too soon, the time came for Bessie and me to leave. Millard accompanied us on our walk back to the trolley station. As we trudged through the snow in the frigid night air, Bessie asked, "Millard, are you planning on performing magic again soon?" I could hear the disapproval in her voice.

He said, "As a matter of fact, my old primary school teacher, Mrs. Beck, just asked me to do a show for her students in a few weeks, and two other people spoke to me about performing at parties."

"Will you continue to work at the lock shop, too?" she asked. "Yes."

I sensed there was something he wasn't saying.

"Locksmithing is much steadier work," Bessie said. "Much more appropriate for someone who should be thinking about settling down soon."

He smiled at me.

"You really enjoy performing?" I asked him quietly, looking up into his handsome face.

He nodded.

I wished I could guess what he was thinking.

When we arrived at the station, Bessie extended her hand to Millard. "It was very nice to finally meet you, Mr. Franklin.

Please come visit us in Boston." In contrast to her welcoming words, her tone was cold and uninviting. She flashed me a stern glance and then climbed the trolley steps.

Millard took my gloved hand in both of his and squeezed it gently. "I am so glad you came to see my show tonight. It really meant a lot to me to have you in the audience. Thanks."

"I happy to see you. You are good magician."

The trolley bell clanged as we stood staring at each other. I noticed that his eyebrows and lashes were much darker than his hair. The bell rang again and I rose to my tiptoes, kissed him on the lips, laughed when his eyes flew open wide in surprise, and then dashed into the car.

*   *   *

At ten o'clock that night, Bessie and I had boarded a train at Providence's Union Station and were now headed toward Boston. My sewing sat idly in my lap as I stared out the window at the gas lamps and the stars.

I'd kissed Millard! I touched my fingertips to my lips, remembering. I knew I'd surprised him, but judging by the huge smile on his face afterward, he'd enjoyed the kiss as much as I had.

I looked over at Bessie, snoozing next to me, her cheek pressed against the cold window. Up until now, she'd been in favor of my relationship with Millard. But after watching him perform his trick today, I was pretty sure that she would guess that he planned to become a professional magician, not a locksmith. She must have noticed how his face had been beaming when he'd emerged from that barrel. Bessie would certainly disapprove of his career choice. How would that affect my future with Millard?

I looked down at Mr. Murphy's vest in my lap and realized I hadn't spoken to Millard about my sewing business. What would he have told me to do? Continue to work for Mr. Miller? Start a dress shop of my own? Or perhaps move somewhere else where I could make a fresh start?

I felt exhausted and confused and wished *Tate* and *Mame* were here in America instead of half a world away. There was no sense in talking to Solomon because I knew what he would say: "Women were put on this earth to get married and have babies," and, "Millard Franklin is not a Jew, so he wouldn't make a good husband or a good father." End of discussion.

But what about the way Millard made me feel…as if anything was possible? And what about the fact that I was sure I was in love with him?

I picked up the vest and my needle and began to sew another brass button into place. Glancing toward the window, I smiled sadly at my own reflection.

Chapter 3: Mixing Business and Pleasure

George McVay

"Can't you make him stop sniveling?" I growled at Edith. We stood in the reception line at the Joy Steamship New Year's Eve Party. Our daughter, Ruthie, now nearly three years old, was excited to meet "Daddy's boss," especially since he was handing out peppermint sticks to all the children. But Raymond, only fourteen months old, was afraid and letting everyone know it by whimpering loudly. Edith scooped him up and whispered reassurances into his tiny ear. I felt guilty about snapping at Edith, but I wished she would do a better job of controlling the children. This was the first time we'd been invited to the company's New Year's Eve party and I was determined to make the most of the opportunity.

Finally, we reached the front of the line. I shook my employer's hand and bowed over his wife's hand.

"My, my, my, who do we have here?" Dunbaugh asked. The smell of pine wafted over from the enormous Christmas tree full of twinkling white candles.

"Mr. and Mrs. Dunbaugh, I would like to present my wife, Edith, and my children, Ruthie and Raymond. They are all very excited to meet you."

Raymond sucked on one of his fingers as a fat tear rolled down his cheek and splashed on Edith's velvet gown. I wished he'd stop acting like such a baby.

Mr. Dunbaugh took Edith's hand in both of his and pressed it warmly. "It is very nice to finally meet you, Mrs. McVay." He turned his attention to the children, holding up one peppermint candy in each of his hands. "Ruthie and Raymond, it's nice to meet you, as well. Have you been good children this year?"

Both children's eyes grew big and they looked toward me.

I laughed nervously. "Of course they've been good—the best!"

"Glad to hear it. What did Santa Claus bring you for Christmas?"

Ruthie carefully slipped the candy from Mr. Dunbaugh's fingers and then recited a list of toys she'd received. I was impressed with her poise.

"And what about you?" he asked Raymond, extending the other peppermint toward him. "Did Santa bring you some nice toys too?"

Raymond looked up at Mr. Dunbaugh's face, took his finger out of his mouth, and howled at the top of his lungs. As everyone at the party turned to find the origin of that terrible sound, I snatched up my son by his armpits. "I'm very sorry!" I said and then hurried through the hallway toward the back of the house. I burst into the kitchen, holding Raymond in front of me. He was still caterwauling louder than I thought humanly possible, especially for someone so small.

A dozen cooks and wait staff, all dressed in white and black, turned to see what the ruckus was about and then frowned, letting me know that guests were not welcome in their domain.

"Oh, my!" one matronly cook said, looking up from a tray of canapés she was preparing. "What seems to be the trouble here?" The room was filled with the conflicting scents of onion and cinnamon.

"My son's afraid of Mr. Dunbaugh," I said.

"Tsk, tsk." The gray-haired woman looked like a quintessential grandmother as she wiped her hands on her apron and then selected an iced gingerbread cookie from a tray on the countertop. "Here, you go, young man. See if this makes you feel better." She waved me toward the chair in which she'd been sitting. "Have a seat."

Raymond stuffed the cookie man's head into his mouth as I plunked down in the chair, with him on my lap. He pulled the cookie away, drool stringing down to his short pants, flashed a big eight-toothed smile at the cook, and returned to gnawing.

In the relative quiet, I noticed the sounds around me: the other cooks chatting and clattering pans as they prepared the food, the servers banging their metal trays, the small

band playing popular music in the dining room, and the partygoers laughing throughout the house. In my lap, Raymond
continued to crunch on his cookie, crumbs and drool falling
from his lips.

"Here," the kindly cook said, handing me a linen napkin.

I used it to wipe my son's eyes and face, while debating what
I should do next. Collect Edith and Ruthie and leave the party as
quietly as possible? Search out Mr. Dunbaugh and apologize for
causing such a disturbance? Wait a few minutes and then return
to the party as if nothing had happened? I dropped the napkin
onto the table and clasped one hand over my eyes.

The cook said, "Don't you worry about a thing, dear. I've
been working these parties for Mr. Dunbaugh for years. Compared to other things that have happened, I'm sure your son's
little fit was nothing."

I looked up at her. "Truly?"

She nodded and smiled. "You should have been here a few
years ago when a certain captain's wife had a bit too much
punch, took off her shoes, and went wading in the fountain."

I chuckled, wondering whose wife that had been.

"And then there was that time—four or five years ago now—
when one of the vice presidents knocked over the Christmas tree
and practically set the whole house on fire."

I laughed again.

"Like I said, your son's crying was nothing." She smiled at
Raymond. "Besides, Mr. Dunbaugh can be a little scary when
you see him up close. Don't you agree?"

Raymond nodded, his hands and face already re-coated in
icing and crumbs.

The kitchen door swung open and Edith peeked into the
room and then entered, pulling Ruthie behind her. "What are
you two doing in here, of all places?" She nodded stiffly to the
cook and then knelt in front of Raymond. "How are you doing,
little man?" He dropped his cookie, reached toward her, and
started bawling loudly all over again. She gathered him into
her arms and paced the kitchen, rocking and swaying, the way
mothers do to console a child.

"Wonderful." I said. "I finally get him calmed down and then you rile him up again."

Edith shot me a hurt look and continued to pace the floor with our son.

Ruthie pointed to the cookie lying in pieces on the floor. "Can I please have one of those?"

"*May* I please have one of those," I corrected.

"Of course you may, dearie," the kindly cook said and retrieved another cookie from the countertop. "What's your name, beautiful?"

"Ruthie," she said. "Thank you." She bit off the cookie's head and stood chewing quietly.

"My, what nice manners your children have." The woman smiled.

I snorted a laugh. "Such great manners that we're now forced to leave the party early because of them."

"And miss my flaming rum torte?" She smiled. "Of course, you must do as you think best, but I'm telling you, you haven't lived until you've tried my torte. It's truly amazing."

"Perhaps we should go back to the party and try to make the best of it," I said, then noticed that Raymond had fallen asleep on Edith's shoulder. "But what about him?"

"I'll take the children home," Edith said.

"I don't want you to leave the party," I said.

The cook discreetly walked to the other end of the kitchen.

"I don't mind," Edith said quietly. "I'm tired and it's well after the children's bedtime."

"But I wanted everyone here to meet you."

"It's been a long day, George. I'm probably too tired to be very good company, anyway."

"But you're always so natural at talking to people," I said. "Much better than I am."

She narrowed her eyes at me. "So you're not worried about missing my company, you just want me here to impress your bosses?"

My face grew warm. "I didn't say that."

"But it's what you meant. Isn't it?" She sighed. "Honestly, George. Sometimes I think you care more about your job than you do about the children or me." She reached for Ruthie's hand. "If you'll please escort me to the carriage, I'll remove our ill-behaved children from the party so you may better spend your time impressing others."

I sighed and looked down at my uniform trousers, covered in Raymond's cookie crumbs. I closed my eyes and took a deep breath. When I looked back at Edith, she was glaring at me.

"To the carriage, please," she repeated firmly. "And don't forget our coats." She turned away from me, still holding Raymond on her shoulder, his drool staining her new dress.

Hardly anyone had seen the dress. Or Edith. They'd just heard our son throwing a fit. Definitely not the impression I'd hoped to make at my first company New Year's Eve party. I pushed through the kitchen door on the way to the front entry to retrieve their coats and summon our hired carriage.

*   *   *

Fifteen minutes later, I had bundled Edith and the children into their coats and had handed them up into the carriage. Edith sat with Raymond, still sleeping on her shoulder, and Ruthie perched next to her, fighting to keep her eyes open. I shut the door and instructed the driver to return for me in an hour.

As I watched the horse trot away through the snow, I wondered if I should have left with them. Edith was upset with me, I knew that. But when would I get another chance to speak to Dunbaugh and the other owners? No, I was right to seize this opportunity. After all, I was doing it for Edith and the children. Surely she realized that.

I returned to the party, rubbing my hands together to warm them. Back in the parlor, I was relieved to see the reception line had finally dispersed and Mr. Dunbaugh was now mingling with guests.

"George McVay," he said. "Where's that pretty wife of yours? And your beautiful children?"

I didn't detect any sarcasm in his tone. "They had to leave, sir. I do apologize again, about Raymond's little fit, though. I'm afraid he was over-tired since it was well past his bedtime."

Mr. Dunbaugh held up a palm. "Say no more, George. My children were young once, too."

"Thank you for being so understanding, sir."

He smiled and nodded.

"If you have a moment, sir, I would like to talk to you about my report on maximizing the cargo space on the *Larchmont*."

He plucked a flute of champagne from the tray of a passing waiter and thrust it into my hand. "You need to learn how to relax, George. Have a drink and, since your wife's gone for the evening, go find some other pretty lady to talk to." He winked at me and walked away.

"Yes, sir," I muttered. I sipped my champagne and surveyed the room. A tall, gruff-looking man with snowy white hair standing nearby caught my eye.

I grinned and held out my hand to him. "Mr. Morse. How good to see you again."

He regarded me with a blank expression.

"I'm Captain McVay," I prompted. "Your sister-in-law introduced us at Mr. Houdini's reception in Boston a few months ago."

Recognition registered on his face as he shook my hand. "Ah, yes. The captain of the *Larchmont*."

"Yes, sir. But, I'm surprised to see you here. Do you still own the International Line?"

He chuckled. "Frank and I might own rival steamship companies, Captain McVay, but we're still good friends."

I nodded and took another sip of my drink. "How has business been lately at International?"

"Passenger travel has slowed down but freight has remained fairly steady, typical of this time of year. It must be the same on the Joy Line."

"Yes, it is. Tell me, Mr. Morse, do you currently have any captain positions available on any of your larger steamships?"

The big man laughed. "You certainly aren't one to beat about the bush."

Had I been too bold? I wished Edith were here to mitigate my social faux pas.

"Frank Dunbaugh and I think of ourselves as friends more than rivals," Morse said. "But that might change if I start poaching his steamship captains from him during his company Christmas parties."

I bowed slightly. "I do apologize, sir. I certainly wouldn't want to put you in such an awkward position. Perhaps I could come speak to you some other time?"

"That would be fine. Why don't you telephone me at my office tomorrow?"

"I'll do that."

He extended his hand to me. "If you'll excuse me, I think I'll go find my wife. It was nice to see you again, Captain."

I shook his hand and watched him walk away. Finding no other important people nearby, I stepped over to one of my own crewmembers, my first pilot John Anson, who stood next to a woman in a drab gray dress. "John, are you enjoying yourself?" I asked.

"Yes, sir. Immensely. We've just spent an hour talking to Mrs. Dunbaugh about our upcoming wedding." He looked sharp in his blue pilot's uniform and his well-polished black shoes.

"Oh, you're getting married?" I continued to scan the crowd.

He nodded. "Yes, sir. Mary and I will be wed this spring. I thought you knew."

I shook my head. "When, exactly?"

"May eleventh," Mary said. She threaded her arm through his and smiled up into his face. I noticed she was rather plain and wondered why John had chosen her as his future wife; a prettier woman would have done more to enhance his professional prospects.

"Have you requested time off yet?" I asked him.

He shook his head. "We still have five months."

"Never too soon." Bored, I nodded to the couple and then walked away. Not finding anyone else I wished to talk to,

I collected my coat and stepped outside to await the return of my carriage.

In the Dunbaugh's cobblestone drive, I mentally outlined what I would say to Morse during our conversation the next day. It was imperative that I make that telephone call count because I *had* to get command of a vessel larger than the *Larchmont*. I felt like my career—and my very life—depended upon it.

Chapter 4: New Year's Eve in Times Square

Anna Jensen

Life with Louise during the past few months had been *intressant*—interesting—to put it mildly.

The day after she and I had come home from Boston, John had gone to speak to her new husband, Hans DeThestrup, at the home he shared with his father and two sisters. John wanted to find out Hans's plans for his future and the futures of Louise and their baby. But instead, John had found Hans drunk and belligerent, threatening to inflict bodily harm on John unless he "got the hell out of South Providence." John managed to placate Hans, and the two of them had a frank discussion, which was surprising, considering how little regard they held for each other. In the end, Hans had confessed to marrying Louise solely for her money. Now that a child was on the way, though, Hans said he was having second thoughts. *Vilken skurk!*—What a scoundrel!

Eventually, John and Hans had come to an understanding: for the sum of $3,000, Hans would allow us to pretend he'd died in an accident, he'd leave town, and he'd never be in contact with Louise again. That way, he'd get some of the money he so desired and we'd get our daughter back without her being shackled to such a poor excuse of a husband for the rest of her life. It seemed like the best solution to a difficult situation. Except for one detail. If Louise ever found out about our involvement in this deception, she'd never trust John or me again. After all, *lögnaren blir bara trodd en gang*—the liar will only be trusted once.

Once the deal had been struck, we had no choice but to see it through. So, that Monday, we'd staged an accident at the greenhouse, pretending Hans had been crushed by a wagonload of fertilizer. To me, that seemed like a fitting death for such an odious person. John bribed the coroner to forge a death certificate for Hans and then paid Henry Roberts of Roberts Funeral Home to bury a casket full of sandbags in Providence's Swan Point Cemetery. We even had a white marble headstone carved, marking the grave as the final resting place of "Hans DeThestrup, Loving Husband." *Vilken lögn!*—What a lie!

Louise sobbed at the funeral and cried again when the headstone was installed a month later, insisting upon attending both ceremonies despite terrible morning sickness. Afterward, she entered a period of deep mourning, wearing black from head to toe and refusing to leave our home or to accept visitors, not even her best friend, Edwina. After a month or so, though, she felt the baby move inside her and told John and me she realized that she needed to return to a full life, if only for the sake of her baby. Just within the past few weeks, she'd become attentive to her dressing and grooming again, looking more and more like the vibrant young woman she'd been before she'd met the vile DeThestrup. "Unless I want to live with you and *Pappa* for the rest of my life, I need to find a new husband for me and a father for my baby," she said wisely. Although I was in constant fear of her discovering our role in Hans's "death," I was proud of our daughter's resilience and was looking forward to becoming a grandmother to her child.

*   *   *

When John returned from a New York City business trip just before Christmas, he told Louise and me of an invitation he'd received from Adolph Ochs, owner of *The New York Times*. In celebration of the opening of his new headquarters in Times Square, Mr. Ochs had been hosting a massive fireworks display on the roof of the building every New Year's Eve for the past few years. This year, he planned to mark the occasion in a special way: by having a large ball made of lumber and electric lights hoisted up a pole by ropes and pulleys and then lowered dramatically at the stroke of midnight. Louise announced that she would come with us to the party, since this would probably be her last chance for a public outing for a while. As she said, her "condition" was becoming too obvious.

*   *   *

Like most days this winter, New Year's Eve morning dawned cold and snowy. The train ride to Manhattan featured vistas of white-capped houses and snow-shrouded pines. We were fortunate enough to once again have the use of a private passenger car, courtesy of my sister's husband, Charles Morse. This train trip, though, was a much more festive outing than the last. John, Louise, and I savored the gourmet lunch of Manhattan clam chowder, flaky buttermilk biscuits, and salmon steaks, which we enjoyed while stretching out on the velvety benches. We appreciated the attentive service of Martin and Maria, our personal steward and maid. Although still somewhat pale—her morning sickness had finally abated just the week before the party—Louise looked gorgeous in her deep purple gown. The Empire-waist dress, all the current rage in Paris, coupled with a mink fur muff, did an excellent job of concealing her slightly expanded belly; she was now five and a half months pregnant. John looked positively handsome in a black silk tuxedo, and I felt rather pretty in my new navy blue taffeta gown, cut just a little lower than usual to show off the large sapphire pendant John had bought me for Christmas. For the first time since the day Hans had "died," we all relaxed and enjoyed each other's company. This gave me hope that perhaps our lives and our relationship with our daughter would return to normal soon.

We arrived at Grand Central Station around dusk and were whisked away to the One Times Square building in Mr. Ochs' private coach, manned by two impeccably attired elderly coachmen and pulled by a pair of very handsome dapple-gray geldings. I felt like the Swedish princess, *Crow-cloak*, arriving at church for my wedding with the prince!

The newspaper owner's penthouse suite was swarming with celebrities, the men in their black tuxedoes and the women swathed in various hues of silk. The guest of honor that evening was none other than the famous magician, Harry Houdini, looking quite dapper with his wavy black hair and well-cut tuxedo. Surprisingly, Mr. Houdini remembered me from September's reception at the Parker House Hotel. I introduced him to John before supper and they strode off together, chatting like old friends.

Mr. Och served a meal of the finest rib eye steak I'd ever tasted at a forty-foot long dining table in the suite's boardroom. Several Remington bronzes decorated the side tables and credenzas and I was fairly certain that the large oil painting of water lilies near the elevators was an original by the talented French Impressionist, Claude Monet. The furniture was walnut and cocoa brown leather and everything felt larger than life, like the city in which they existed. Huge potted poinsettias were scattered throughout the room, adding color and a reminder that we were still in the Christmas season.

As I nibbled on my salad, I was gratified to see Louise chatting with the handsome young man seated next to her. I hoped he might turn out to be someone special to her. I glanced across the table to catch John's eye, but he was deep in conversation with a beautiful young woman, whom I recognized as an actress from Victor Herbert's *The Red Mill*, currently appearing on Broadway. Ah well, as long as he *letat, men berörde inte*—looked, but did not touch.

At eleven o'clock, the elevator carried us up one floor to the roof of the building, where the snow had been shoveled away and chairs had been set out in even rows with strategically spaced portable heaters. Perched high atop a flagpole, an iron and wood sphere, five feet in diameter, was illuminated by a hundred electric lights. It waited to mark the arrival of the year 1907. I thought it was an ungainly structure, unfinished wood and bare light bulbs with wires running every which way, but Mr. Ochs stood proudly, directly beneath it, discussing its features with anyone willing to listen.

Even dressed in my warmest woolen coat, hat, and mittens, I found it to be bitterly cold on the roof, so I stood huddled near one of the portable heaters. John wandered off to speak to a group of businessmen as Louise brought me one of the fur stoles the employees were distributing to guests.

"An outdoor event in New York City in December? Whose brilliant idea was this?" she asked with a laugh, draping the fur over my shoulders.

I accepted two china cups full of hot chocolate from a waiter and handed one to Louise. "The fireworks, they are scheduled to begin in a few minutes. Then the lighted ball is to 'drop' at midnight. Hopefully, we'll be back downstairs, in the warmth, within the hour. Unless we freeze to death first." I smiled. "Who was that boy you were speaking to at dinner?"

Louise blew on her chocolate, her diamond necklace and earrings sparkling in the lamplight. "Robby O'Sullivan. According to him, his father owns half of Manhattan."

"It's good to see you enjoying yourself again." I gave her shoulder a gentle squeeze. "*Jag* älskar *dig*, Louise."

"I love you too, *Mamma*," she said absently while staring across the roof, frowning. "I could have sworn I saw someone," she mumbled.

I followed her gaze. "Who, *min kära?* Who do you think you saw?" I pointed toward the base of the flagpole. "*Pappa*, he is over there talking to Mr. Houdini and Mr. Ochs. They are all now the best of friends."

"No, not *Pappa*," she said, patting my arm. "I'll be right back." She walked toward the elevators.

My maternal alarm clanged loudly, so I followed her.

We approached a group of a half-dozen people standing around another portable heater, laughing and drinking. One of them did look quite familiar from behind.

"Hans?" Louise said.

The man turned slowly, a look of shock on his handsome face. He was, in fact, none other than Hans DeThestrup.

Louise emitted a high-pitched scream and dropped her cup. The china smashed on the asphalt roofing, splattering cocoa on our shoes and gowns. Many other partygoers turned toward the noise.

"Hans? What? How?" Louise's chest rose and fell rapidly.

I grasped her shoulders and guided her toward the elevator, at the same time crying out, "John, *hjälp, jag behöver dig!*"

He appeared and immediately comprehended the situation. "Join us," he said to Hans and ushered the four of us into the elevator. We returned to the penthouse suite, one floor below.

I crossed my arms over my chest and glared at Hans De-Thestrup. I wondered where he'd gotten his fashionable suit and overcoat. Stolen, perhaps? I certainly believed him capable of theft and much worse.

Louise stared at him as if he were a ghost. To her, I supposed he was.

I motioned us all toward some armchairs grouped around a table displaying a bronze statue of a horse rearing away from a snake. The statue seemed ironically appropriate to the situation.

We sat.

John clenched and unclenched his hands in his lap, obviously quite upset. But, once again, I could tell he was going to be of no assistance in this dreadful situation.

I felt compelled to break the tense silence. "What do you have to say for yourself, Mr. DeThestrup?"

Hans shrugged. "I promised you I'd never return to Rhode Island and wouldn't contact Louise. I've done neither, so I don't see that you have any basis for complaint against me."

"What are you doing here?" I asked.

"I was invited."

"By whom?"

"Probably the same person who invited you, Adolph Ochs."

"How do you know Mr. Ochs?"

"It just so happens that I'm engaged to marry his daughter."

"What?" I gasped. "You can't marry her. You're still married to Louise."

He shrugged. "Not as far as I'm concerned."

"What do you mean?"

"*Sanningen ligger i betraktarens* öga."

I must have looked shocked because Hans sneered, "Yes, I know some Swedish, too, Mrs. Jensen. The truth is in the eye of the beholder. Correct?"

"You're alive?" Louise asked him quietly.

Hans laughed at her.

I felt like slapping him. Hard.

John stared intently at the bronze statue as if trying to memorize its every curve and angle.

Louise shook her head. "What about the accident? The funeral?" She looked so pale and fragile. I wanted to wrap my arms around her and hug away her pain, but I was afraid that she'd push me away.

"We can explain," I began.

She held up one trembling hand. "No. I think I'm beginning to understand well enough." She looked at Hans. "You married me to get to *Pappa's* money?"

Hans shrugged and glanced toward the elevator.

Louise looked at me. "So you and *Pappa* offered him a bribe to make him go away?" I hated the look of betrayal on her face.

"It wasn't like that, *min kära*," I said. "Hans, he said he didn't want you or the baby. He wanted to leave. He asked for money."

"So you paid him off. And then you pretended that he died?"

"We tried to keep you from getting hurt."

"By lying to me?"

"By giving you another chance for happiness, the chance for true love. *Det bästa du någonsin kommer att lära dig* är *att älska och bli älskad tillbaka*—the greatest thing you'll ever learn is to love and be loved in return."

"But you lied to me," Louise repeated.

The thing that I'd feared most had happened: Louise had found out about our deception. What were we going to do now? How could we ever repair our relationship with our daughter? Such a blatant betrayal. Such boldfaced lies. Our intentions had been good, but they wouldn't matter. Now, Louise would just remember the lies.

Through the window, I saw a colorful explosion of fireworks and realized the new year had begun without us.

Hans stood abruptly. "I'd love to stay for this little chat, but I have a fiancée waiting for me on the roof."

"What about Louise?" I asked. "Legally, she is still your wife."

"The Ochses are very eager to have me marry their daughter. I'm sure their attorney will be able to find a judge to disavow my marriage to Louise. After all, we never lived together as husband and wife. Isn't that grounds for an annulment?"

"Annulment?" Louise whispered. "As if our marriage never happened?"

Hans nodded.

"But what about our baby?" she asked.

Hans shrugged. "There are ways to get rid of unwanted pregnancies."

I leapt to my feet. "*Försvinn!* Get out of here!"

Hans laughed and then strode through the lobby. "Have a nice life," he said over his shoulder, and then banged open the door to the stairwell and disappeared.

The three of us stared as the door swung shut behind him.

Louise rose and placed her palm on Hans' chair, tracing the imprint of his body. "He never really loved me. Did he?"

I looked at the wool rug and shook my head.

"And then you made up the story about him dying? You even had Dr. Adams fill out a fake death certificate and had Mr. Roberts bury an empty casket?"

I saw the pain in my daughter's face. "We were just . . ."

She silenced me with a pain-filled glance. "Where did he go after he supposedly died?"

"We bought him a ticket to New York City. Maybe he was here the whole time."

"You bought him a train ticket? You helped him leave me?"

"We wanted him out of your life," I said. "We did what we thought was best for you and the baby."

Louise was crying now, silent tears streaming down her cheeks and falling onto her beautiful purple gown. "I would like to go home now," she whispered as she picked up her coat. She walked to the elevator, pushed the call button, and stood waiting, her back to John and me.

Chapter 5: Career Announcement

Millard Franklin

I didn't take the direct route home from the trolley station New Year's Eve, but instead meandered down the snowy side streets and alleys of North Attleboro, gradually working my way north toward our home on Park Lane. As I walked, I kept replaying the events of the evening because, oh, what an evening it had been!

First had come my performance in the church variety show. Everything had gone absolutely perfectly and the audience had loved me. I'd never received such an ovation before—an entire minute. For the first time in my life, I felt like a *real* magician, someone Mr. Houdini would be proud to have in his vaudeville show.

And then, after my performance, dinner with Sadie had been wonderful. I loved having her sitting next to me, introducing her to people. She kept smiling at me with her dark eyes and adorable, tiny, white teeth, and telling me how much she enjoyed the show.

Everyone at the church hall had said such nice things to me tonight. And Reverend Foster had nicknamed me the Boy Houdini. Imagine *me* being compared to the Great One.

And, to top off the evening, Sadie had kissed me. From her letters, I'd *thought* she might be growing to like me at least a little bit, but I had no idea she felt as strongly as I did. I could still feel her soft lips pressed against mine, her small hands squeezing my arm.

As I turned onto Park Lane and then into our driveway, I realized that I never wanted to return to work at the lock shop again. I was tired of living a double life, with my hands doing locksmithing while my head and heart were doing magic. Tonight's performance had solidified my resolve. Somehow, I had to tell my family and Uncle Henry. I had to make them understand that I had to accept the job with Houdini. I had to do magic. My very life depended on it.

How would Sadie feel about me being a magician? Would she rule me out as a potential suitor, thinking I could never provide for a wife and family? Would I have to choose between magic and her? I sure hoped not. I'd write to her tonight and try to make her understand my career choice.

I opened the door to the kitchen and encountered three things simultaneously: a blast of warm air, the smell of fresh-baked pecan pie, and a dozen voices yelling, "Surprise!" My whole family—including Aunt Hattie, Uncle Henry, and four of my cousins—were gathered in our dining room, waiting to congratulate me on my magic performance in the church show.

Mom bustled forward, wearing the biggest smile I'd seen on her face in a long time. She enfolded me in a tight hug and kissed me noisily on the cheek. "We're all so proud of you, Milly!" she said with tears in her eyes. Then, one by one, all of my relatives stepped forward and offered their own words of praise.

Even Uncle Henry. "Although I don't approve of magic as a profession," he said, "I must admit, I was quite impressed with your performance this evening." Aunt Hattie, standing by his side, smiled and bobbed her head repeatedly.

I hadn't even been aware that they were in the audience.

Uncle Henry thrust his hand forward. "Congratulations, son. Job well done." As we shook hands, though, he frowned and said, "Just don't let me catch you practicing at the lock shop."

I had to tell him—to tell all of them—the truth. Now. I cleared my throat. "Hey, everyone…"

A few people turned around expectantly, but most kept on talking.

"May I have your attention?"

Still, most continued with their conversations.

An ear-splitting whistle filled the room. Everyone turned to see Thomas taking his fingers out of his mouth. He winked at me. "Works every time." Loudly, he announced, "Milly, our star of the evening, has something he'd like to say."

Logs popped in the fireplace and filled the room with a flickering orange glow.

Suddenly, I felt awkward and unsure. What if everyone disagreed with my decision? What if they all thought I'd be better off taking over Uncle Henry's business, as planned? Everyone was staring at me, waiting.

"Umm…I guess the first thing…umm…"

"Speak up!" My cousin Frank shouted from the back of the room.

He was right. It was time for me to speak up. I pulled back my shoulders and cleared my throat again. "First of all, I'd like to say thank you." I found my younger brother's face in the crowd. "Chester, thanks for your expert assistance."

My family clapped and hooted as Chester took a bow.

"And thank you all for coming out to support me at the church tonight. It really meant a lot to me to have you all there."

More applause and cheers erupted.

I located my mother and uncle. They weren't going to like this. "There is something that I've wanted to tell you for quite some time now," I said.

Mom darted an anxious glance at Uncle Henry. I wondered if they had any idea what I was about to say.

"I wanted to make sure that I was one hundred percent positive before I said anything. And now, after the show at the church tonight, I am." I paused to select my words carefully.

Then I talked to my family. I explained how my fascination with magic and locks had grown steadily, how what was once just a hobby had turned into the main focus of my life. I finished by announcing, "In March of this coming year, I will be returning to Boston to begin touring in a vaudeville show with Mr. Harry Houdini."

My declaration was met with a stunned silence. Not even my brothers or sisters said anything. Finally, my uncle stroked his too-skinny moustache and asked, "So, your mind is made up?"

"Yes."

"And nothing we say is going to change how you feel?"

"No."

He thudded his fist down on the arm of his chair, his thin face growing redder by the second. Looking at Mom, he said, "Well, Laura, now you see what comes from mollycoddling the boy. I warned you that we needed to be firm with him. But did you listen to me? No."

"What do you mean?" Her face was white, in stark contrast to the festive green dress and bonnet she wore.

"When Millard insisted on fooling around with all of that magical nonsense, I told you it was a bad idea. But you disagreed. 'The boy needs his hobby,' you said. Well, look at where his hobby has gotten him, now. He intends to run off and become a magician." He was talking about me as if I wasn't there.

"I am seventeen years old," I reminded him.

"I don't care how old you are. As long as you're apprenticed to me, you'll live by my rules."

"But I won't be your apprentice anymore. I'll be touring with Mr. Houdini instead."

"And where will you live?" my uncle asked. "How much will he pay you?"

I picked up the fireplace poker and jabbed it at a log in the fire. "We haven't discussed the particulars yet."

"You're giving up a well-paying, steady job at my shop for a position with a man you hardly know, to live who knows where, and for an unknown amount of money? And—to make matters that much worse—he's a Jew." He laughed mirthlessly. "Sounds like a well thought-out plan to me."

"But it's what I want to do," I said.

"Grow up, Millard!" he shouted. "We don't always get to do what we want!"

I glanced toward my mother for intervention, but she wouldn't meet my eyes.

"You know," Uncle Henry said, "if you decide to take this course of action, I won't hold your job for you. Since your aunt and I have no children of our own, I was planning on turning the shop over to you in a few years. That wouldn't happen, either. You'd be giving up your entire future with me."

"I understand," I said. "And I want you to know how grateful I am to you for letting me work for you for the past year. Because of you, I met Mr. Houdini and all of this happened." I sighed and looked into the fire for a moment. "Mom, Uncle Henry, everybody… If I don't accept this offer, I know that I'll spend the rest of my life thinking, 'What if?' Look at me. I'm a teen-aged kid from North Attleboro, Massachusetts. When am I ever going to get another chance to tour with the greatest magician who ever lived, to learn what he knows, and to see the world? This is the opportunity of a lifetime. I can't pass it up, and I can't believe that you would honestly want me to either." I searched my uncle's face, hoping to see some glint of understanding.

From across the room, my littlest sister said, "Milly's gonna be a real magician."

Uncle Henry whipped his head around. "What did you say?"

Ethel walked over to me, her shiny black Sunday shoes clicking on the wood floor. Taking my hand, she tipped her head back and looked up at me. "You told me you're gonna be a real magician, and one day you're gonna make me float just like that lady in your book. Right?"

I smiled down at her big brown eyes, full of admiration and love, and nodded.

My mother quietly said, "She's right, Henry."

Everyone turned to look at her as she stood behind me, resting her hands on my shoulders. "Millard was born to be a magician. It's in his blood, in his bones. Anyone can see that. He's good at it, too. Just look at how everyone loved him in the variety show tonight." She squeezed my shoulders. "And this job offer from Mr. Houdini is the biggest thing to ever happen to anyone in this family, maybe to anyone in this town." She smiled at her brother-in-law. "Everything you said is true, Henry, about the uncertainty of the whole thing. But that doesn't erase the fact that this is an amazing opportunity for our boy here. You said that we don't always get to do what we want. But why not? Why shouldn't Milly get this chance to fulfill his dreams? What's the worst that will happen? His job with Mr. Houdini won't work out and he'll have to come home?" She shrugged. "I understand that you can't hold his job for him, that you'll have to hire someone else in his place. So? Milly can always go back to painting houses with Thomas and Chester. Would that be so bad?" Mother walked over and stood before Uncle Henry's chair, her hands clasped in front of her as if she were praying. "Milly's a good boy and he's always worked very hard. If he wants to tour with Mr. Houdini, we shouldn't stop him."

For a moment, no one said a thing; the only sound in the room was the log crackling in the fire grate.

Then Uncle Henry stared down at the wood floor and shook his head slowly. He sighed and glanced at his wife. "Hattie, I guess I'm not going to retire as soon as we'd planned."

She leaned over and kissed him on the cheek. Turning to my mother, she asked, "Didn't I hear you say something about pecan pie?"

"Coming right up," Mom said, hurrying into the kitchen.

Chapter 6: Out With the Old, In With the New

Sadie Golub

On the train ride home from Millard's magic show, somewhere between the Canton Depot and Boston's South Station, I had decided that the time had come for me to stop sewing for Mr. Miller and to strike out on my own. I already had plenty of clients. I just needed to make the leap of faith required to be entirely self-employed. Yes, I was a woman. And no, I wasn't even an American citizen—not yet. But I was sure if I worked hard enough, I could succeed in my own sewing business. I resolved to start my new life the very next day: New Year's Day 1907.

Unfortunately, Solomon, my brother and guardian, obviously did not agree with my resolution, because the following afternoon found me sitting at our kitchen table, knitting a pair of socks for his son, while he overplayed his role as my older brother. Bessie sat next to him, bouncing Morris on her knee. I wondered whose side she'd take in the discussion.

Solomon said, "They have a saying in this country that you probably don't know yet." He stood in front of our kitchen sink, his large hands resting on his narrow hips.

I hated when he talked to me in such a condescending tone. Yes, he'd been in the United States for three years longer than I had and, yes, he spoke English far better than I did, but I was learning the language quickly and I didn't appreciate him constantly pointing out my shortcomings. I struggled to keep my tone neutral. "What is this saying?"

"Don't bite the hand that feeds you. It means…"

"I know what it means." I stabbed my needle into the sock's heel.

"…It means, since Mr. Miller pays you to sew for him, you shouldn't go into business for yourself."

Instead of haranguing me like this, I felt like Solomon should be praising me. I was now giving him twice as much money each week as I used to when I'd been working exclusively for Mr. Miller. Because of my increased contribution, Solomon no longer struggled to pay his bills every month and we'd been able to send enough money to Russia to fully finance our younger sister's trip to America; Esther was due to arrive in Boston when the weather broke in the spring.

But apparently Solomon didn't approve of my self-sufficiency. "No man will marry you," he said. "You'd make him feel like half a man, since you don't need him to support you."

I finished a row of knitting and started on the next one. "I am a woman. I will meet a man soon."

"You think so? Then where is he? I don't see him." Solomon opened the apartment door and pretended to peer out into the hallway. He returned to the kitchen table, wearing a smug smile.

I wanted to tell him about Millard, who, far from being threatened by my burgeoning dressmaking business, had been extremely encouraging, filling his letters with suggestions of ways for me to advertise my business and to attract more customers. I wanted to show my stupid brother that not every man was as backward thinking as he was about women and their rights. But I knew he wouldn't listen, so instead I decided to be contentious. "Maybe I not ever have husband. I not need one."

Bessie stopped bouncing the baby and gasped. "Sadie! Every woman needs a husband."

"Why?"

She nodded toward her son. "So you can have children, of course."

"Maybe I not have children." I replaced my knitting supplies in my sewing basket.

"But you have to," she insisted. "That's why women were put here on this earth."

I shrugged as I stood and tied a piece of twine around the large brown paper-wrapped packet of clothing, the last packet I ever planned to take to Mr. Miller. "It not matter. I not have time to sew for me and for Mr. Miller. I make more money to sew for me, so today I tell him that I not work for him anymore."

I put on my coat, gloves, and hat, and strode to the door, the wrapped parcel tucked under one arm and my purse tucked under the other.

"I am warning you, little sister, you will never get a husband as long as you pretend to be a businessman, and you will never be happy without a husband."

"If man not marry me because I run a business, then I not want him for a husband." I stepped out into the hallway and slammed the apartment door behind me.

*   *   *

Twenty minutes later, I stood in the gray snow in front of Mr. Miller's tailor shop. As I paused to catch my breath in the frosty air, I heard people in a nearby tavern singing loudly, "Should old acquaintance be forgot, and never brought to mind…" I was so nervous about speaking to Mr. Miller that I'd forgotten today was New Year's Day.

Squaring my shoulders and smoothing the front of my dress coat—designed and made by me, of course—I twisted the cold brass doorknob and stepped into the warm shop that smelled of starch and sewing machine oil, two of my favorite scents.

As I entered, Mr. Miller's round, red face looked up from his sewing machine. "Ah, Miss Golub, have you finished those aprons for the textile mill owner?" He strode to the front counter. Five middle-aged women, all wearing headscarves, looked up and then returned their attention to their sewing machines.

I handed Mr. Miller the paper-wrapped bundle. He untied the string with his pudgy fingers and inspected my work. "I suppose this is acceptable."

I smiled as I realized this was the last time I'd have to put up with his lack of praise for my high-quality work.

He reached under the counter, picked up an envelope, and handed it to me. "Here are your wages for the week."

"Thank you." I withdrew an envelope from my purse and handed it to him.

He looked confused. "What's this?"

"Thirty-four dollars for sewing machine. I buy it."

He held the envelope out to me. "You don't have to buy the machine from me, Miss Golub. You can just keep borrowing it like you've been doing." The tone of his voice was the same tone someone would use when speaking to a small child. I resented that.

I held up a palm. "I not want to borrow machine any more. I want to buy it. If you not want to sell, I will give it back to you and buy new one at store."

"As long as you are working for me, you can simply use that one. There's no need for you to purchase it."

Pulling myself up to my full height, I said, "Thank you for letting me work for you. But now I work for me."

He blinked rapidly. "For you? I don't understand."

"You said I could use sewing machine in my spare time. So, I sewed clothes for other people and now I have enough work that I not need to sew for you anymore. I work for me now."

His normally red face turned an alarming shade of purple as he leaned over the counter, his hands and arms shaking. "Why, you little…!"

I gasped and took a step back while the other women in the shop stopped sewing, turned, and stared.

"Where did all of your customers come from, Miss Golub?" Mr. Miller yelled. "Did they just magically appear?"

I shook my head. "I took in dress for Mrs. Houdini. Then she have me sew four traveling dresses for her. Then she tell other women about me. And they tell other women. Now I have dress-making business. But thank you for your…"

"A fine way you have of thanking me! By stealing my customers!"

All of a sudden, I was tired of other people telling me what to do: my brother, Bessie, and now Mr. Miller. I was an adult woman, perfectly capable of making my own decisions. And I certainly wasn't going to let Mr. Miller bully me into continuing to work for him. I placed my purse on the counter and leaned toward his perspiring face. "I not steal your customers."

"Oh, yes, I forgot. You said that the wife of a world-famous magician hired you to make some clothing for her and then recommended you to her friends. Why would she do that for you, a stupid Russian Jew?"

I heard gasps from several of the other women in the shop, many of whom were also recent immigrants from Russia. I picked up my purse and tucked it under my arm. "I not stupid, Mr. Miller. Mrs. Houdini says she like my work—you never say that—and she pays me good money. And then her friends pay, too."

He scoffed, "I gave you a job when you needed it and you thank me by stabbing me in the back."

I pointed to the envelope on the counter. "You want money for sewing machine or want me to give machine back?"

He snatched up the envelope. "I'll take the money. Although that machine is probably worth more than $34."

I withdrew a newspaper clipping from my purse and placed it on the counter. "Singer 66 sewing machine at Sears Roebuck Department Store for $34, brand new. I pay you $34 for one-year-old machine. Yes?"

Mr. Miller waved one hand. "Fine. Go ahead and take the damned thing."

I withdrew another paper from my purse. "Sign this."

"What is it?" His eyes squinted suspiciously.

"Paper that say you sell me sewing machine for $34."

Mr. Miller grabbed a pen from the counter, dunked it in the nearby inkwell, and scrawled his signature across the bottom of the paper. "Now, get out of here!"

I calmly blew the ink dry, refolded the paper, and tucked it into my purse. Re-buttoning my coat, I said, "Mr. Miller, thank you for…"

"Just get out!" he roared.

As the women in the shop smiled at me and nodded their approval, I slowly walked out the door and closed it firmly behind me.

"Get back to work!" I heard Mr. Miller growl to the other women.

I slopped through the slushy sidewalk snow for a block and then paused. Slowly, a smile spread across my face. I'd done it! I'd quit my job and now I was self-employed. Sadie Golub:

Dressmaker. Out with the old and in with the new. Happy New Year to me!

Humming "Auld Lang Syne," I walked home.

Chapter 7: Missed Connection

George McVay

The day after the Joy Line New Year's Eve party, I telephoned the steamship office and reported in sick; some other captain would have to guide the *Larchmont* to and from New York City Harbor that evening in my stead. In the four years I'd worked for the Joy Line, I'd never called in sick before, but today I needed to telephone Charles Morse at the International Steamship Line and I couldn't do that from on board my ship. Something about Morse's facial expression at the party the night before had made me nearly certain that today he was going to offer me a captainship on one of his larger vessels. He was a man who recognized my true potential. At last, I was going to get the command—and the increased salary—that I deserved.

Despite the cold and the snow, I'd arranged for Edith and Matilda to take the children out for a walk that morning so the house would be quiet for my telephone conversation. I wished the damned contraption wasn't mounted in the house's main hallway. Why couldn't it be located in a more secluded room, like the parlor? I'd heard stories of people in Newport with telephones installed in several different rooms of their homes. That seemed a bit excessive to me, but I wouldn't mind having ours located in a quieter spot.

I'd decided on ten o'clock as the ideal time to telephone Morse. Starting at nine forty-five, I paced the hallway, checking my pocket watch every few minutes. At nine fifty-five, I removed the telephone earpiece from its cradle and briskly turned the crank on the side of the wooden box six times.

"Good morning, Providence operator," a woman's voice said.

Speaking into the funnel-shaped receiver, I said, "Good morning. Would you please connect me to the Boston office of Charles Morse, President of the International Steamship Line?"

"Yes, sir. And who may I say is calling?"

"Captain George McVay."

"Just a moment."

As I waited for her to connect me, I listened to the whirs and pops of static on the telephone line. I'd been up most of the night, pacing our bedroom floor, considering exactly what I was going to say to Morse. I wanted to sound self-assured but not overly confident, enthusiastic but not childish. While Edith slept, I'd stood before our dresser mirror and rehearsed my lines, guessing at Morse's responses. I'd practiced many different scenarios and felt fairly sure I'd be able to react appropriately, no matter what he said or asked.

I heard the Providence operator speaking to the Boston operator, requesting the connection, and my heart beat faster.

I wondered if Morse had asked my boss about me. If so, what had Dunbaugh said? As far as I knew, Dunbaugh held me in high regard. Otherwise, he wouldn't have promoted me to captain so quickly. But that'd been two years ago. And the *Larchmont* was one of the smaller steamships in the line. Why hadn't I been promoted again? Suddenly, I was worried.

"Good morning, International Steamship Line," a distant feminine voice said. The Boston operator announced my call. The Providence operator said, "Go ahead, sir," and completed the connection.

"Good morning, Captain McVay," the International operator said. "I'm afraid I cannot connect you to Mr. Morse."

"Why not?"

"He's not in his office today, sir. Actually, nobody's here but me. The office is closed for the celebration of New Year's Day."

"The office is closed? Was that a last-minute decision?" Just last night, Morse had told me to call him today.

"No, sir. The International is always closed on New Year's Day. The ships don't run, either. May I take a message for Mr. Morse?"

Why had he said to call if he wasn't going to be in the office? Had he forgotten about the holiday? Or had he deliberately misinformed me, just to get me to stop bothering him at the party? I was stunned, but I recovered sufficiently to leave my name and telephone number. I replaced the earpiece in its cradle and sat heavily on the bench in our front hallway.

The front door swung open and Ruthie, Raymond, Edith, and Matilda trudged in, snowflakes dusting from their coats and hats onto the floor. Matilda gathered the children and ushered them through to the kitchen.

"Hello, dear," Edith said to me, unbuttoning her coat. "How was your telephone call? When are you going to meet with Mr. Morse?" She unwound the red wool scarf from her neck.

"I didn't speak with Morse. The office was closed for the holiday."

"Oh." The look she gave me was full of pity and I didn't like it.

I frowned at her. "I'm sure it was just an oversight on his part. He simply forgot that today was a holiday. He's a very busy man, you know."

She nodded rapidly. "I'm sure that's the case, dear. He'll probably telephone you tomorrow and apologize." Now she was patronizing me, I could tell.

"I'm sure he will." I stood and then realized I had nowhere to go. I'd called in sick to work and therefore had the entire day before me with nothing scheduled. I immediately resolved to write a letter to Morse; at least I'd be sure to reach him that way.

"George, I was wondering…" Edith removed her coat and hung it in the hall closet.

"What?" I said impatiently. I wanted to get started on my letter.

"When I phoned Father last week, he mentioned that Captain Duke was retiring this spring. Would you like me to ask about his position for you?"

"Me, a captain on the Bangor-to-Boston line? Those captainships are even less prestigious than the command of the *Larchmont*."

"I just thought that you might be interested."

"Do you really think so little of me?"

Her cheeks, already pink from being outside, flushed even more. "No, dear. I'm sorry. I thought it could be an alternative to your current position."

"No, thank you." As the daughter of a steamship captain, she should have known better than to even mention such an option.

"Fine." She slammed the closet door and climbed the stairs toward our bedroom.

I strode into the parlor and slid the doors closed behind me. I had a letter to write. And I needed to make it a good one.

Chapter 8: Unanswered Prayers

Anna Jensen

"*Mamma*, wake up! Something's wrong with my baby!" Louise stood next to our four-poster bed, her face bathed in sweat. She was clutching her little belly with tears streaming from her eyes and a terrible red stain spreading across the lower part of her blue flannel nightgown.

After the brutally silent train ride home from New York, I'd finally climbed into bed, exhausted, just as the sun was peeking over the Providence skyline. Now, instantly awake, I sprang to my feet, reaching for my robe lying on a nearby chair. "What is it, honey? What's wrong?"

"I don't know," Louise said. "I was sleeping and then I had this terrible pain in my back."

I reached to touch her shoulder, but she pulled away from me. "Just one pain?" I asked.

"No. They keep coming, every ten minutes or so. And there's all this blood."

I heard the panic in our daughter's voice and reached across the bed to roughly shake John's shoulder.

"What? What's wrong?" He sat up and raked his fingers through his silver hair.

"John, it's Louise. Her baby's coming."

"It's too early," he mumbled.

"A baby doesn't consult a calendar, *min kära*. Send Moses to get Dr. Adams. We need the doctor here—now." With the tone of my voice, I tried to convey the urgency of the situation without alarming Louise.

John threw back the quilt and grabbed his own robe. "I'll go fetch Adams myself." He looked at Louise's blood-stained nightgown and gasped. "Get back to bed," he said and then strode away, calling for Moses to help him dress.

I put my arm around Louise. "*Pappa's* right. Let's put you back to bed."

Her beautiful blonde hair, pulled back in a braid for bed, had begun to unravel and hung in long curly strands around her face. "But what about the baby?" she pleaded.

"*Pappa* is getting Dr. Adams." I led her down the hall, dimly lit by one gas lamp. In her bedroom, I helped her change into a fresh nightgown and then tucked her under her covers. "Sometimes babies arrive a little ahead of schedule, but they are just fine."

"But my baby's not due until spring!"

"I know," I soothed. "We'll just have to *vänta och se*—wait and see." I poured a glass of water for Louise and said a silent prayer.

God, Louise has been through so much lately. If anything happens to this baby, I don't think she could take it. Please keep them both safe. Amen.

As Louise moaned with her next contraction, I gently wiped her forehead and repeated my prayer, over and over again. I would make God listen to me this time.

*   *   *

An hour later, John returned with Dr. Adams, who examined Louise, his eyebrows drawn together in a bushy, gray vee. Casting off his overcoat, he called for some soap, hot water, and towels. In a fatherly voice, he said to her, "The next time you feel a contraction, go ahead and push."

"But it's too early!" Louise pleaded.

"Early or not, that baby is coming now. Go ahead and push."

As Louise lay there, I was struck by how young she was. Too young to give birth. Too young to be a mother. Tears and sweat mingled on her cheeks as she lifted her head from her pillows and bore down. Her contraction subsided, but then, only a minute later, she was overcome with another, stronger one. She screamed as if she was being torn in two and tears sprang to my eyes as well.

God, please help Louise and her baby! Please!

"Here it comes," the doctor said calmly, reaching out with a clean bath towel. One more prolonged yell from Louise and Dr. Adams was wrapping something up in the towel. "Hold him," he said, handing me the bundle.

I cradled the smallest baby I had ever seen. From the top of his head to the bottom of his feet, he could have fit entirely in one of my hands. As much as I could see of him, he was perfect—ten fingers and ten toes and a clump of curly dark hair—but he was tiny...so tiny...too tiny. I could see his little chest rising and falling rapidly. His miniature hands were balled into tight fists. His skinny legs were tucked up to his tummy. And his skin was a dusky blue color.

"*Mamma*, I don't hear the baby," Louise called out weakly. "Where's the baby?"

I tucked the towel closer around the tiny infant and brought him to the head of the bed. "Here he is, Louise. It's a boy." I tried to smile at my daughter, but my lips wouldn't lie.

Louise reached out with trembling arms as I handed her the baby. She cuddled him to her damp chest. "He's so small, *Mamma*, and he's so quiet. Why is he so quiet?"

I shook my head slowly, tears running down my cheeks and dripping onto my bathrobe. I stroked Louise's hair as she stroked her son's. Together we watched as the baby gradually breathed slower and slower, his skin turning a deeper blue. He didn't open his eyes or wave his arms or kick his legs. He just breathed, slower and slower.

And then he stopped breathing.

"Dr. Adams," I said loudly.

He took the baby from Louise and hurried over to the desk. We watched as he laid the baby on his back and then on his stomach, patting him firmly and blowing into his tiny mouth. After a few minutes, the doctor wrapped the baby in the towel again and brought him back to Louise's bedside where he handed her the bundle with a sad shake of his head.

Louise bent and kissed her son, hugged his little body tightly in her arms. Then she cried as only a mother bereft of her child can cry: a keening that came from her very soul. I gathered the two of them into my arms and rocked them back and forth, back and forth, still praying for a miracle.

But the miracle didn't happen.

Sometime later, Dr. Adams placed a gentle hand on my back.

I turned and found John standing by his side. I let go of Louise and clung to my husband, releasing my own sobs. John picked me up like a child and sat with me on his lap in the rocking chair next to Louise's bed, holding me with his strong arms. Gradually, the room quieted.

Dr. Adams returned to Louise's bedside. "Would you like to say goodbye?" he asked her.

She nodded and kissed the baby's forehead once more, closed her eyes, and rocked him, a small smile playing across her lips. After one more kiss on his forehead, she handed him to the doctor.

Dr. Adams brought the baby over to the rocking chair and I took him in my arms for the second and final time. I unwrapped him just a little so that John could see him, could see how perfect he was. Perfect...and tiny...and dead. I kissed the baby's forehead, John kissed him, and then I handed him back to the doctor.

"I'll take him right over to Roberts Funeral Home," Dr. Adams said as he picked up his bag and walked from the room. John followed him into the hallway.

I tucked the covers in around Louise's sweaty body and brushed damp blonde curls away from her forehead.

"He was so beautiful, *Mamma*," she whispered, her eyes closed.

BOOK 3:
THE *LARCHMONT* DISASTER, FEBRUARY 1907

Chapter 1: Magician on Board

Millard Franklin

Despite the heavy snow and bitter cold, on the afternoon of February 11, I decided to walk from Union Station to the Joy Line pier at the Port of Providence. I wasn't sure of the trolley schedule in that area and didn't want to risk missing the boat. I carried a duffle bag of clothes over my shoulder and dragged my trunk of magic gear behind me. As I trudged down the drift-filled streets, though, I doubted the wisdom of my choice. The snow fought against me, stinging my cheeks and forming huge mounds for me to plow through with my heavy luggage. And it was so cold. I wondered if we'd even sail in such bad weather.

I'd deliberately timed my arrival at the pier to be several hours prior to the *Larchmont*'s scheduled departure at six-thirty, hoping I'd be able to get a tour of the ship before we left. Of course, that depended upon Captain McVay remembering me and the offer he'd made at the Houdini reception five months ago. As I recalled, the captain had been much more interested in impressing Mrs. Jensen than in becoming my friend.

Arriving at the steamship's gangplank, I set down my trunk and handed my ticket to the tall officer standing there. He looked cold despite the thick blue woolen coat he wore over his uniform. Now, the snow was coming down so hard I could barely see the outline of the ship, bobbing up and down in the turbulent bay. The young officer quickly examined my ticket and handed it back to me. "Very good, Mr. Franklin. You may go aboard. Make sure to see a steward about selecting a sleeping cabin."

I hesitated.

"Is there something else I may do for you?" he asked.

"Yes. I met Captain McVay last September at a party in Boston and he told me that, if ever I had the chance to stop by his ship, he might give me a tour." I stumbled to a stop.

"So, you want me to tell the captain that you are here and ask him if he has a few minutes to show you around?"

"Yes." I smiled. "If that's not too much trouble."

"No trouble at all. Please go on into the main saloon, and I will meet you there once I speak to Captain McVay."

"Thank you." I picked up my luggage and carefully climbed the slippery wooden gangplank. I dragged everything through the ship's narrow doorway, down the carpeted hallway, and into the main saloon. Once there, I parked my trunk against one wall, deposited my duffle bag on top of it, and plunked myself onto the first empty space on one of the long wooden benches. Glancing at my trunk, I smiled as I saw that my mother had carefully stenciled "The Boy Houdini" on all six sides.

Two pre-teen boys approached me. The taller one said, "My brother, Bobby, and I have a bet. I say you are that magician guy—the Boy Houdini—but he says you're not."

I smiled and pulled off my felt cap, soggy with melted snow. "So, how much did you bet?"

"A nickel."

"Hmm. That's a serious bet," I said, noticing the patches sewn on the boys' trousers and jackets.

"Yeah. So, are you that Houdini guy or not?"

I pointed to my trunk.

The taller boy read my mother's stencils and threw both arms up in the air. "Yeah!" The smaller one, Bobby, solemnly fished in his pocket, pulled out a nickel, and paid his brother.

Feeling sorry for Bobby, I summoned them closer. "Would you like me to show you a trick?"

The boys' eyes grew big. "Yea!" they said in unison.

I withdrew a pack of cards from my pocket, shuffled them, and fanned them. "Pick one."

The tall boy selected a card and showed it to Bobby.

"Okay, now put it back in the deck anywhere you'd like." I reshuffled the deck. Tapping it with my index finger, I said, "*Abracadabra!*" and indicated that the boys should look at the top card.

When they saw it was the card they'd selected, they were just as amazed as I'd been the first time I'd seen the trick ten years earlier. "How'd you do that?" they asked in unison.

I smiled. "A good magician never reveals his secrets, but watch carefully." I repeated the trick twice again, each time more slowly. Then I handed them the deck of cards. "Take these. I'll bet if you practice with them for a little bit, you'll be able to figure it out."

The boys said, "Thanks!" and scampered off while I sat back on the bench. A moment later, though, they were back, staring down at their scuffed-up shoes.

The taller boy thrust the deck of cards toward me. "Mom says we can't take these from you. She said that you probably stole them. I told her that she was wrong, that you were a good guy, but she said we had to give them back to you, anyhow."

I looked up to see a dark-haired woman glaring at me from the other side of the saloon.

I smiled sadly at the boys as I accepted the playing cards. "Please tell your mother that I didn't steal these cards or anything else. I'm a magician, not a thief."

"I told her that!" the older boy said.

I nodded sadly to the two brothers and they shuffled away.

I was only momentarily upset, though. A quick glance around the room reminded me that I was on my first-ever steamship ride. A wide grin overspread my face. I had to be one of the luckiest men alive!

A moment later, I felt even luckier when the officer who'd checked my ticket on the gangplank strode up to me and said, "Mr. Franklin, as the saying goes, I have good news and bad news. The bad news is that the captain is currently occupied and cannot take you on a tour of the ship. The good news is that he said I could be your guide."

"That would be great. I mean, if you aren't too busy."

He held out his hand. "Assistant Steward Jefferson Barnes, at your service. You can call me Jeff, unless the captain is around. Then I'm Mr. Barnes, sir."

I laughed and shook his hand. "Hi, Jeff. Please, call me Millard. I really appreciate you taking the time to show me around. I've never been on a steamship before."

"Well then, follow me. We'll start in the hold and end up in the pilothouse." He pointed toward my trunk and duffle bag. "But let's first find a place for you to stow your gear."

We descended to the *Larchmont's* main deck, where we selected an empty private cabin and dropped off my luggage. Then I followed Jeff down another steep flight of stairs into the belly of the ship, which was rocking violently back and forth, despite still being tied up to the pier.

"These are the parts of the ship that most passengers don't get to see," Jeff reported, as we walked through the crew's quarters with berths stacked from floor to ceiling. Many of the men lying on the bunks greeted Jeff, some in English, some not.

We stepped through a bulkhead into a room where Jeff told me "firemen" shoveled coal into furnaces that powered the ship's boilers. The room was incredibly hot, even on this frigid winter's day, and the men working were stripped to the waist, with sweat pouring from their bodies.

The next room, the engine room, was crammed with giant, odd-looking equipment full of rivets and gears and smelled of hot oil. I began to appreciate all of the technology and people necessary to run a two-hundred-and-fifty-foot-long side-paddle steamship. An older man in a ship's uniform—the head engineer?—frowned at Jeff and me as we entered the engine room, so we hurried through to the opposite side, where we stepped into the men's dorm room. Jeff explained that this was where male passengers could sleep for no additional charge during overnight trips. Bare cots filled half the room and long wooden benches took up the rest of the area.

Back up on the main deck, we walked by dozens of doors to private and semi-private cabins. The saloon deck contained the main saloon, the dining saloon, and another array of sleeping cabins.

Outside on the freezing hurricane deck, a double-row of small white cabins extended from the huge paddle wheels to the back of the ship, with large covered lifeboats, swinging slowly from metal brackets, mounted on the cabins' roofs. Two massive black smokestacks towered above the cabins and the small pilothouse. From that vantage point, I noticed that the snow had slowed down a bit, but as the sun dipped lower in the winter sky, the temperature had dropped even more. What a night to be out on the water!

Inside the pilothouse, Jeff and I hugged one wall, trying to stay out of the way of the four men preparing the ship for departure. We stomped our feet and blew on our hands to warm ourselves as Jeff continued narrating the tour. "That's the ship's wheel." He pointed to a massive structure housing two large, spoked, wooden wheels. "And that's where the captain stands." He indicated a worn spot on the deck next to the large windows, which looked out over the ship's bow.

"How many people does it take to sail the *Larchmont*?" I asked.

"Tonight, we have a crew of fifty-two. Here in the pilothouse, Captain McVay has at least one pilot and two quartermasters with him at all times. It takes both quartermasters just to turn the ship's wheel, never mind to operate all of the other controls you see there." Jeff indicated a bank of switches and dials that lined the front of the pilothouse. He turned around and pointed to a closed door at the rear of the room. "That's the door down to the captain's cabin, so even when he's not on duty, he isn't very far away."

I stood in the center of the room, turning around to get a good look at everything. Looking down at the gangplank, a female passenger boarding the ship caught my eye. "Sadie?"

Jeff looked over my shoulder. "Do you know that girl?"

"I'm not sure." Turning back to him, I shook his hand. "Thank you very much for taking the time to show me around the ship. I'm truly amazed." I swirled my wrist and bowed in the same way I did at the end of my magic shows and then walked toward the door.

I heard Jeff gasp. He grabbed my arm and spun me back around to face him. "Wait a minute! I just realized that you're Millard Franklin, the Boy Houdini! My cousin Frankie caught your act in Pawtucket last month. He said you were great."

I smiled. "Thanks. I really love performing."

"Hey, would you consider doing a show for the other passengers tonight after dinner? The Salvation Army Band is going to perform a few songs, but I'm sure everyone would enjoy a magic show afterward. And it'd earn me some major points toward my promotion."

"Sure thing, Jeff. Just let me know when and where." I hurried out into the cold.

Chapter 2: Traveling Day

Sadie Golub

On a cold February day, Solomon insisted on accompanying me from Boston to Providence, saying, "It's bad enough that you will be on the steamship alone. I don't want you to ride the train alone, too." Even now that I was moving out of his home for good, he was still determined to fulfill his commitment as my big brother and guardian.

Mid-afternoon, we arrived at the Port of Providence in the middle of a howling snowstorm. At the bottom of the snow-drifted gangplank, Solomon handed my bags to a porter and then reached out and pulled up my woolen scarf to cover my cold ears.

I smiled up at him through the snowflakes, wondering when I'd see him again. Tears burned the backs of my eyes. As he turned to leave, I caught his sleeve. "Solomon, thank you for being big brother. I know you and Bessie did your best for me. Maybe I fit in better with Katerina's family."

He laughed. "Maybe our sister will teach you to act more like a lady."

I chuckled.

"And maybe in New York City you'll forget about that *goy*, Franklin."

I gasped.

"Yes, I know all about him. Bessie told me."

I was instantly angry at Bessie for betraying my trust. She'd been my best friend long before she'd become Solomon's wife. "Why you not say anything about Millard before now?"

"Every time I told you not to do something, you did it even more. So, this time, I didn't say anything."

"Millard is good man, even if he not Jewish."

"And maybe he would have been a good husband as a locksmith, but not as a magician. What kind of life could he make for you or for a family?"

An exciting one, I thought, but I said nothing. I didn't want to start another fight now.

He shrugged. "Now that you're going to New York City, you might not see Franklin ever again."

"I'll see him." Sooner than my brother knew. I darted a glance at some other passengers boarding the ship.

My brother shrugged again. "It's not my problem now." He kissed my cheek. "Make sure to write." After one last squeeze of my arm, he turned and walked away.

I watched him disappear into the swirling snow and then pivoted to look at the steamship. It was huge: more than two hundred and fifty feet long and as tall as a four-story building. It was made of wood, painted white, and had two tall black smokestacks. Just in front of the gangplank, I could see one of its large wooden paddlewheels with "Larchmont" painted in tall gold letters. Although much smaller than the trans-Atlantic steamer I'd sailed on from England, this ship looked quite capable of transporting us to New York City despite the heavy weather.

I pulled my ticket from my pocket and handed it to a man in a blue uniform. Then I followed the porter, also wearing a blue uniform, up the slick gangplank and through a drafty carpeted corridor to the toasty main saloon, dimly illuminated with just a few small electric lanterns. The porter found me a seat on a long wooden bench and deposited my luggage at my feet and I handed him a coin. "Where I find passenger named Millard Franklin?"

"You'd have to ask a steward, miss."

"Steward?"

"Yes, miss. They've got red blazes on their uniform. One of them should be coming through the saloon in a few minutes to help passengers select their cabins for the evening."

I nodded my thanks, wondering what a red blaze was. Then I opened one of my satchels and withdrew my sewing kit and a christening outfit I'd been making for Katerina's new baby. Looking around at the other passengers, I was surprised to see someone I thought I recognized. Setting aside my sewing, I walked over to the young woman and tapped her on the elbow. When she turned, I was delighted to see that she *was* Louise Jensen, or rather, Louise DeThestrup, the young lady I'd met at the Houdini party in September. But I was also shocked by her drastically altered appearance. In Boston, Louise had been a beautiful young woman, who seemed capable of conquering the world. Now, she was painfully thin, her skin was blotchy, and her hair was dull and arranged in a messy, unattractive style. Even her dress, bonnet, and shawl—all black—were wrinkled and fit her poorly. She looked like a shadow of her former self.

I smiled uncertainly. "Hello, Louise. Remember me, Sadie Golub? We met at Houdini party in Boston."

She stared at me with a blank expression and then shook her head slowly.

"Oh. Sorry." I turned to leave when Louise's eyes flew open wide and she clutched my sleeve.

"Wait. I do remember you. You were going to sew some maternity clothing for me."

I nodded. "But you send note not to come. You get sick?"

"Sick in the heart, maybe." Louise sighed, letting her hands fall to her sides. Two tears rolled down her cheeks. "Oh, Sadie, everything in my life has gone so wrong." She looked at least ten years older than she had in September.

I sat down next to her on the bench and handed her my handkerchief.

She shook her head slowly. "My husband is gone. So are my friends. And my parents lied to me." She twisted my handkerchief into a thin rope in her lap. "And the baby. He's gone, too." Her tears began flowing in torrents now, dripping from her face to her lap.

Tears sprang to my eyes as well. "I so sorry." I hoped that she would explain more about what had happened to her, but instead we sat side by side in silence.

A few minutes later, a porter appeared. "Miss Jensen, your mother asked me to show you to your cabin now, so you may dress for dinner with the captain."

She rose slowly, patted my cheek, and followed the porter out of the saloon, looking like a lost lamb.

I walked back to my luggage and felt a knot of dread settle in my stomach. How could so many tragedies have befallen one person in such a brief time? And, if that could happen to someone like Louise DeThestrup, what bad things could happen to me? I stared out one of the windows at the driving snow.

A moment later, I heard a familiar voice. "Sadie?"

I turned to find Millard Franklin standing before me, looking every bit as confused as I'd expected him to be. I wanted to jump into his arms and kiss him—my cheeks flushed just thinking about it—but the ship's saloon was filled with other people, some of them watching us curiously, so instead I reached out and squeezed one of his strong hands.

"How in the world did you get here, on this ship?" he asked. He was nicely dressed in the same suit he'd worn in the Houdinis' hotel suite the first time I'd seen him. His blond hair was slicked back and his eyes were bluer than I remembered. Even in the room's dim light, he looked quite handsome.

"You are surprised?" I asked.

"Yes, very surprised and very happy. But, please, tell me why you're here."

I pulled him down to sit next to me on the bench, enjoying the solid feel of his arm in my hands. "Two weeks ago, I get letter from Katerina, our sister in New York City. She say she has baby boy, but he sick. She ask me to come help with baby and two other children. I say yes. So, now I go to start new life in New York. I plan to open dress shop there. Hillel, Katerina's husband, found store near their house for me to rent. My sister say she has friends who will sew for me. I be shop owner, like Mr. Miller."

Millard reached over and gently squeezed one of my hands. "That's wonderful, Sadie. What an opportunity!" His whole face was beaming. I wished Solomon could see him.

I added quietly, "And, I want to see you." I looked at our hands intertwined in my lap, afraid to meet his gaze. "You wrote in a letter that you be on this boat this day. So I bought ticket. I want to talk to you about the future. Maybe we be together. Maybe not. But, we talk. Yes?"

He lifted my hand to his lips and kissed it, sending shivers down my arm. I looked into his eyes as he said, "Yes, we definitely need to talk." Just then, the ship's whistle sounded, announcing our departure. Millard pointed to my satchels. "Are you planning on getting a cabin?"

I blushed. "No. I will stay here tonight." I didn't want to spend any of my hard-earned money to rent a room with a bed for the overnight trip so I'd planned to just sit up all night in the main saloon and then to sleep once I got to Katerina's apartment in the morning.

He smiled. "The people who hired me to perform in New Jersey paid for me to have a cabin here on the *Larchmont*, but I'm doing a magic show for the other passengers after dinner and then I was hoping to explore the ship, so I'm not going to use my cabin much. Why don't you take it, instead?"

"I not steal your room!"

"You wouldn't be stealing it. You'd be doing me a favor. Otherwise, it'll just sit there empty." I frowned at him, but he just laughed. "Come with me." He picked up my luggage and led us a short distance down the corridor to a cabin door. Fishing a key from his trouser pocket, Millard opened the door to reveal a cabin with two bunks suspended from one wall, a large blue upholstered sofa against another wall, and a bath stand with a mirror positioned on the short wall in between. The walls and ceiling were made of wood planks painted white, the floor was blue carpeting, and the whole cabin felt cozy and comfortable. He placed my suitcases on the lower bunk. "Would you mind if I leave my stuff here too until—"

He was interrupted by an announcement on the ship's public address system. "Ladies and gentlemen, please note that supper will be served in the dining saloon immediately after we depart from the pier. We hope to see you there."

Millard smiled broadly at me. "Would you be so kind as to join me for supper this evening?"

I smiled and nodded, wondering where our mealtime conversation would take us.

Chapter 3: Captain's Duties

George McVay

Five months after Houdini's reception and five weeks after the Joy Line's New Year's Eve party, I was still employed as the captain of the lowly *SS Larchmont*, shuttling passengers and cargo from Providence to New York City and back again on overnight cruises, six nights a week. Despite two letters and four telephone calls to Charles Morse at the International Line, nothing had come of my acquaintance with him. He did not respond to my repeated attempts to contact him and I was beginning to believe he was avoiding me.

Which was why I was surprised to see the names of Anna and Louise Jensen, Morse's sister-in-law and niece, listed as passengers for that evening's cruise. I summoned one of my assistant stewards and gave him specific instructions for their reception. Then I rose, buttoned my jacket and overcoat, and headed for the ship's cargo hold.

As I climbed down a ladder from the pilothouse to the hurricane deck, I assessed the weather conditions. Although the week-long blizzard that had wreaked havoc on the region had finally abated, the weather was still far from ideal for that evening's trip. Snow was falling heavily, the wind was gusting, and the air temperature had plunged far below freezing. But I was expected to sail, if at all possible. If I didn't, the Joy Line would lose money and the cancellation would be noted on my permanent record, something I certainly wished to avoid.

I knew the *Larchmont* would probably have a full load of passengers for this evening's cruise, since the other Providence to New York line did not sail on Mondays. But, because of the Joy Line's policy of only recording the names of those who had reserved special sleeping cabins, I didn't know the total number of passengers who would be aboard. The International Steamship Line was much more organized, compiling a complete passenger list and registering a copy with the home office for every voyage prior to pushing back from the pier. And their ships each contained a new Marconi Wireless Telegraph Device to maintain constant contact with the shore. Two more advantages to working for them rather than for the Joy Line.

Ironically, the Joy Line did insist on a full accounting of all *cargo* prior to departure, which was to include many details: the name of the sender, the name of the receiver, the nature of the cargo, and its approximate weight and value. This morning, I had assigned the arduous task of creating the cargo manifest to my chief mate, Anatole Theophilus. Unfortunately, the assignment had proven too taxing for the Greek native, with his limited grasp of the English language. And so it was that at 3:30 in the afternoon of February 11, I found myself, the captain of the *Larchmont*, in the vessel's cargo area trying to decipher Theophilus's illegible scrawl and match it with the various crates and barrels of freight stowed there.

Finally, I checked off the last crate of cargo, marking the manifest so vehemently that I accidentally tore a hole in the paper. Perfect! Now I'd have to rewrite the whole list again. Tucking the clipboard under my arm, I trudged up two flights of stairs to the saloon deck and then, bracing myself, dashed outside into the bitter cold and climbed back up to the pilothouse, the navigational heart of the ship. Slamming closed the pilothouse door, I returned the salutes of the officers there but didn't stop to chat, instead hurrying through the space and descending the ladder to my own private cabin. I shed my hat, gloves, and overcoat and flopped into my desk chair, preparing to copy the cargo manifest. But instead, I dropped my head into my hands and groaned quietly, overcome with a sense of helplessness. I simply *had* to figure out a way to get off this insignificant ship and onto something bigger and better. I felt like I was dying aboard the *Larchmont*, one monotonous trip after another.

A knock sounded on my cabin door.

"Come in."

A Mediterranean-looking steward opened the door and descended the ladder. I didn't recognize him, but this did not surprise me; the personnel turnover on the Joy Line was horrendous, probably due to the insufficient salaries they offered.

"Sir, you asked me to inform you when Mrs. and Miss Jensen came aboard."

"Very well, Mister…?"

"Núñez, sir. Assistant Steward Juan Núñez."

"Mr. Núñez. Did you show the Jensens to our best cabin and invite them to dine at my table this evening?"

"Yes, sir. Mrs. Jensen said they'd be delighted to join you."

"Very well. That is all."

As Núñez climbed the ship's ladder to the pilothouse, I smiled in anticipation of dinner. Maybe, just maybe, Anna Jensen would have some sort of communiqué from Morse. Dare I hope…a job offer? If only the damned weather would cooperate and not confine the passengers to their cabins with seasickness. Even tied to the pier, the ship was pitching and rolling enough to make my stomach feel queasy.

Refocusing on the papers in front of me, I growled in frustration at the menial task.

If I were a captain for the International Line…

*   *   *

As soon as I finished with the cargo manifest, I put on my overcoat and hat and headed up to the pilothouse. With windows on all four sides, the structure did little to protect us from the cold wind howling down the Narragansett Bay that afternoon. The officers inside, performing their pre-trip checklists, were all bundled in woolen overcoats, hats, and gloves, but they still appeared to be suffering from the arctic chill.

Nodding to my first pilot, I said, "Mr. Anson, a report on the current weather conditions."

Anson, who was even younger than I was, saluted me and then hurried to a bank of dials mounted along the forward wall of the pilothouse. "Sir, it is now three degrees Fahrenheit. The wind is out of the northeast and is currently gusting up to 26 knots. As you can see, it's still snowing heavily, making visibility practically zero."

I nodded. "And what is your recommendation pertaining to tonight's voyage?"

"I would say that conditions are extremely dangerous at the moment, sir. I suggest we cancel this voyage, or at least postpone it until tomorrow morning when the weather clears."

Addressing the mustachioed man standing next to him, I said, "You see, Mr. Wyman, that is why I am the captain of the *Larchmont* and Anson here is not."

My second pilot looked up from his clipboard. "Sir?"

Speaking loudly so as to be heard by all four men in the space, I said, "Gentlemen, unlike young Mr. Anson here, I know that delaying this trip is unnecessary. Based upon my experience, I know that this snow will abate soon, visibility will improve, and we will be able to pilot out of the bay safely."

Anson's face flushed bright red. "What about the wind and the cold, sir? Won't the passengers be too uncomfortable?"

"Quite the contrary, Mr. Anson. The passengers will be asleep in their warm cabins and will hardly notice the inclement weather. They want to get to New York City and would be quite upset if I let a little wind and cold interfere with their plans."

"Yes, sir," he mumbled.

Turning to one of the ship's quartermasters, a solid, beefy man who always wore his cap at a sharp angle, I asked, "Mr. Moreland, what's the word from the engineering department?"

"Mr. Gay reports that we will have plenty of steam to power the turbines and enough left over to keep our passengers warm."

"Mr. Kannaly," I said to my first mate, "Are all of the ship's hands present and accounted for?"

"We were missing quite a few, sir—'tis the flu season—but I managed to roust up enough replacements for almost a full crew."

"Is there anyone of importance missing?"

"Just Swenson, one of the bow watchmen, but I'll try to have someone else take his shift."

"Okay then, gentlemen. I am anticipating an on-time departure at six thirty, but I'll be here a half-hour prior to reassess the situation. In the meantime, I'll be in my cabin if you need me."

I turned on my heels and strode back toward my cabin door, glad to have been able to teach Anson a thing or two. He'd been getting a little too cock-sure of himself lately and I think he had his eye on my captaincy. As if he had what it took to replace me! I'd done well to cut him back down to size a bit.

*   *   *

At seven o'clock that evening, I stood at the open center window of the *Larchmont*'s pilothouse. Even though it was well below freezing outside, the window was ajar to keep it from frosting over and so we could hear the bow watchman if he called out a warning, but it sure made it damnably cold in there. I watched as a tugboat pushed our steamship away from the pier. Because the northern portion of the Narragansett Bay was so narrow, I was forced to wait a full half hour for a break in the snow to provide us with the visibility necessary for a safe passage. The delayed departure would be noted on my record.

I personally piloted the ship for over an hour, guiding her from her pier, south through choppy water, all the way to Sabin's Point, where the bay opened up into the Block Island Sound. Here we found that the storm's persistent winds had churned the waves to monstrous proportions, some rising as high as the ship's upmost deck. We bobbed up and down like a child's bathtub toy. My stomach lurched violently and I certainly would have vomited had I not wisely skipped lunch. As it was, I had to clench my jaw to avoid retching. Why had I never grown used to the pitching and rolling of life aboard a ship? After all these years of service, I should be acclimated by now. I knew the crew joked about my continued seasickness, much to my embarrassment.

Seeing the huge swells in the Sound, I considered turning back to Providence. It'd be another black mark on my record, but at least we'd be safe. Peering through the windows, though, I saw stars twinkling in the night sky. If the stars were out, the storm must be passing and the seas would soon calm.

"Very well, Mr. Anson," I said. "Carry on."

"We're continuing to New York, sir?" He seemed surprised.

"Are you afraid of a few waves, Mr. Anson?"

One of the other officers chuckled.

"No, sir." Anson's face was bright red.

"Very well. Then I'm off to supper. Afterward, I'll make my rounds and return here before retiring for the evening. If conditions deteriorate, have someone summon me immediately."

I left the bridge at around eight-thirty.

Chapter 4: On Board Ship

Anna Jensen

On the evening of February 11, in our overnight cabin on the steamer *Larchmont*, I saw my reflection in the mirror mounted over the vanity table and frowned; I had aged terribly over the past five months. My hair, which had once earned me the nickname *Guldlock*, was now more silver than blonde and was falling out at an alarming rate; I feared I might be completely bald by the end of the year. My milky-white Scandinavian complexion now showed deep lines and wrinkles, making me appear much older than my forty-six years. Even my posture, formerly beautifully erect, was now bowed, as if all of the problems and worries I'd encountered over the past half-year were literally pressing down on my shoulders.

I unlatched one of my kid leather suitcases and withdrew my toiletries, placing them on the small vanity. I knew we'd be aboard the ship for only twelve hours, but I still liked my things arranged neatly so I could find them. Louise's luggage remained jumbled on her narrow bed where she'd dropped it before wandering out of the cabin without saying a word to me.

She hated me. That was plain. But why? What had I done wrong? From the moment I'd brought her home from her boarding house in September, married and pregnant, John and I had done our best to help her, but nothing had gone according to our plans. First Hans DeThestrup had proven to be much more of a *skurk*—scoundrel—than we'd anticipated. Then we'd run into him at that New Year's Eve party. What were the odds that we'd decide to go to the same party? And then the baby, Johan… My eyes teared up again, just thinking about the poor little boy. *Den dagen, den sorgen*—that day, that sorrow.

In the mirror, I studied the details of our cabin, supposedly the nicest one on board the *Larchmont*. But the thick blue and gold drapes that framed the two brass portholes were frayed at the edges, one of the curtain rods drooped down sharply, the dark blue carpet was worn and spotted near the door, and the walls—

once painted bright white—were now a dull gray. The shabby accommodations did little to improve my melancholy mood.

I stabbed a few more pins into my raven-feathered hat, securing it to my thinning hair. Even though I'd never publicly acknowledged the death of little baby Johan, my soul just couldn't bear to wear bright colors, not yet. So, my shoes were black, my dress was black, and even my hat was black. I dropped a pile of pins into my small black handbag to secure Louise's black hat, too. Louise, *min kära...*

As difficult as the events of the past few months had been for John and me, they'd been positively brutal for Louise. Our eighteen-year-old daughter, once effervescent and beautiful, now looked like a lost little lamb: skinny, rumpled, and without hope. For a short while, just before Christmas, she'd rallied and had almost returned to being her happy-go-lucky self, but since running into Hans at that party and the death of her baby in January, she'd abandoned all effort at life. For the past month and a half, she'd shown no interest in anyone or anything and seemed to be simply biding her time here on Earth.

John and I desperately wanted to help Louise feel better in any way possible. Tonight, she and I were aboard this steamship on our way from Providence to New York City, where John was to meet us and join us for a trip across the Atlantic to Sweden. According to John, "Returning to the Old Country should fix what ails Louise. Remember—*blott Sverige svenska krusbär har*— only Sweden has Swedish gooseberries." I just hoped that Swedish gooseberries were the medicine that Louise needed.

Responding to a sharp rap on the cabin door, I found a uniformed, colored man standing in the corridor. "Excuse me, Mrs. Jensen. My name is Abraham White and I'm your porter for this trip. Is there anything I may do for you? Unpack your suitcases, iron some clothes, polish your shoes?"

The man reminded me of Moses, our butler at home. I smiled. "*Tack*, Mr. White. I don't require any of those services, but if you would go to the main saloon and ask my daughter to come dress for dinner, I would appreciate it. We've been invited to dine at Captain McVay's table, and I don't want to be late."

"Yes, madam. I'll fetch Miss Jensen right away." He tipped his hat and hustled away.

*   *   *

An hour later, Louise and I were seated across from each other at the captain's table in the *Larchmont*'s dining saloon. Brass electric lights hung from the beamed ceiling and red carpeting covered the deck. The foul weather rocking the ship, caused the chairs and china to shift continuously and forced me to hold my water glass tightly to avoid wearing its contents.

Looking across the table, I was dismayed to see how loosely Louise's black lace dress hung on her skeletal frame. When we arrived in Sweden next week, I'd buy her a whole new wardrobe—*nya kläder för ett nytt liv*—new clothes for a new life. For now, I tried to catch Louise's eye to encourage her to smile and be sociable, but her gaze remained fixed morosely on her empty plate, as if she was trying to memorize the image of the crossed flags bearing the initials *J* and *S*, the emblem of the Joy Steamship Line.

The ship's officers arrived in the dining saloon *som en grup*—all together—including Captain McVay, who looked sharp in his gold-trimmed uniform. "Mrs. Jensen, Miss Jensen, how nice to see you both again," he said, placing his napkin in his lap.

I nodded.

"I believe we met in Boston last September at a lovely party at the Parker House Hotel, made even lovelier by the presence of you and your beautiful daughter."

"How kind of you to say so." And how insincere. As I remembered the occasion, neither of us had enjoyed the other's company one wit. He had seemed to regard me as a snobby socialite and I'd thought he acted like a fawning sycophant.

As the waiters served steaming bowls of New England clam chowder, Captain McVay leaned toward me. "Mrs. Jensen, I was wondering if your brother-in-law might have spoken to you about me?"

"You mean Charles Morse. *Ja?*" I shifted in my chair.

The captain nodded, his eyes darting to the nearby members of his crew. He lowered his voice even further. "At one point, Mr. Morse and I had discussed the possibility of me applying to become the captain of one of his larger ships."

I nodded sadly. Dealing with wearisome people like Captain McVay always seemed like such a waste of time and energy to me. Didn't he realize that I had no intention of helping someone like him to achieve his over-lofty career goals? "Charles didn't say anything about you when I saw him a few weeks ago. However, he didn't know that I'd be on your ship this evening."

"No matter." He quickly turned and spoke to the woman seated on his other side. I noticed he wasn't eating his meal. A seasick captain? I grinned.

Glancing over at Louise again, I was encouraged to see her listening attentively to a young officer.

She looked up and smiled, taking my breath away. The young man appeared to notice her gorgeous smile too, and redoubled his attentions to her.

I tapped the captain on his sleeve. "Who is that officer talking to my daughter?"

Captain McVay frowned at my interruption of his conversation. "My Second Pilot, John Wyman."

"Is he married?"

"I don't believe so. Why do you ask?"

I smiled. "No reason." I sipped my watery soup while watching my daughter converse with Officer Wyman and allowed myself to feel slightly more hopeful about life.

Chapter 5: Planning the Future
Millard Franklin

Sadie and I followed our noses through the steamship's corridors to the dining saloon, where Jeff Barnes showed us to a private dining table, covered in a white tablecloth and set with all manner of silverware and china dishes. Everything seemed so luxurious that—except for the violent rocking of the ship—I felt like we were back at the Parker House Hotel. Luckily, neither Sadie nor I was seasick, so we happily dined on fresh scrod and potatoes. Judging by the number of empty tables, however, many of the other passengers were not as fortunate.

Sadie and I started the meal talking about nothing much: the unusually cold weather that winter, being on board a steamship, and the delicious food. But, very soon, we found ourselves discussing our futures…together.

As we munched on our warm dinner rolls, she asked, "You want to work for Mr. Houdini?"

I nodded, wiping my mouth with a napkin, wondering how much I should tell her. I really wanted her to understand the way I felt about becoming a magician, wanted her to see that I really had no choice. I'd never been very good with words, but I had to try. "This magic is like a drug," I said. "The more I try it, the more I want to do it. And once I start performing with Mr. Houdini and the other magicians, they'll be able to teach me so much." I hoped that, rather than focusing on my poor choice of words, she'd hear my excitement.

"How much he pay you? Where you live?"

Practical questions for which I had no answers. "We haven't talked about those kinds of details, yet. I imagine we'll be moving all over, traveling to wherever the shows are."

How would that work with Sadie? Would she wait for me to come back to her? The Houdinis did own a house in Harlem, so hopefully we'd stop by the city often.

The waiter cleared our dinner plates and served dessert: cherry cobbler, steaming in white china bowls decorated with tiny ship's flags.

I broke off a corner of the cobbler with my fork.

"You do not follow my plans." She frowned.

"I didn't know…"

"…That I have plans? Yes, Mr. Franklin." She flashed a flirty smile. "I plan for future just like you. I go to New York City now, take care of Katerina's baby, and open my own dress shop. I even know what I call it: Precision Tailoring and Dressmaking."

"That sounds very professional."

"Thank you. I find the words in big dictionary in Boston Public Library."

"I can tell that you've been thinking about your future a lot." I put down my fork and took her hand, my heart pounding in my throat. "Do you think there's any room in your future for me?" I asked.

"You want to be in my future?"

"Very much."

She stared up at me with her dark eyes.

On the other side of the dining room, someone tapped a spoon against his water glass to get everyone's attention. We turned to see Jeff Barnes standing on the small stage with six men and women in uniforms arranged in a row behind him: three carried musical instruments and three held songbooks.

"Ladies and gentlemen," Jeff said. "This evening, we are fortunate to have not one but two different forms of entertainment to offer you. First, as you can see behind me, some good folks from the Salvation Army have volunteered to sing a few of their favorite songs for us. And then, as a special treat, Millard Franklin, the Boy Houdini, has agreed to amaze us with some incredible magic tricks." Jeff directed a big wink in my direction. "So, please help me welcome the Salvation Army Band from Worcester, Massachusetts." The audience clapped politely and settled back in their chairs, ready to digest their food and be entertained.

As the band began playing "Nearer My God to Thee," I leaned toward Sadie and whispered, "I need to go get ready for my show."

"I help?"

I was happy she offered. "Sure. I could use a pretty assistant." Mostly, I just wanted to be with her.

We slipped out a side door and retrieved my trunk from "our" cabin. After a brief search, we located an empty saloon in which to practice the simple tricks I planned to perform; the ship was rocking too hard to attempt anything very difficult.

After going through the tricks twice, Sadie said, "Wait!" and hurried from the room. A few minutes later she returned, wearing a form-fitting chocolate brown gown. "I made this sample for my dress shop. Would it be good for show tonight?"

I opened my mouth to answer but no sound came out. I cleared my throat and whispered, "Wow," suddenly feeling quite warm, despite the cold weather.

Sadie smiled and squeezed my arm.

We went through the magic routine one more time. Just as we finished, we heard prolonged clapping coming from the dining room down the corridor.

"Sounds like we're on," I said.

She became very pale, covered her mouth with one hand, and leaned heavily against a table.

I clasped her arm. "What's wrong? Are you seasick?"

She laughed weakly. "No. I nervous. I never perform in front of people before."

I smiled, relieved. "Don't worry. You'll be fine. You are much prettier than any assistant I've ever had. Remember my last assistant, my brother Chester? The audience will look at you and won't pay any attention to the magic. If we make mistakes, no one will even notice!"

Sadie laughed more heartily.

I fastened the cape around my neck. "Come on. It's show-time! We mustn't keep our audience waiting."

Chapter 6: On Stage

Sadie Golub

Oy vey! I was standing on a stage in front of a whole crowd of people. When I'd volunteered to help Millard with his magic act, I'd thought it would be fun. But now that I was up here with all these people looking at us, I was finding it difficult to breathe.

Millard leaned over to me and whispered, "If you'd rather not do this, you could just sit down. I'll be all right by myself."

I shook my head rapidly. I'd told him I was going to help him and I always kept my word.

"Ladies and gentlemen and children of all ages," Millard began.

The ship lurched to one side and some audience members gasped. Others giggled. Millard smiled confidently and everyone quieted.

"As Assistant Steward Jefferson Barnes said"—he paused and winked at Jeff—"my name is Millard Franklin, but many call me the Boy Houdini, because, by carefully observing the Great Houdini and other talented magicians, I've learned to do many feats of amazing magic."

People leaned forward in their dining chairs.

Millard looked at me and raised his eyebrows.

I tried to smile back at him but my cheek muscles wouldn't cooperate.

He smiled at me and then pointed to the podium.

Oy! I was supposed to do something! I quickly grabbed the deck of cards and spread them out in a wide fan with their faces toward the audience. I hoped my shaking hands wouldn't detract from the trick.

"Now, if one of you would be so kind as to select a card. How about you, Madam?" He nodded toward a woman wearing a diamond necklace at the captain's table. It was Mrs. Jensen, Louise's mother. I wondered if Millard recognized her. Like Louise, she looked so much older than she had just a few months ago.

I walked over to her. My knees felt wobbly and my lips were stuck to my teeth.

Mrs. Jensen pulled a card out from the middle of the deck and the rest of the cards tumbled from my hands. "I'm so sorry," she said.

I quickly stooped and started gathering the cards into a pile.

Millard laughed and handed me another deck from the podium. "Try again, please."

I fanned the second deck, spreading the cards a little farther apart, and then offered them again to Mrs. Jensen. My hands were shaking even more violently this time.

She pulled this card out much more gently.

I smiled at her in thanks.

"Very well," Millard said. "Madam, would you please show your card to the other members of the audience, taking care not to allow me or my beautiful assistant to see it?" He smiled at me.

Mrs. Jensen did as instructed.

"Good. Now kindly return the card to the deck, anywhere you'd like."

I held out the deck to her and she slid in her card.

I closed up the fan and handed the cards to Millard. He tapped the deck with his magic wand and then threw the cards into the air, catching a single one in his silk top hat while allowing the rest of them to scatter on the carpet. He walked over to Mrs. Jensen. "Would you please see what card I caught?"

The light reflected off a diamond ring she wore on her middle finger as she reached her hand into the hat. She pulled out the card and showed it to the audience. Everyone gasped and then clapped enthusiastically because, evidently, it was the card she had selected.

I took a deep breath and closed my eyes for a moment. We'd made it through one trick. *Gut.* Maybe this wouldn't be too bad.

The next several tricks involved Millard making bright-colored scarves and flowers appear from his sleeves and hat. My "job" was to direct the audience's attention, causing them to look at Millard sometimes and elsewhere at other times. Despite my nervousness, I performed just as we had rehearsed, and the audience clapped even louder.

I was beginning to enjoy myself. I smiled at Millard and he smiled back, looking relieved.

For the following set of tricks, he manipulated some small plastic balls, making them appear and disappear from various places throughout the dining room. Whenever he completed a stunt, I smiled and put my arms up in a gesture Millard had called a "tada." A man in the audience hooted and yelled out, "Pretty lady!" and I smiled even bigger. This was beginning to be fun.

By the time Millard pulled out his metal hoops to perform his final tricks, I was prancing around the stage, swishing the skirt of my gown, and having a good time. When we took our final bows, I blew kisses to the audience and they applauded wildly. The crowd loved us!

As the people filed out of the dining room, Millard gathered up his magic equipment and stowed it carefully in his trunk.

"I like that!" I said. "First, I afraid. Then you do tricks and people clap and I have fun!"

"Uh oh!" he laughed. "I think you might be a natural-born performer, too."

"What you mean?"

"Just that you belong on stage. With me." Millard looked surprised at what he'd said.

"I your assistant?"

"Maybe. Though, I doubt Mr. Houdini expects me to bring my own assistant with me at first."

"Because you are—how you say—a starter act?"

"A warm-up act, yes. But then, in a year or so…Who knows?"

"Maybe then we perform together?" I was starting to like the idea more and more. Touring the country—maybe even the world—with Millard.

He closed his trunk. "Why don't we put this back in the cabin and then go up on deck?"

"Outside? Is freezing and the ship is bumping up and down!"

"Just for a few minutes. I've never been on a steamship before and I want to see everything. We'll get your coat from the cabin."

I was not thrilled with the idea of going outside, especially not in this frigid weather, but I nodded since I wanted to be with Millard, wherever he was.

A few minutes later, as we stepped through the door to the icy deck, a bitter wind swirled around us. Apparently, the *Larchmont* was now out of the shelter of the Narragansett Bay, so the wind was fiercer, the waves were higher, and the ship was rocking even more wildly.

"*Oy!*" I said. My brown silk gown swirled around my ankles.

Millard smiled, took my gloved hand in his, and pulled me against the wall next to the door. "Come on. Just for a minute."

We stood together and spotted a light twinkling in the distance. Looking across to the other side of the ship, we saw the sweeping beam from a lighthouse several miles away.

I shivered violently. Millard unbuttoned his blue woolen pea coat and held it open. "Come here."

As he looked down at me with eyes full of warmth, I turned around and snuggled my back against his chest. He wrapped his arms around me and gently rested his chin on top of my red knitted hat. We stood like that in silence for several minutes before I began to shiver again. He turned me to face him.

"Why don't we plan on talking more tomorrow morning? Inside, somewhere warm." He smiled down at me and I was amazed at how deep blue his eyes were, even in the dim light. My breath caught in my throat and my heart thumped against my ribs.

He tipped my chin up with his thumb. I could feel his breath on my face as he bent and gently kissed my lips. I reached up and wrapped my arms around his neck. He encircled my waist with his strong hands and our kiss went on and on. I no longer suffered from the cold. I didn't notice the ship rocking. I just felt as if I were floating on a warm cloud. When the kiss finally ended, we both stepped back and smiled, not saying a word.

I shivered again. "I go in now." My lips were still tingling.

He nodded. "I'll see you tomorrow morning?"

"Yes. We eat breakfast on boat?"

"I read a notice that said food will be served just before we get to New York City, so shall I meet you at our table in the dining room?"

"When?"

"Is seven too early?"

"Seven is good." I reached out and cupped his cheek with my gloved hand and then opened the door and stepped back into the relative warmth of the ship's interior. As I pulled the door closed, I looked back over my shoulder and saw him watching me, smiling.

Chapter 7: Making the Rounds

George McVay

I left the *Larchmont*'s dining saloon, extremely disappointed with my unfruitful conversation with Mrs. Jensen. She had no message for me from Morse, she knew nothing about any possible opening for a captain on his line, and I was pretty sure she still bore a grudge against me for asking her to introduce me to Morse at the Houdini party. All she'd wanted to talk about at supper tonight was whether or not my second pilot was married. She was probably looking for a husband for that pasty-looking daughter of hers—so typical of a woman.

After dinner, I climbed down to the freight deck, where I spoke to the cargo watchman for a few moments. Then I descended to the engine room to make sure the turbines truly could cope with the rough seas we were experiencing. After a brief stop at the quarterdeck to speak with the saloon watchman, I visited Oscar Young in the purser's office. At each of these stops, I found everything shipshape. I congratulated myself for running the *Larchmont* so efficiently.

My customary final stop before retiring to my own quarters for the evening involved a trip outside to the bow of the ship to visit the night watchman. Pulling up the collar of my woolen pea coat, I stepped through the door to the hurricane deck and immediately slipped on the icy planking and crashed into the ship's white-painted rail, grabbing onto it just in time to keep myself from plunging into the foamy sea.

"Are you all right, sir?" the watchman called out.

"Yes, Mr. Anderson." I was embarrassed that he'd witnessed my clumsiness. I made my way forward, holding tightly to the ship's railing.

Anderson stood completely unsheltered at the very prow of the ship, stomping his feet on the ice-coated deck and swaying back and forth with his multi-mittened hands tucked into his armpits. Even with all the layers of hats, scarves, and coats he currently wore, he was obviously freezing. "It certainly is cold tonight, sir," he said, his voice muffled by his scarves.

"What time are you relieved of duty?"

"Not until we dock in New York, sir."

"You're scheduled to be here all night?" Duty rosters were drawn up by my first officer, Kannaly, but I tried to be aware of all my crew members' schedules. "Don't you and Swenson usually share this duty?"

"Aye, sir, but Swenson's sick—the influenza. He didn't even make the trip from Providence." Anderson chuckled. "But don't worry about me, sir. I'll be all right. Farnsworth said he'd bring me some hot coffee when he came off his shift at midnight."

I made a mental note to speak to Kannaly before I retired for the evening. "Have you seen any other ships?" I asked Anderson.

"Aye, sir, but not many. I think some might have decided to wait in port for calmer weather."

"Unfortunately, we didn't have that luxury." The *Larchmont* plowed through another tall wave causing a curtain of frigid water to splash down on both of us.

Anderson wiped his face.

I shook the water from my eyes and glanced aft, where I saw a young couple snuggling near the main saloon doorway. Why didn't they go inside where it was warm? Seeing them together reminded me of Edith. Lately, she'd been avoiding me and I missed the closeness we once had. If I got a promotion and raise, maybe we could afford to take a vacation somewhere, just the two of us. A hotel in Newport for a weekend?

I sighed. "Well, Mr. Anderson, try to keep yourself warm and be sure to shout out clearly if you see any other ships nearby."

"Aye, aye, sir." He touched the brim of his hat and then resumed swaying back and forth in his dance to stay warm.

Carefully picking my way across the ice-encrusted deck, I climbed the ladder to the pilothouse and ducked inside. "Send the word for Mr. Kannaly."

"Aye, aye, sir," Wyman responded.

I turned to Anson. "Any change in weather or conditions?"

"It's now four degrees Fahrenheit, sir, with thirty-five knot wind gusts out of the northeast."

"Have you spotted any other craft nearby?"

"None closer than a half-mile, sir."

"Very well. Send Mr. Kannaly down when he arrives and have a steward send some coffee." I descended the ladder to my quarters.

In my cabin, I shucked my winter wear and huddled next to the small propane heater, frowning at the pile of paperwork that still awaited my attention: the projected cargo manifest for the return leg of the journey, a recommendation for promotion for Assistant Steward Jefferson Barnes, and various other documents that required my signature—in triplicate, of course. I was so tired of all of this ridiculous busywork. I sighed and picked a page off the top of the stack.

Chapter 8: Honesty

Anna Jensen

Throughout supper and the subsequent concert and magic show, Louise sat next to Second Pilot John Wyman, often smiling and chatting with him. Now, as we made our way back to our cabin, I was pleased to see a little color in her cheeks. I fervently hoped this might portend her return to health and happiness.

Back in our sleeping cabin, I mused aloud, "That Boy Houdini and his assistant, they looked familiar. We have seen them perform somewhere before. *Ja?*"

"No, *Mamma*. But we've met them before, at the hotel reception in Boston last fall, the same party where we met Captain McVay."

"That's right. You and she got along well at the party that day. Have you spoken to her on board the ship tonight?"

"Sadie and I talked briefly while you were freshening up in the cabin," she said quietly. "We spoke about Hans and the baby."

"Oh." I busied myself at the vanity, unpinning my hat and brushing my hair.

Louise took the silver-handled brush from my hand and ran it through my thinning locks. I closed my eyes and savored her touch, an all-too-infrequent occurrence lately.

"*Mamma*, may I talk to you about something?"

I stiffened but met her eyes in the mirror and nodded.

She placed the brush on the vanity and put one hand on each of my shoulders, squeezing gently. "This past year has been so terrible for our whole family. Me sneaking around to see Hans and then marrying him without your knowledge was an awful thing to do. And then he turned out to be such a terrible person. I truly am sorry that I put you and *Pappa* through that."

I turned around and pulled her into a fierce hug. "Your father and I, we are so sorry if we hurt you, *min kära*. We love you so much."

She nodded and sat on the lower bunk. "I'm ready to listen to you now, *Mamma*. Please explain to me why you and *Pappa* did what you did with Hans, so I can understand."

Carefully choosing each word, I told Louise exactly how the situation with Hans DeThestrup had unfolded, from John going to talk to him, to Hans asking for a payoff, to us putting him on the last train south that night, explaining not only *how* everything had transpired but also *why* we had made the decisions we had. I told Louise everything, believing this might be my one and only chance to win back my daughter's trust and love. No more secrets. No more trying to protect her feelings or mine. Just the honest truth.

Louise sat on the bunk and listened, asking no questions, expressing no emotion. When I was done, she said, "Thank you for telling me that. I'm sure it wasn't easy."

And then I burst into tears.

Louise hugged me. "Why are you crying?"

I withdrew a lace handkerchief from my purse, wiped my eyes, and blew my nose. "I hate what it's done to our family! But if I had to live the past six months over, I'm not sure what I would do differently. Your father and I, we tried to do what was best for you, but we failed."

Louise patted my hand. "Whatever happened to Hans? I mean after the New Year's Eve party."

"We received those papers from the Ochs' solicitor . . ."

"Those annulment papers?"

I nodded.

"Nothing else?"

I shook my head.

"So he doesn't know about the baby?"

"No." I squeezed her hands, so glad she was allowing me to touch her again. "Louise, I've always believed in fate and I still think God has something wonderful planned for you."

"*Tro på Gud den Allsmäktige*—have faith in the God Almighty?"

"Because *det som inte dödar, harder*—what doesn't kill, hardens." I smiled.

"*Efter regn kommer solsken*—after rain comes the sunshine." She laughed.

"And *nya kvastar sopar bäst*—new brooms sweep the best!" I said. We both laughed.

Louise smiled a true smile, rose to her feet, and wrapped her arms around me, giving me the best hug of my life. We clung to each other and rocked back and forth, matching tempo with the undulations of the storm-tossed ship.

Chapter 9: Ship—Dead Ahead!

Millard Franklin

Out on the icy deck of the *Larchmont*, I watched as Sadie stepped back inside, my lips still warm from our kiss. As she disappeared through the doorway into the ship's interior, I heard a familiar voice.

"She sure is a good-looking one."

I turned to find Jeff leaning casually against the ship's wall on the other side of the door, his overcoat unbuttoned, seemingly oblivious to the ridiculous cold. Until he'd spoken, I hadn't been aware that anyone else was around.

"Where'd you meet her?" Jeff pulled two cigarettes from his pocket, offered me one, and then struck a match on the bottom of his shoe, providing a light for both of us.

"Sadie and I met at a party in Boston last September."

"Sadie, huh? A pretty name for a pretty girl." He drew smoke deeply into his lungs and looked up at the stars now visible in the clear night sky. A thin crescent of moon was just appearing on the horizon. He exhaled a puff of smoke. "Have you asked her to marry you?"

The idea surprised me; after all, I'd only known Sadie for five months.

Apparently my shock was obvious because Jeff laughed. "I'm sorry to scare you, pal. With the way the two of you were kissing, I thought you were definitely headed to the altar."

I smiled. "Actually, marriage to Sadie sounds like a good idea. It'd have to wait a couple of years, though. Starting this spring, I'm going to be doing a lot of traveling, so I won't be able to support anyone for a while."

"Don't miss your chance with her, pal. A girl like that won't stay single for long."

I nodded and stared up at the night sky, smoking my cigarette.

Jeff looked out across the turbulent sea. Cocking his head to one side, he said, "That's strange."

"What do you mean?"

"See those lights?" Jeff pointed in front of the *Larchmont*. "See how one of them is red and one of them is green?"

I nodded.

"That means there's a boat coming straight toward us. If we were going to pass port-to-port, the way we're supposed to, we'd only see her red light."

From the front of our ship, a man's voice called out, "Ship—dead ahead."

Our bow swung gently to the right.

"Good," Jeff said. "We're turning to starboard. That should fix things."

We watched as the red and green lights started to drift slightly to our left. But then they shifted and were coming our way again.

The bow watchman called out with much more urgency, "Ship—dead ahead! Approaching fast!"

"Look at that!" Jeff said. "She's headed right for us again!"

The steamship turned sharply to the right again, but it was too late. As four blasts sounded from the *Larchmont*'s warning whistle, Jeff and I saw a large sailing ship loom into sight with her three canvas sails flapping wildly. We watched in horror as she plowed directly into the port side of the *Larchmont* with the force of a freight train. Our steamer lurched violently, throwing us off our feet. The sounds of crashing wood and breaking glass were deafening. Sitting on the ice-coated deck amid pieces of debris from both vessels, Jeff and I looked at each other in utter disbelief.

Chapter 10: Love and Collision

Sadie Golub

Returning from my brief visit on deck with Millard, I closed the door to my cabin and flicked the switch for the electric lights, splashing the room with a yellow glow. As I slipped off my coat, hat, scarf, and shoes, I found myself smiling. I was in love with a good man, he loved me too, and I was on my way to a new, exciting future in New York City. My life was finally going somewhere.

I slid off my gown, corset, and petticoats and breathed deeply, glad to be free of all that fabric, even if it was rather chilly in my cabin. Carefully folding my clothes, I tucked them into one of my satchels, at the same time retrieving my white flannel nightgown. I tugged it on over my head and flopped onto my back on the dark blue cotton duvet covering the lower berth, continuing to smile. With my eyes closed, I happily relived my time tonight with Millard: talking, dinner, rehearsing, the magic show, standing on deck, and our first long kiss.

I was jolted awake by a tremendous crash that threw me from my berth into the wooden bath stand on the opposite wall. Dazed, I reached up to find a small bleeding cut on my forehead. The whole steamship shuddered and groaned, and many voices screamed.

With trembling hands, I shoved my shoes back onto my feet. Snatching my coat, hat, and scarf from the top bunk, I put all of them on over my nightgown and then slowly opened the door to the corridor, afraid of what I might find.

A porter appeared in front of me, his dark brown face sweating profusely, his uniform jacket buttoned incorrectly. He was the same man who had helped me with my luggage earlier. "Miss, there's been a collision. You'd best get yourself upstairs to the lifeboats as quickly as you can."

"A collision? Are we sinking?"

The porter looked into my eyes, his fear evident. "Just take your lifebelt and get yourself to the boats right away. You hear?"

I nodded and he hurried down the corridor and pounded on the next door.

"Millard!" I yelled.

No response.

I ran back inside my cabin and grabbed one of the lifebelts from beneath the bottom bunk. Not bothering to close the cabin door behind me, I rushed toward the stairs, tying the lifebelt straps around my waist as I ran.

Chapter 11: John Anson, What Have You Done?

George McVay

I was doing paperwork at the small desk in my cramped cabin when I felt the ship pull to starboard. Why we were adjusting course? I stood and put on my uniform jacket. As I bent to retie my shoes, the ship swung hard to starboard, toppling me to my hands and knees. Four loud blasts from her warning whistle vibrated through her hull. I jumped to my feet, yanked open my cabin door, and bounded up the ladder to the pilothouse. The men there were frozen in place, all eyes staring intently through the portside windows. My own eyes adjusted to the dim light in time to see the lethal prow of a sailing vessel rapidly approaching from that direction. It was going to hit my ship!

"John Anson, what have you done?" I cried. With a deafening crash, the smaller vessel smashed into us, forward of our portside paddle wheel box, hitting with the force of an explosion. Terrified screams filled the night air. Then I heard splintering and grinding as the sailing vessel broke free of us and drifted aft, cooking pots and chinaware from our kitchen and dining saloon littering her deck. Her three luffing sails quickly disappeared into the inky darkness, as if she had never existed. The whole thing was over in a matter of seconds.

Thrown against the ship's wheel by the impact, I righted myself, out of breath and bruised. The pilothouse was full of cries of pain and I heard many more coming from elsewhere on the ship.

Wyman knelt next to my first mate, who was prostrate on the deck on the other side of the ship's wheel. "Kannaly, do you hear me?" Wyman asked.

No response.

I rushed out of the pilothouse and leaned over the ice-encrusted rail to view a ten-foot-wide jagged gash in the ship's port side. Roiling steam poured from the wound in a deafening roar as seawater rushed in.

I skated back to the pilothouse and slammed the door behind me. Glancing around frantically, I realized that my five officers were cut and bleeding. Kannaly still lay on the deck motionless. The others, who were less seriously hurt, seemed to be awaiting instructions from me. I wanted to scream at them, "Don't look at me! How in the hell would I know what to do? I've never been in this situation before!" They were moaning and talking excitedly and making so much noise that I found it difficult to think clearly. The ship was already listing badly toward the port bow.

Damage reports. I should gather damage reports. I turned a small brass crank fastened to the wall, ringing a bell that signaled for an engineer to pick up the other end of the speaking tube that snaked its way from the bridge to the engine room.

"Hello?" I heard a voice respond.

I picked up my end of the tube. "This is Captain McVay." My voice sounded high and squeaky, like a teenage boy's. I cleared my throat and lowered my tone. "How bad is the damage? Are the turbines functional?"

No response.

I rang the bell again just as the pilothouse's electric lights flickered and went out.

Someone lit a small gas emergency lantern fitted with red glass panes, casting a bloody light throughout the pilothouse. I shuddered as I studied my officers' faces. Wyman still knelt next to Kannaly, who remained unconscious. Staples leaned against the portside instrument panel, grasping one of his legs. Moreland, my other quartermaster, stood gripping the ship's wheel and peering intently toward the bow, even though the engines had stopped and we were no longer moving. And Anson stared vaguely out the portside windows, squinting and shaking his head.

At the other end of the speaking tube, an engineer said, "Hello?" again.

"Damage report, please!" I shouted.

Once again, no reply. I slammed down my end of the tube. "Mr. Wyman and Mr. Staples, go below and determine the extent of the damage. And find out from the engineer whether or not we are capable of making headway."

Even though Wyman's right eye was swollen shut and Staples was limping badly, both men immediately touched their hats in obeisance and hurried out the door.

My first pilot still stared through the windows at the black night, obviously in shock.

"Mr. Anson, what happened here?" I pointed in the direction of the gaping wound in the *Larchmont*'s hull.

He shook his head.

"Mr. Anson, I asked you a question!"

He slowly focused on my face, tears welling up in his eyes.

"Get a hold of yourself, man!" I said and then decided to alter my tactics with him. More calmly, I said, "Let's concentrate on dealing with our current situation. Right now, I want you to…" My eyes lit upon the brass telescope rolling across the deck near his feet. I pointed to it. "Take that glass outside and look for any nearby ships. Several other steamers should be in the area."

Anson groped for the telescope and stumbled through the doorway, banging his shoulder on the doorframe on his way out. I started to consult the chart on the navigation table to determine our exact position, but before I could fully plot the angles, Anson had already returned to the pilothouse, shaking his head.

"The waves are too high," he mumbled.

The ship lurched violently beneath my feet and I realized the *Larchmont* was sinking fast. How was that possible? A ship I captained could not possibly be sinking. It would ruin my reputation.

Wyman and Staples returned, their faces red and their eyes watering. Wyman couldn't speak at all, making only rasping sounds. But Staples croaked, "Main steam line is cut. Steam pouring out. Scalding people alive. Engineer said we're taking on water. Got to beach her, now."

"Do we have any power, Mr. Staples?"

The quartermaster looked confused and glanced at Wyman who shrugged.

"Good God, men! You were supposed to determine if the turbines are still functional." I turned to my first pilot. "Mr. Anson, get down to the engine room and report back to me immediately." Anson stumbled out of the room as a gust of wind picked up the chart off the table and flung it into the instrument panel. I stalked over to the door and slammed it closed. Through its window I saw people, both crew and passengers, climbing stairs and ladders up to the icy boat deck, some of them wearing only nightclothes.

The lifeboats! How could I have forgotten about them? I pointed to everyone inside the pilothouse. "All of you get to your lifeboat stations and prepare your boats. Alert the rest of the crew, too. Do all you can to save all you can." Everyone who was physically able rushed out of the pilothouse, leaving Kannaly, still insensible on the deck, and me, standing beside the ship's wheel.

I took off my cap and ran my fingers through my hair. What had happened? One moment we'd been sailing through the Block Island Sound, business as usual, and then the next moment we'd collided with another ship and were sinking. How was that possible? I was going to demand a full account from Anson when he came back from the engine room, no matter how upset he was. But right now, I had to concentrate on getting the passengers off the ship. If everyone made it into lifeboats and was rescued, I'd still have to deal with the monetary loss of the ship and her cargo and the shame of a mid-sea collision, but at least there wouldn't be the added complication caused by loss of life.

The ship groaned and dipped further to port. She was going down very quickly.

I suddenly realized if I didn't get off this ship soon, I could actually die; I'd never see Edith or the children again.

There was no way I was going to let that happen.

Chapter 12: A Very Bad Feeling

Anna Jensen

After my soul-baring discussion with Louise, I breathed freely for the first time in months. We sat in the cabin, comfortable together in silence, holding each other's hands. I felt ten pounds lighter and ten years younger.

Finally, I rose. "I am exhausted, *min kära*. I need to go to bed. Do you want the top bunk or the bottom one?"

Louise giggled, a beautiful sound. "As if you could climb up to the top bunk, *Mamma*."

"I was a good gymnast when I was young. Still, I might be able to vault my way up there…"

My words were interrupted by a horrible, shuddering crash that tossed us both across the room and under the vanity table as if we were mere rag dolls. The whole ship shook violently, and the sounds of wood splintering and glass breaking filled the night. Then we heard screams—terrible, pain-filled screams.

Louise pushed away a toppled chair and one of my empty suitcases and reached for my hand. "Are you all right, *Mamma?* Are you hurt?"

"I don't know. My leg hurts." I pulled myself up next to the vanity and tried to stand but found that my left ankle hurt terribly and wouldn't support my weight. "*Ånej!* It may be broken."

"Just stay where you are." She helped me settle back onto the floor, my injured limb extended in front of me. "I'll find someone to help us." She hitched up her black lace gown and crawled across the slanted floor to the berths and used them to pull herself to her feet. Just as she stood, the cabin's electric lights flickered once, twice, and then went out, plunging us into total darkness.

A woman in the cabin next door shrieked.

"Be careful, *min kära*," I cautioned Louise.

I heard her feel her way to the cabin door, followed by a series of rattles and small grunts.

"What's wrong?" I asked.

"The door's jammed." Her voice trembled. She banged on the door repeatedly, each time a little longer and a little louder, and called out, "Is there anybody out there? Can someone help us?"

The only response was the sound of rushing water. The ship listed more and more.

"*Mamma*, I have a very bad feeling about this," she said quietly.

"So do I, *min kära*."

She crawled back to where I sat, underneath the vanity. Side by side, with our backs against the wall, we clasped each other's hands and stared into the inky blackness.

Chapter 13: Lifeboat No. 4

Millard Franklin

Jeff and I climbed back to our feet in time to see the sailing ship break away from the *Larchmont*, leaving her bowsprit behind, stabbed into the heart of the steamship. We could hear voices howling in pain, water pouring into the hull, and steam hissing out of ruptured pipes into the frigid night air. Jeff leaned out over the rail and then whistled. "That's a big hole and it goes down beneath the waterline." He turned to me. "Pal, this ship is sinking. If I were you, I'd find that pretty lady of yours and meet me at Lifeboat No. 4 as soon as you can." He pointed to a small boat, sheathed in a canvas cover, hanging suspended from two metal arms.

I didn't have to be told such terrible news twice. Slipping and sliding on the icy deck, I hurried through the door and jumped down the ladder to the main deck, where I found a few people leaning their heads out of their cabins. I rushed past, yelling, "The ship is sinking! Go up to the lifeboats, now!" But no one moved. Why? Did they think I was joking? Hadn't they heard and felt the collision?

I reached Sadie's cabin only to find the door swinging open and no one inside. I thought about grabbing some of my more expensive magic equipment from my trunk but rejected the idea. There was no time. I needed to find Sadie now. I ran out of her cabin just as the ship's lights flickered and went out. The ship was listing badly to one side and scalding steam from the broken pipes was swirling up stairways, filling the corridors. I could hear the horrible screams of people being burned on the deck below. I ran as fast as I could back the way I had come, my arms outstretched, feeling my way. I collided with someone with a beard. "Go up to the lifeboats!" I urged, but he muttered something and walked the other way.

I dashed up the stairs to the main saloon and scanned the crowd, illuminated by gaslight. No Sadie. Back up on the hurricane deck, I found Jeff Barnes struggling to pull the frozen cover off his lifeboat.

"Where's Sadie?" he asked.

"I couldn't find her. She wasn't in her cabin."

"She'll show up, don't worry. Everyone will be coming up on deck in a minute or two, as soon as they realize the ship is sinking. Look." He pointed to the saloon deck, one level down. As I watched, the deck railing dipped into the ocean. The *Larchmont* was going down fast.

"Help me with this lifeboat, will you?" Jeff asked me. "One of the saloon stewards is supposed to be here but he hasn't shown up."

"Have you ever done this before?"

"We have lifeboat drills every month. I've never actually lowered one into the water, but I think I know how to do it."

I followed his instructions and together we coaxed the ropes through the pulleys and lowered the little boat toward the rough sea.

Two dozen passengers, half of them wearing only their nightclothes, rushed up the stairs to the hurricane deck. Many of the men were carrying bags or suitcases and some of the women held small children. All of them looked cold and terrified. Jeff and I exchanged wary glances but continued to lower the lifeboat, bringing it even with the deck so it could be boarded.

One of the passengers pointed to it. "There's one!" They all turned and rushed toward us.

Jeff dropped his rope and stepped in front of them, his palms forward. "Now everyone, just be calm. There's plenty of room, but we have to do this in an orderly fashion."

The passengers, yelling and screaming at each other, elbowed Jeff and me aside and climbed into the lifeboat, shoving others out of their way in their panic to get aboard. I saw a young woman carrying a bundled-up toddler grab an older woman by the back of her coat and pull her off her feet. Then the young woman leapt into the already crowded lifeboat, landing on top of two other passengers. The lifeboat, still attached to the supporting arms, overturned, spilling the men, women, children, and their luggage into the freezing ocean. I watched in horror as the young woman fell, still clutching desperately to her child, and disappeared into the icy water.

Jeff grabbed armfuls of cork and canvas lifebelts from a nearby closet and shoved some at me. Together we tossed them to the people in the water, since we had no way to pull them back onto the ship. "They'll have to climb into the lifeboat once we launch it," Jeff said as he shoved the lifeboat with his foot, spinning it upright again. He paused to catch his breath and pointed again to the deck below. "Look at that."

I turned to see the tops of the windows disappear under the black, foam-covered water.

Jeff caught my eye. "We'd better hurry."

Chapter 14: Looking for Millard

Sadie Golub

Rushing down the corridor, I was surprised to see no one but the porter. Where were all the other passengers? Why weren't they running to the lifeboats, too? I scrambled up the nearest ladder. One flight up, I reached the enclosed saloon deck where about two dozen people huddled together in the main saloon. I called out, "Millard!" several times, but he didn't answer. I hurried outside into the bitter cold. Even my winter coat and the bulky lifebelt did little to block the cutting wind. I considered going back to my cabin to dress myself more warmly, but just then the rest of the ship's lights blinked and went out, plunging us into near-blackness. The only illumination now came from the twinkling stars, the thinnest sliver of moon, and a few gas lanterns. I groped in front of me for a ladder up to the next level where I was relieved to find some people in blue uniforms readying lifeboats. Maybe Millard was there with the assistant steward. I rushed over to the nearest boat and tapped an officer on his shoulder. "I look for my friend... Maybe he with Jeff Barnes. Do you know where is Jeff?"

The man turned and scowled. "Not here. Try one of the boats on the other side of the ship." He turned back to his lifeboat, elbowing me out of his way.

I hurried across the slippery, sloping deck to the other side of the ship calling, "Millard!"

I had to find him.

A large cloud of white steam belched from a nearby pipe, forming a scalding cloud around me. I coughed violently and stumbled against a metal ladder that led up to the roof of a row of cabins. Thinking that maybe I'd be able to find Millard more easily from a higher vantage point, I gathered the bottom of my nightgown and climbed the slippery ladder to the rounded wooden roof where I found nearly two dozen other passengers already huddled, bracing themselves against the angry wind. As I stepped over the top rung of the ladder, the *Larchmont* tipped violently to one side and I dropped to my knees to keep from sliding off the roof's slick surface.

A loud cracking noise, like a hundred trees snapping in half, filled the air and vibrated through the ship. The row of cabins upon which I was perched lurched wildly, throwing some people off. I could hear their terrified screams and then their bodies thudding onto the deck below. I grasped the top of the ladder with all my might. With another ear-splitting crack, the cabins separated from the ship and the whole structure was tossed into the turbulent ocean. A large wave immediately crashed over us and drenched us. I cleared the seawater from my eyes with one shaking, gloved hand and was horrified at the pandemonium surrounding me. People were everywhere: thrashing around in the icy water, clinging to all manner of flotsam and jetsam, and calling out in the most pitiful voices.

What manner of hell was this? I closed my eyes. I just couldn't bear to see any more.

Chapter 15: I'm Finished

George McVay

I left the relative shelter of the pilothouse and hurried across the slanted, icy deck toward Lifeboat No. 1, the forward boat on the starboard side, the one assigned to my command. As I skated the length of the ship, clutching tightly to the rail with every step, I saw that only four of the eight lifeboats were being prepared to launch. I grabbed the shoulder of a porter working on one of the lifeboats. "Where are the other officers and crew members? Where are the passengers?"

"Don't know, sir." His words appeared in white puffs. Icicles hung from his dark mustache. "We knocked on the cabin doors and told everyone to come up to the lifeboats, but I don't think they believe the ship's sinking."

"Oh, she's sinking, all right. Go back to the cabins and tell them they're almost out of time. Within five minutes—ten at the most—the *Larchmont* will be lost."

The porter's eyes grew wide and he hurried away.

I counted fewer than a dozen passengers on the starboard side. Should I personally go below and encourage them to come up to the lifeboats? No! Damn them if they were too stupid to save their own lives. I wasn't going to die for a group of imbeciles out of some misplaced sense of duty. I wanted to get home to my wife and children.

I rushed forward to Lifeboat No. 1 to find that Quartermaster Staples had already drawn back its cover and was working the ropes and davits, lowering the boat toward the churning ocean. Assisting him were Purser Young, waiters McFarland and Vann, and two firemen. In the dim starlight, I saw that the saloon deck was already awash and the bow of the hurricane deck was now almost even with the ocean's frothy surface. "Hurry, men," I urged.

The lifeboat splashed down and the seven of us stepped in, spacing ourselves evenly on the thwarts. I ordered the men to push off and row us away from the ship.

"But what about the passengers, sir?" McFarland asked. "Shouldn't we try to fill up the boat?" Each lifeboat had a capacity of thirty-five.

"There's no time!" I yelled. I'd heard too many tales of lifeboats being sucked underwater by the vortex caused by a sinking ship; I would not let that happen to mine. "Do as I command."

With a mighty shove, the two firemen pushed us away from the sinking steamer.

Almost immediately, floating debris knocked violently against the sides of our boat. "Fend off that wreckage with your oars," I ordered. I didn't want something smashing a hole in our lifeboat's thin wood plating and sending us to the bottom of the Block Island Sound even before the *Larchmont*.

I looked back at the floundering steamship and was horrified to realize ours was the first—and, so far, the only—lifeboat launched. How would that look at the inquest? The captain abandoning his poor helpless passengers? Good God! Shouting so as to be heard above the crashing waves, I said, "Bring this boat around to the other side of the ship. The passengers must be over there, trying to stay warm."

As McFarland and one of the firemen manned the oars, straining toward the far side of the crippled steamer, I saw two other lifeboats being launched from the ship. The first one, commanded by Chief Engineer Gay, was loaded with at least twenty-five crew members and passengers. If the other lifeboats were likewise full, nearly everyone would be saved. That hope was quickly dashed, however, when I saw that the other boat carried only ten people.

As our lifeboat rounded the bow of the steamer and emerged from her lee, we were slammed with gale-force winds and fifteen-foot high seas, ruthlessly pushing us away from the sinking ship. We could see people clinging to the *Larchmont*'s superstructure and could hear them frantically calling out for assistance, but we couldn't get to them.

"Row harder, men!" I yelled, but we made no headway. Instead, we were forced to watch in horror as people tumbled into the ice-filled water and were pushed away into the darkness by the relentless wind and waves. We couldn't save anyone—not one soul.

I covered my face with both hands and groaned, "I'm finished."

Chapter 16: Mother and Daughter

Anna Jensen

In our cabin, the hissing noise became progressively louder as steam seeped in through the cracks around the door. At first we could feel the steam hovering near the ceiling, like a hot cloud. Then, gradually, it filled the cabin. The temperature rose alarmingly and it became harder and harder to breathe. The sound of rushing water was now audible as well, leaving no doubt: the *Larchmont* was indeed sinking.

Emitting a terrible groan, the ship dipped violently to one side, jarring my injured leg and causing me to gasp in pain.

Louise squeezed my hand in the dark.

I was filled with an overwhelming feeling of sadness. Not for me. I was forty-six years old now—an old woman. I'd lived a full life and could face death without regrets. No, my sadness was for Louise. She was only eighteen and her life had just begun. There were so many things she had yet to experience. Like having a real husband and a loving family, climbing the Great Pyramids, or floating in the Red Sea. I sighed and encircled my beautiful daughter with my arms, pressing a kiss into her blonde hair that smelled of roses. With tears filling my eyes, I said, "*Min kära.*"

Louise, her voice full of tears as well, said, "The ship is sinking, isn't it?"

I nodded in the dark, still holding her tightly.

"And no one's coming to rescue us." She spoke so calmly, so peacefully.

I shook my head.

Louise squeezed my hands. "*Allt händer för en anledning*—everything happens for a reason."

"What reason? Why should you have to die before you've even lived?" I coughed from the steam burning my throat.

"I've lived, *Mamma*. I even got to see the Great Harry Houdini perform. How many people can say that?" Her voice was growing hoarse, too.

"If only Mr. Houdini could be here, now, to help us escape."
I stroked my fingertips across her wavy hair, my cheek still resting
on her head. "I wanted you to have a real husband, one who
truly loves you. And children." I coughed.

"I did have Johan for a little while. He was so perfect. Just too
small." I felt her hiccup a sob.

"He was beautiful." I squeezed her and rocked her.

She coughed several times. "Will I see him again?
In heaven?"

"Yes—definitely."

"Would you pray with me?" she asked.

I nodded and we held hands, praying silently together for
several minutes. Then I sighed. "Your father will blame himself
for this. For not being here to save us. Poor man."

I felt Louise nod her agreement.

"Let's write a note," I said. "There was paper on the desk."

After some scrambling in the dark, Louise found some
paper, a pen, and an inkwell. Together we blindly wrote
a short note to John, reassuring him of our love and
wishing him happiness. I folded the message tightly,
wrapped it in one of my makeup pouches, and tucked it into
my corset.

The steam now completely filled the room, making the air
heavy and difficult to breathe. Louise snuggled closer to me and
laid her head on my shoulder. I could feel her straining to pull air
into her lungs, too.

"I'm glad we talked tonight," Louise croaked.

"Me too." I kissed her hair once again. "You are *ljuset i mitt
liv*—the light of my life."

"*Jag älskar dig, Mamma.*"

"*Jag älskar dig också, kära.*"

She squeezed my hands again as the ship groaned loudly.
We were simultaneously struck with prolonged coughing fits as
freezing seawater began pouring in under the door and quickly
flooded the room. Louise calmly helped me up onto the bottom
berth and then, as the icy water rose, we held hands and floated
to the top berth.

As we shivered violently with our faces pressed against the cabin ceiling, collecting our last breaths, I held my daughter as close as I possibly could.

She hugged me. "I hope we'll be together in heaven."

I kissed her cheek tenderly. "We will be," I promised.

Chapter 17: Howling in the Darkness

Millard Franklin

On the hurricane deck, Jeff and I wanted to avoid another mob scene like the one that had caused the lifeboat to overturn, spilling all those poor passengers into the frigid sea. So, this time we quietly rounded up those closest to the lifeboat and helped them to board, one at a time, distributing their weight to keep the boat balanced. Once we had collected around fifteen people—we left room so we could rescue the others from the water—Jeff nodded to me and we used the pulleys and ropes to lower the boat down to the roiling ocean. We unhooked the lifeboat from the supports and Jeff hopped in with the passengers, rising and falling with the mountainous waves. He motioned for me to join them.

"But what about Sadie?"

"We'll have to find her from the lifeboat. If we don't get away from the ship before she goes under, she'll pull us down with her and we won't be able to find anyone."

I took one more frantic look around me and then jumped in. We pushed away from the *Larchmont* just as the ocean swamped her hurricane deck. A loud cracking sound like a dozen shotguns being fired filled the air as a row of cabins broke off the ship and plopped into the sea. I saw people clinging to the roof of the wreckage. They must have been freezing. And one of them looked like…

"Sadie!" I cried.

Desperately clutching the top of a ladder, she turned her head and stared at me. She was only twenty or thirty feet away and, even in the dim moonlight, I could see the sheer panic in her eyes.

"We have to save her, Jeff!" I screamed.

We dove under the seats of the lifeboat to retrieve the oars only to discover they'd fallen out when the boat had flipped over. A frantic search revealed that we had absolutely nothing we could use to propel the boat: no oars, no sail, no supplies whatsoever. And I didn't know how to swim.

I looked back to the floating cabins. "Hold on, Sadie! Don't let go! I'll find you…somehow!"

Within seconds, she was blown out of sight.

"Sadie!" I howled into the darkness.

I sent up a prayer to God, asking him to watch over her. She'd looked so scared.

Since Jeff and I had no way to help Sadie or the others atop the cabins, we scanned the sea around our lifeboat for any survivors. We could only see about twenty feet around us, but within that distance, we saw no one in the water—at least no one still alive; just a few dead bodies, face-down amidst chunks of ice-covered wreckage, being tossed about by the huge waves. The bodies were already coated with a thin layer of ice that made their skin appear shiny and plastic, making them look more like mannequins than actual people. We could hear voices further away in the darkness, calling out for help, but without oars, we could do nothing for them, either. Frustration burned in my chest. I couldn't save Sadie, I couldn't help those people calling out, and I couldn't even row our lifeboat to shore. All I could do was sit there and grow colder and colder.

I thought about Houdini and his Great Shackled Water Escape from the Charles River and wondered what he would do in our situation. Surely there must be some magic trick that could free us from this terrible predicament. If only I were a more experienced magician.

Jeff and I sat side by side in the middle of the rocking lifeboat with the other passengers all around us. In the dim light, I recognized a few of them: the two brothers I had taught the card trick, their mother who thought I was a thief, and three members of the Salvation Army band still dressed in their uniforms. The other seven passengers—two men, three women, and two little girls—sat shivering in their nightshirts and nightgowns.

We were all cold, though, no matter what we were wearing. The wind was blowing hard, whipping the ocean into huge swells that dwarfed our tiny boat. Spray blew off the tops of the waves and soaked us, immediately freezing our clothing and skin. I was glad to have my coat, hat, and gloves, but I was still colder than I'd ever been in my life. My feet and hands felt numb and clumsy. My elbows and knees were stiff, locked at right angles. And I couldn't turn my head more than a few degrees in either direction; my neck bones seemed to be fused together.

I counted fifteen people in the lifeboat, including myself. How many people had been on the *Larchmont* that night? Close to two hundred? How many of them had managed to board lifeboats? Did Captain McVay send out a distress signal? I hadn't seen any flares, but maybe he'd been able to radio a report to someone on shore. I wanted to ask Jeff these questions, but I was afraid the answers might upset the other people in the boat with us, so I kept silent.

A huge wave broke over us, drenching us all and filling the boat with a foot of icy water. Wiping the seawater from my eyes, I was horrified to find that two of the Salvation Army band members were now missing, washed overboard. Their remaining friend frantically called out for them to no avail. I looked left and right but couldn't see them in the water.

Everyone in the lifeboat huddled in groups of twos and threes, trying desperately to keep warm. Since the buckets for bailing had been lost with the oars, we couldn't empty the seawater from the bottom of the boat, so we were forced to sit with our feet and lower legs submerged. I could no longer feel my legs below my knees. When we'd first boarded the lifeboat, many people had been talking excitedly to each other, recounting their harrowing escape from the sinking ship. But gradually, the voices had grown quieter and quieter and by now had ceased altogether. Another wave crashed over us and I watched as it stole a man and a woman clinging to her daughter, all three of them disappearing into the churning sea.

How many of us were left, now? Fifteen take away two is… is…thirteen. Thirteen take away three is…is… My brain felt fuzzy.

Jeff Barnes suddenly stood and pointed toward the Rhode Island coastline, causing the lifeboat to rock dangerously. "Look!" he yelled. We saw a large steamer ship passing not far away. Her lights were glowing brightly, and snippets of music from a brass band drifted across the turbulent water.

"Help! Help us!" we all screamed, waving our arms wildly in the dark. But the wind blew our pleas away from the other ship, sending them southward, unheard. We watched in despair as the steamer sailed away, completely unaware of our terrible plight. Everyone slumped in their seat, eyes focused on their own personal misery.

Sometime later, Jeff looked over at me and flashed a lopsided grin, icicles hanging from his hair. "So, what did you think of your first steamship ride?"

"I think I'll stick to trains," I said, trying unsuccessfully to grin, too. My face was stiff, frozen underneath a mask of ice that clogged my nose and burned my skin. "How long have you been on the *Larchmont*?"

"I'm not on her anymore, matey."

I stared, amazed that he was still able to joke around. I was finding it more and more difficult to speak at all. "How long *were* you on the *Larchmont*?"

"Three years." He fumbled in his stiffly frozen coat pocket—looking for cigarettes maybe?—only to come up empty-handed. They'd probably been lost during the struggle to launch the lifeboat. He sighed. "How 'bout you? Do you have a job?"

I nodded. "Locksmith. But I'm quitting in March to join a vaudeville show."

"What show?"

"Harry Houdini's Great Magical Spectacular."

"Lucky dog!" Jeff bumped his shoulder against mine. "Can I come see you?"

"Sure."

My body began shaking from head to toe. Icicles hung off me like I was a Christmas tree. Everything felt numb or burned with pain. I was extremely tired, but I knew that if I fell asleep I'd be swept overboard by the next big wave. I kept talking to stay awake. "You have a girlfriend?"

Jeff laughed weakly. "She dumped me."

"Why?"

"I was fooling around with other girls."

"Did you love her?"

Jeff shook his head. "No. Do you love Sadie?"

"Yes." I closed my eyes and warmth flooded through me as I remembered kissing Sadie earlier that night. Was that really just a few hours ago? It seemed like a lifetime. Opening my eyes, I said, "Jeff?"

He didn't respond.

"Jeff?" I said a little louder. When he still didn't respond, I bumped my shoulder into his, knocking chunks of ice from our clothing.

"W-what?" he said groggily.

Speaking softly, I asked, "Are we going to make it?"

"Sure."

"Really?"

He was silent for so long that I was afraid he might have fallen asleep again. Finally he said, "No. No flares, so no one knows we're in trouble. And they won't know where to look for us." He sighed. "Doesn't matter, though. We won't last until daybreak. If the cold doesn't get us, one of those waves will."

Another huge wave—this one at least fifteen feet high—crashed over our lifeboat and carried away more of its occupants. There were far fewer of us now, only six or seven, and everyone looked the same: soaked, frozen, and miserable.

Jeff whispered, "I'm so tired. Can't keep my eyes open."

I could see that he was truly suffering. "You sleep. I'll hold on to you."

"Thanks, pal." He slumped down in his seat, his chin on his chest, and, within moments, I heard his breathing slow and felt his body relax.

"Goodnight, friend," I mumbled. "Sleep well."

Chapter 18: On the Roof

Sadie Golub

I counted two dozen other passengers with me, clinging to the cabins' barrel-shaped roofs. Mostly men, a few women, but no children. What had happened to all the children that had been aboard the ship? Were they all dead? Drowned? Maybe that was better than slowly freezing to death like we were, desperately clutching to anything we could find. Two men and I held fast to the top of a metal ladder. Others held vent pipes and light fixtures. But the waves were relentless. Every few minutes another one crashed over us, drenching everyone yet again and adding another layer to the coating of ice that encased us all. I felt like I was being buried alive under heavy, salty sheets of frozen seawater. After a few more huge waves, there were less than twenty people on the roofs. The others had simply disappeared, like the multi-colored feathered flowers in Millard's magic act earlier this evening.

Millard... I hoped he was safe in that lifeboat.

One of the people clinging to the ladder with me, a big hairy man wearing a red and white striped nightshirt, said with authority, "Be sure to keep moving, everyone. If you stop moving for too long, your arms and legs will freeze. And don't fall asleep because you won't wake up."

Another man croaked, "How do you know these things?"

The big man answered with a wry grin, "I'm Harris Feldman of the Russian Navy and I've been here before. I was shipwrecked on the Baltic Sea back in '96. Twelve of us floated around in a lifeboat for two days before we were rescued. But we kept awake and kept moving and most of us made it."

I leaned my head against the ladder and closed my eyes.

Mr. Feldman reached over and vigorously rubbed my legs and arms. "Sorry, Miss. But you have to keep your blood moving."

I shifted as far away from him as I could while maintaining my grip on the ladder. I tried to speak but my words came out as a whisper. "Someone will rescue us?"

He flashed a smile. "Yes! There're probably boats looking for us right now."

I couldn't tell if he meant what he said or if he was just trying to bolster our spirits. Meanwhile, my eyes drifted closed again. I knew I'd feel better if I slept and forgot the painful cold, just for a few minutes. More rough hands chafed my arms and legs as the man on the other side of me tried to help me, too. I wished they'd both leave me alone. What was the sense? No one was going to find us out here. Eventually, we were all going to freeze to death or drown. Why wouldn't they leave me alone so I could fall asleep and be done with it? I wished Millard was with me, with his warm arms around me as they'd been earlier that evening.

A few minutes later, when Mr. Feldman rubbed my arms and legs again, I didn't react at all. I just didn't care anymore.

Chapter 19: Mr. Staples Tells His Tale

George McVay

Bobbing on the white-topped waves in our lifeboat, I stared at the spot where the *Larchmont* had disappeared. "My God, I can't stand this!"

"Sir, look!" Purser Young cried, pointing behind me.

I turned to see a steamer—the *Kennebec*—less than a mile away, her cabin lights dancing brightly on the water's surface.

"Grab those oars!" I shouted. The boat rocked violently when Vann and the second fireman jumped to the thwart nearest the rowlocks. They pulled on the oars with all their might, while the rest of us called out in unison, "Ahoy, there! Help us!"

It only took a minute for us to realize that our efforts were useless. The howling wind was out of the north, forcing both our boat and our cries for help away from the Rhode Island coastline and away from the steamer. Discouraged and freezing, we slumped down into the lifeboat and helplessly watched the *Kennebec* sail out of sight. A few minutes later, when the big Fall River Line steamship, the *Providence*, appeared on the horizon, we didn't even attempt to hail her, accepting the futility of our situation.

In the dim starlight, I could see none of the *Larchmont*'s other lifeboats, and there was no one visible in the water around us. Where had they all gone? The seven of us sat huddled together, miserable, waves crashing over us, coating us in ice. Frigid water pooled on the floor of the boat, numbing our feet and ankles. Every few seconds, a chunk of ice or a piece of debris from the ship knocked against the hull, renewing my concerns about springing a leak.

I'd seen only two other lifeboats leave the ship. So how many people had been trapped below deck? How many had been scalded to death by the steam? And how many had ended up in the ocean? Those in the freezing water would last only a few minutes before succumbing to hypothermia. So, unless they'd managed to climb into a lifeboat already, they were dead. But how many?

I gasped when I realized I'd forgotten to order the launch of signal flares before the ship sank. So no one on shore knew we were sitting there in the lifeboats, freezing to death. No one would come looking for us until tomorrow morning when we didn't arrive in New York. By then, we'd all be frozen to death. Our only hope for survival was that perhaps someone from the sailing ship that collided with us had reached shore and notified the authorities. How likely was that? I shook my head and groaned.

I asked my quartermaster, "Mr. Staples, how did this happen?" He'd been at the ship's wheel at the time of the accident.

He shook his head, revealing a nasty gash below his left eye. Blood coated his cheek and stained the shoulder of his uniform jacket. "I've been trying to wrap my mind around it, sir, but it just doesn't seem to make any sense."

"What do you remember?" I tucked my gloved hands into my armpits in a vain attempt to warm my fingers.

"We were cruising southwest by a quarter west, sir, just passing Point Judith, when Anderson called out that he saw a ship dead ahead."

"Did you see any lights?"

"Yes, sir. A red and a green one."

"Both red *and* green?"

"Yes, sir. That's why it doesn't make any sense. That would mean that a ship was coming straight toward us. So, Mr. Anson told me and Moreland to port the wheel a bit."

"Swinging the ship to starboard."

"Yes, sir. So, we did that and everything seemed to be okay for a few moments. We only saw the other ship's red light."

"Indicating that we would pass her port-to-port, as we should."

"Yes, sir. But then, all of a sudden, we saw both her red and green lights again."

"Had we changed course again, Mr. Staples?"

"No, sir. Not since first porting the wheel like Mr. Anson told us to do."

"So the other ship must have altered her course."

"It would appear that way, sir."

I contemplated this information for a moment. "And then what happened?"

"Anderson called out his warning again, so Mr. Anson sounded the alarm whistle and ordered us to haul the wheel over to port as hard as we could."

"Did you?"

"Yes, sir. Immediately. But it was too late. The other ship was too close and she rammed us. There was nothing we could do to prevent it."

"Do you know the name of the other ship, Mr. Staples?"

"The *Harry Knowlton*, sir. I saw it painted on her hull as she slipped away aft after the crash."

"And what manner of craft was she?"

"Some sort of schooner, sir. Three masts—maybe a collier?"

"Did you happen to notice how badly she was damaged?"

"No, sir. I was too busy dealing with affairs aboard the *Larchmont*."

"Very well, Mr. Staples. I'll have to question Mr. Anson about the accident later, but it sounds like he did everything correctly."

"Begging your pardon, sir, but I don't think you'll get the chance to question Mr. Anson."

"Why is that?"

"Remember you sent him below deck to find out the condition of the boilers? Well, he never came back up."

This latest news stunned me. Judging by the small number of people I had seen boarding the lifeboats, Anson certainly wasn't the only one who was dead, but he was the one who'd been in charge at the time of the accident.

I gasped.

If Anson were dead, the blame for the collision would rest entirely on my shoulders.

Oh God!

Chapter 20: In Love

Millard Franklin

Throughout the rest of the dark, frozen night, I sat in our lifeboat, clutching my seat with one hand and Jeff with the other, while the wind and the waves tried their best to pry my fingers loose from both. I know I dozed off a few times, but somehow I managed to stay just conscious enough to maintain my grip on the boat and my friend. My hands cramped, and my arm muscles ached, but still I didn't let go; I knew our lives depended upon it.

Finally, I saw the sun rise in a surprisingly clear, blue sky. I closed my eyes and lifted my chin, hoping to feel some warmth from its rays. When I opened my eyes, I was startled to see Sadie sitting in the boat with me, wearing the pretty pink gown she'd worn to Houdini's party. She was smiling and looking beautiful, with her black hair cascading down her slim back. Glancing around, I noticed the sea had calmed completely. The water was gone from the bottom of the lifeboat, and the air was so warmed by the bright sunshine that I no longer felt cold at all. Even my clothes were dry and ice-free. Thank God!

I took Sadie's delicate, little hands in mine and stared into her huge, dark eyes. "When I saw you floating away on that piece of wreckage, you looked so small and frightened. I was worried about you."

She squeezed my fingers and smiled again. "You say you will find me...and you do."

"Are you well?"

"Soon I will be. But first I talk to you. I say two things."

I gazed at Sadie, content to be with her and to be able to hold her hands.

"First, I say that you are a good man and that you would be good husband. Even though you pick being a magician instead of being a locksmith, you would make sure to provide for your family. And I think life with you would be fun!" She paused and kissed me sweetly on the lips. Our third kiss.

She sat back and smiled. "Second, I tell you I love you."

"I love you, too." Even though we were in a lifeboat, I stood up, drew Sadie into my arms, and kissed her warm lips. She reached up and wrapped her arms around my neck and pulled me even closer. I kissed her again and again, pulling her tighter to me until I couldn't tell which arms were hers and which were mine. Together we were surrounded by a cloud of warmth, and I was happier than I'd ever been.

Chapter 21: Rescued

George McVay

Everyone in our lifeboat had grown too quiet. We were all freezing to death. Whenever a wave crashed over the boat, it coated us with a salty spray that quickly froze into a glaze of ice. The ice was like a thousand needles stabbing into our skin, while it mummified us and made it difficult for us to move.

I knew I had to do something quickly or we'd all die of hypothermia before the sun came up. I saw the oars still in the rowlocks, their blades sitting idly in the water pooled on the lifeboat's floor. Shouting to be heard over the crashing waves, I said, "All right, men. We'll form three teams of two rowers each. Ten-minute shifts. I'll man the steering oar. We won't make much headway, but at least we'll keep our bow into the wind and we won't capsize." I pointed to two of the men. "Staples and Young, first shift; McFarland and Vann, second; and you two firemen, third. Move it." The men grumbled as they rearranged themselves into the rowing teams.

Hour after hour, I forced the men to row through the enormous waves. We were tossed from the towering crests to the cavernous troughs, but we kept rowing and fighting, and somehow we stayed afloat. Twice I relinquished the steering paddle to Staples and took up an oar myself, partially to maintain morale—I didn't want them to think I was shirking the hard work—and partially to keep myself warm. Within minutes my arms and shoulders were painfully sore.

Finally, the eastern sky turned from black to dark blue to metallic gray. As the sun broke the horizon, the bottom of the boat scraped across sand and came to rest. "What's happening?" I mumbled through numb lips. It took me several moments to realize that our lifeboat had washed up on a beach somewhere. "We have to go get help," I croaked to Staples, the only other man in the boat still conscious. With supreme effort, the two of us rolled ourselves over the side of the boat and fell face-first into frigid shallow water. Our legs, numb and frozen, would not support us, so we crawled through the freezing surf to a sandy beach that led to a dirt road. We lay next to the road for several minutes, mustering our energy. Then, leaning on each other, we rose to our dead feet and stumbled down the road, falling frequently.

A man hurried toward us. Thank God! Supporting me on his right and the quartermaster on his left, he half-walked, half-dragged us down the road a quarter mile to a life-saving station. There, Staples and I were quickly ushered inside, stripped of our clothing, tucked into cots, and layered with piles of blankets.

"Where are we?" I muttered, my mouth and tongue feeling large and clumsy.

"You're on Block Island, sir," a man replied. "It's an island off the coast of Rhode Island."

"I know where Block Island is," I growled. "The others... Have you found the others?"

"What others, sir?"

"The five other men in our lifeboat!"

"Oh! We'll go get them right now."

I nodded and then drifted into blissful unconsciousness. Later, one of the surfmen told me they'd returned to the beach and had rescued the others in Lifeboat No. 1. All seven of us had survived; I was proud of that fact. But what about the *Larchmont?* My ship!

*   *   *

Later that morning, one of the rescuers must have recognized my rank by my discarded uniform. He dragged a cane-backed chair over to my bedside. Leaning close, he said, "Captain, I'm Surfman Charles Mitchell of the Block Island Life-Saving Service. Do you feel well enough to answer some questions?"

I kept my eyes shut and shook my head.

"Just a few questions," he insisted, drawing his chair even nearer. "At six o'clock this morning, a young man named Fred Hiergesell stumbled up to the Sandy Point Lighthouse and knocked on a window. The poor lad, nearly frozen to death, said he was from the steamship *Larchmont* and that there'd been a terrible accident. But after warning us that more survivors would be arriving on our beaches, he collapsed and was unable to give us any further information."

"Hiergesell? I don't know him," I murmured. He must have been another new employee, like that steward. What was his name? I blinked my eyes open. Everything around me was blurry, and halos of light framed the windows. I could see that Mitchell was a large man with sandy brown hair, but I couldn't focus well enough to make out his facial features.

"By his clothing, sir, I'd say he was a passenger."

"Oh, a passenger." I was so exhausted. I just wanted to sleep.

"Sir, was the lad correct? Are you from the steamer *Larchmont?*"

I nodded.

"And what is your name, sir?"

"McVay." My eyes drooped shut. I heard a pencil scratching on paper.

"What happened to your ship, sir?"

"Not my fault," I mumbled. I heard more pencil scratches. Then, something he'd said struck me. "One boy?" I gasped, forcing my eyes all the way open. Mitchell's face swam in and out of fuzzy focus.

"Excuse me?"

I struggled to sit up. "One survivor? No others?"

He shook his head slowly. "All the others in Mr. Hiergesell's lifeboat were dead—frozen—as were the people in the two other boats that washed up after his. But the men from your boat seem to be doing well. And I understand that one or two men from another lifeboat were found alive, as well."

I collapsed back onto my cot. "How many?"

"How many what, sir?"

"Survivors."

"That's hard to say, sir. Boats continue to wash up on the beach. And many more survivors probably landed at Point Judith and other spots on the Rhode Island shore."

I shook my head. "Not the mainland. Not with the wind and the tide." I tried again to focus on the surfman's face. "How many here on Block Island?"

Consulting his notebook, he said, "So far, there're ten."

I groaned and turned my face to the wall. All those passengers—dead. And the crew, too. "Not my fault, not my fault." I mumbled, over and over again.

"Captain, what happened to your ship? Where did the accident occur? Was another ship involved? How many people were aboard the *Larchmont?* How many lifeboats were launched?"

I said nothing.

Mitchell roughly shook my shoulder. "Captain McVay, please."

I lay with my eyes closed, pretending to be asleep.

I heard another man walk into the room. "I'm sorry, Charles," he said. "But this man is clearly suffering from nervous exhaustion. I must insist you allow him to rest up a bit before you ask him any more questions."

"But he's the captain, Dr. Larabee. He's the one who would best know what happened and where to find other survivors."

I wanted to scream at the idiot, to tell him there weren't going to be any more survivors.

The doctor said, "I understand that, but right now I must insist that you let the poor man sleep at least a little before you talk to him anymore."

I opened my eyes just enough to glimpse a tall man with white hair, wearing a dark gray suit.

He pulled a small, square bottle from his bag. Shaking it vigorously, he removed the stopper and poured a generous amount of its contents into my mouth, some of which dribbled down my chin, much to my embarrassment. After a few minutes, the doctor repeated the dosage and I immediately fell into a troubled sleep, full of images of sinking ships and frozen bodies.

Chapter 22: A Living Nightmare

Sadie Golub

My living nightmare went on, hour after hour after hour. Adrift on the sea, the wind froze my bones while the water tried to drown me. My arms and legs, which had initially been painfully cold, were now completely numb and felt like a mannequin's limbs, pinned to my torso. I should have been glad that I couldn't feel the pain anymore but, instead, I was worried. What if I was never able to feel them again? How would I walk? How would I sew?

Mr. Feldman, our self-proclaimed leader, never gave up hope, shouting encouragement every few minutes, long after the rest of us would have gladly quit. He and another man took turns rubbing the ladies' legs and arms and engaging us in conversation in a futile attempt to keep us awake.

When the sun finally broke over the horizon, I peered around through blurred eyes and was horrified. Those passengers nearest the outer edges of our raft were all dead, coated with a two-inch layer of ice. They looked like glass statues. Only the ten or twelve passengers who comprised the inner circle, including myself, were still alive, even though we were also ice-coated. Looking past the mountainous seas around us, I couldn't see any land. I closed my eyes again, relieved. No one would rescue us now, and pretty soon this would all be over. I immediately allowed myself to drop into a gray sleep full of jumbled images.

First, I dreamed of Millard and me sitting in a small boat together, smiling and holding hands. I told him that I loved him, and he said he loved me, too. I felt so warm and happy.

Then I imagined a sailing ship circling around us and men in a small rowboat. When they tried to take me off the cabin roof and into their rowboat, I fought them.

"Please, just let me sleep!" I begged.

But they didn't. They dragged me into the rowboat and then onto the deck of their ship.

My next image was of being laid in a soft bed with warm blankets piled on top of me and a kindly woman leaning over me saying, "That's right, dear. Just go to sleep." Then I dreamed I snuggled down into the bedding and fell into a blissfully deep slumber, thinking it was funny I was dreaming about sleeping.

*   *   *

The terrible pain in my arms and legs awakened me. Hundreds of straight pins pierced my skin from my fingers to my shoulders and from my toes to above my knees. I moaned in pain. Opening my eyes, I saw fuzzy images of lights and darks. When I tried to speak, I discovered my tongue was so swollen it nearly filled my mouth and my lips were too chapped to move. I felt the pressure of many layers of blankets piled on top of me, yet I shivered violently. Where was I? What had happened to me? I smelled the salty-fish scent of the sea and heard the raucous call of seagulls, so I knew I must still be near the ocean. Taking deep breaths, I tried to remember.

I clearly recalled the train ride to Providence with Solomon, boarding a steamship, and talking to Louise DeThestrup, the girl I'd met at the Houdini party. I'd felt so bad for her and had wished there was something I could do to help her; she seemed so sad. Then I was with Millard—talking, eating dinner, performing magic, and kissing. I smiled as I relived our warm embrace. After that, I remembered going back to the cabin and laying down on my bunk. And then…

The crash, the panic to escape the ship, being stranded on the cabin roofs, and being colder than I'd ever been in my life. I moaned at the painful recollections.

A blurry, middle-aged woman's face appeared before me. "There, there, you poor dear. Just try to lie still. Dr. Larabee will be back to see you as soon as he can." The woman slipped her arm behind my shoulders and helped me raise my head to drink some warm tea, but my tongue wouldn't work and most of the liquid ran down my chin. Using a soft, white towel, the woman gently mopped up the dribbled tea and tucked in my blankets again. I couldn't make my eyes focus. "Where am I?" I croaked in a whisper. The effort split open my lower lip.

The woman dabbed at my bleeding mouth. "You're in the life-saving station on Block Island."

"How?"

"Some of the local fishermen found your raft floating off the coast and brought you here."

"Millard?" I asked in a slightly louder whisper. "Millard Franklin?"

"Who's that, dear? Was he on the steamship with you?"

I nodded several times.

"There are some people from your ship here at the life-saving station and others at the lighthouse. Bobby Johnson was here a few minutes ago collecting the names of all of the survivors. Which reminds me, I was supposed to ask you your name as soon as you woke up."

"Sadie Golub," I whispered.

"And where are you from, Miss Golub?"

"Boston." Whenever I spoke, my lips split and bled more.

The woman wrote my name and town on a scrap of paper. "By the way, my name is Mrs. Milliken. You just rest and I'll be right back." She bustled out of the room and returned a few moments later. "I asked Mr. Johnson about your Millard Franklin and he said that, so far, he hasn't met anyone with that name, but hopefully more passengers will be found. He promised to ask around to see if anyone knew of your friend's whereabouts."

I nodded and closed my eyes, moaning softly. The pain in my limbs was excruciating.

"You poor dear," Mrs. Milliken said. "I know you must be quite uncomfortable, what with your hands and feet nearly frozen. But Dr. Larabee said that pain in your arms and legs is actually a good sign. It means they might not be too badly hurt and that they will probably recover. How awful that must have been, though, floating around in the freezing water on that little piece of boat. It's a wonder you're alive at all! It seems like many of your fellow passengers might not have been as fortunate."

I opened my eyes and tried to focus on her face. "How many?"

"How many what, dear?"

"Rescued?"

I heard her sharp intake of breath. "Not very many have arrived here on Block Island, but I'm sure others have made it to the Rhode Island shore."

I could tell that she didn't want to upset me, but I needed to know the truth. "How many here?" Blood dripped down my chin from my cracked lips.

Mrs. Milliken dabbed it with a soft cloth.

"I'm not quite sure," she said hesitantly. "I believe Bobby said that now there are twenty."

"Total?" Such a small number! There must have been nearly two hundred people aboard the ship. "Millard!" I whispered.

"There, there! Now, Miss Golub, I'm sorry I've upset you." She gently patted my shoulder. "Like I said, many more passengers—including your Millard—probably made it to the mainland. Right now, though, you really must rest. You've been through quite an ordeal, and you need to regain your strength."

I closed my eyes and almost immediately drifted into unconsciousness.

Chapter 23: Onto the *Kentucky*

George McVay

I was awakened that afternoon by the sound of heavy objects being dragged across a floor. "What's happening?" I mumbled.

A middle-aged woman bent over my cot. "Captain McVay. How are you feeling, sir?"

"Not well." I struggled to sit up only to discover that I was tired and dizzy. But I could see better than earlier, which gave me some hope. "What's that noise?"

The woman supported my shoulders and propped two pillows behind me. "The surfmen from the life-saving service are transferring all of you to a steamship anchored just off the beach."

"What ship?"

"I believe she's called the *Kentucky*."

I peered through the frosted window but could not see clearly enough to identify the ship. "Why are we being taken there?" I asked.

"Your steamship line sent her here, full of doctors, nurses, and medical supplies to take care of the injured."

"Me, too?" I was afraid that I might be sent to jail, instead. Two years ago, the captain of the *Slocum* had been sentenced to ten years in prison for a steamship fire in New York City Harbor in which a thousand passengers had died. Just like me, he hadn't been at the helm of his ship at the time of his disaster, either, but that hadn't saved him.

"Yes, sir," the woman said. "You're due to be transported to the *Kentucky* in a few minutes. But Charles Mitchell has asked to speak to you before you leave. Do you feel up to talking to him now?"

I shook my head.

"Well, I'll get you a cup of tea and then maybe you'll feel stronger. He's been waiting for quite some time." She returned with the tea and then disappeared again only to be replaced in the chair by Mr. Mitchell. The man reminded me of a fly pestering an open wound.

"Hello, captain. Are you feeling any better?"

I shook my head.

"Well, hopefully you'll still be able to assist us." He opened his notebook.

"How many?" I asked.

This time, he knew right away what I meant. "Nineteen survivors. So far."

"How long since you found the last one?"

"A few hours. But there are still some local fishing boats out looking for more."

Fifty-two crewmembers and approximately one hundred passengers had been aboard the *Larchmont* last night. If only nineteen of those survived, then nearly one hundred and thirty-three people had died.

"I'm going to be sick!" I rasped.

Mr. Mitchell hurried from the room. A nurse arrived just in time to provide me with a basin. Afterward, she helped wipe my face and settled me back underneath the covers, where I fell into another fitful sleep.

A short time later, I was vaguely aware of my cot being lifted and carried out to an awaiting cart, which transported me to a large dory that carried me to the *Kentucky*. I was placed in a well-apportioned private cabin—the captain's own quarters?—where I slept on and off for the remainder of the day and night. From time to time, someone came in to check on my condition or to give me drink or food, but, mostly, I was allowed to sleep. I was grateful for the oblivion.

Chapter 24: Millard Found

Sadie Golub

The next time I awoke, I heard voices. Men appeared as blurry shapes milling around my cot. Were my eyes permanently damaged? Would I ever be able to see clearly again?

"Oh good, you're awake, miss," one of them said. "We were just about to transport you to the *Kentucky*, a steamship anchored just off shore."

"No ships," I croaked. I felt a bubble of panic rise into my chest, threatening to choke off my breathing. Thousands of pins continued to accost my arms and legs.

"There's nothing to worry about, dear," I heard Mrs. Milliken say from nearby. "The steamship line sent the *Kentucky*, with doctors and nurses on board, waiting to help you and the other survivors."

"No, please!"

"Miss Golub," another man said, "you'll be able to receive much better care on the ship. All of the other passengers have already been put on board. You're the last one."

"No!" Tears coursed down my chapped cheeks as blood oozed from my cracked lips. "Please! No ships! No!"

"All right, dear," Mrs. Milliken said, gently pulling up the blankets and tucking them in around my shoulders. "Shhh. Calm down."

"But she can't stay at the life-saving station," one of the men said with an air of authority.

"Then I'll take her home with me," Mrs. Milliken replied matter-of-factly. "Would that be all right with you, Miss Golub?"

"Yes, please!" I sat up, causing the blankets to slide down and reveal my grossly swollen arms and hands, the skin mottled in unnatural hues of red and gray. Even with my poor eyesight, I could see how grotesque they were. I burst into great wracking sobs.

"Now, what's all the ruckus about in here?" asked a man with pure white hair as he entered the room. The other men left quickly.

"My arms!" I cried.

"Don't you worry about them, young lady. I suspect they look much worse than they are."

"Miss Golub, this is Dr. Larabee," Mrs. Milliken said.

"Can you feel this?" The doctor squeezed my arm just below the shoulder.

I screamed, sobbed, and nodded. Even though he'd been extremely gentle, his touch was excruciating.

He squeezed below my elbow. "How about that?"

I screamed again, tears coursing down my cheeks.

Finally, he lightly grasped my hand. "What about that?"

I shook my head. "What does that mean? Why can't I feel my hand?"

"Just hold on one moment. Let's see how your other arm is doing, shall we?" He repeated his tests on my left arm. This time, when he squeezed my hand, I could painfully feel his touch there, too.

He nodded thoughtfully. "I suspected that your right arm might be worse off than your left. But I think that with a bit of patience, both of them have a good chance of recovery."

"What about my eyes?"

He lifted my eyelids and peered into my eyes. "Once again, time will tell."

I glanced down at my feet, bundled under layers of woolen blankets. "What about my legs?"

The doctor smiled. "Did I hear that you will be a guest of Mr. and Mrs. Milliken?"

Mrs. Milliken and I both nodded.

"Okay. Then we'll wait until tomorrow to evaluate your legs. And we'll recheck your arms and eyes then, too. The more time they have, the more they'll heal."

I smiled through my tears, grateful for his encouragement.

"But remember," he continued, "patience is the key here."

Mrs. Milliken coaxed me to lie back again and re-tucked my blankets. "Very well, Dr. Larabee. We'll see you tomorrow."

"I'll stop by the house before noon." He patted me on my head and strode from the room.

Mrs. Milliken rose. "If you think you'll be all right here by yourself for a few moments, I'll go fetch my husband and son so they can carry you to our home."

"What about Millard Franklin?" I asked.

The corners of her mouth pinched into a tight frown as she sat down on the edge of my cot and laid a hand on my shoulder. "I'm afraid I have some bad news for you, Miss Golub."

Oh no, oh no, oh no...

"One of the surfmen found your Mr. Franklin about an hour ago. His body washed up on North Beach, near the lighthouse. I'm so sorry."

Chapter 25: Sunday's Sermon

George McVay

On Sunday, six days after my ship sank, I awoke in my own bedroom to the sound of something being dragged across the floorboards over my head. Dust sifted down through the cracks and coated my pillow. Why was someone tramping around in our attic so early in the morning? I pushed aside layers of bed quilts, stuffed my feet into slippers, and groaned as I shoved my swollen hands into my bathrobe sleeves. Nearly a week after the accident and I was still feeling its ill effects. As I shuffled across the room, I noticed that Edith's side of the bed was empty once again.

The bedroom door creaked as I opened it. I trod across the hallway carpet to the bottom of the stairs. Just then, the attic door opened and Edith appeared with Matilda, each carrying a large satchel. The maid gawked at me with eyes wide. Edith saw me and likewise froze for a moment, her hair framing her lovely face. Then she turned around and slowly backed down the steep stairs with Matilda at her heels, both women careful not to trip on their long skirts. As Edith stepped down onto the hallway runner, she said, "Good morning, George." She usually called me "dear" or "darling" so right away I knew something was wrong.

"Good morning, Edith. What's this about?" I tipped my head toward our beat-up old suitcases. "Are we going somewhere?"

She handed her bag to Matilda. "Please take these into the children's room. I'll join you there in a few moments." Edith frowned at me. "May I talk to you?"

Back in our bedroom, she pulled open a drawer of her dresser, removed a stack of petticoats, placed them on our bed, and returned to the dresser for another load. Waiting for an explanation, I gathered one of the bed quilts around my shoulders and sat down in the chair near the door. Ever since the accident, I just couldn't seem to get warm enough.

Edith withdrew another bundle of clothes from the dresser. "I spoke to Father on the telephone this morning, discussing our situation." She closed the drawer with her hip and placed the pile on the bed next to the first one. "He thought it would be best if I brought the children up to Maine for a visit. Mother agreed."

"But you know we can't leave town now," I said, frowning. "I'm waiting to hear about my reassignment. And then there's the inquiry."

"I'm talking about taking the children to my parents' home… by myself. Just me and Matilda."

I felt as if I'd been punched in the stomach. "You're leaving me?"

She tossed a handful of hosiery onto our bed. "No, I'm not leaving you, George. I just want to get the children away from here for a little while, until things settle down a bit."

I shook my head. "Call it what you want. The truth is that you're leaving me—just when I need you the most." I pulled the quilt closer around my shoulders and stared out the window to my right, watching the wind swirl the snow on our neighbor's roof.

She sat down on the edge of the bed, facing me. "I am not going on this trip for my own benefit. I can handle whatever insults people want to hurl at me. But when old ladies at the market ask Ruthie and Raymond how it feels to be the children of a murderer, responsible for the deaths of scores of people, I have to put my foot down. They are too young to understand why everyone is so upset. And I'm afraid for their safety, too. Many families around here lost a loved one in the accident and most of them blame you. Who knows what someone might do to retaliate? I refuse to subject our children to such danger."

"My co-workers have turned against me, the owners of my steamship company won't return my telephone calls, and my neighbors glare at me as if I were Jack the Ripper. But instead of standing by my side and supporting me in my time of difficulty, you're taking the children and going to Maine." I swallowed. "How do you expect me to live without you?" I couldn't remember ever having felt so alone in my whole life.

Edith knelt on the worn carpet at my feet. Squeezing my knees, she said, "You'll be fine, dear. You're a strong man and you know you weren't to blame for the disaster."

"But what if I was?" I whispered.

Two years ago, I had been in charge of the *Tremont* when she sank. Yes, the stupid cook had started the fire, but since I'd ordered him to make breakfast, I ultimately been responsible and Jones had died.

Now, with the *Larchmont* accident, so many more people had died and, once again, I'd been in charge. I knew the weather was bad that night. Very bad. Why hadn't I canceled the trip? Or why hadn't I ordered us to come about when we reached the mouth of the bay and saw how rough the seas were? I don't know if the storm contributed to the accident, but it sure made the situation dire after the ship sank. It had been so cold. Even now I shivered, just thinking about it.

The doorbell rang in the hallway downstairs. Edith looked at me quizzically. A moment later, Matilda knocked at our bedroom door.

"Come in," I called as both Edith and I rose to our feet.

The door squeaked open. "Sorry to disturb you." Her eyes darted from Edith to me.

I smiled tightly. "What is it, Matilda?"

"There's a boy here from the steamship office. He brought this." She held out a white envelope embossed with the blue Joy Line logo. "And he says he's to wait for your reply." She curtsied and left.

I ripped open the envelope and quickly skimmed the note from Mr. Dunbaugh.

Edith put her hand on my forearm. "What is it, dear? Is that your reassignment?"

I finished reading the note a second time and sank down onto a chair, the paper slipping to the rug between my feet.

Edith picked it up and quickly scanned its contents. Frowning, she turned to me. "I don't understand. What does this mean?"

"It means that the gentlemen in the front office have decided to suspend me from being a ship's officer of any kind, until further notice."

She glanced down at the letter. "Without pay?"

I nodded, already striding to the writing desk where I quickly wrote a strongly-worded letter to Mr. Dunbaugh, informing him that they'd made the wrong decision and encouraging him to reconsider. When I finished, I stuffed it into an envelope and hurriedly dressed in my best uniform. I hustled down the stairs with Edith behind me. There I found a scrawny boy slumped on a settee near our front door. Seeing me, he leapt to his feet, his eyes huge, as if he was seeing a monster.

I had a strong urge to slap back the boy's ears, but instead I handed him my letter and a nickel and smiled at him pleasantly. "Please see that Mr. Dunbaugh receives this note personally."

He nodded and hurried out the heavy front door, which I slammed, causing the dishes to rattle in the nearby china cabinet.

Edith squeezed my shoulder. "I'm sorry they decided to suspend you, dear. It isn't fair." She patted my arm. "But maybe, now that you'll be here to help me deal with the neighbors and the reporters, the children and I could stay…not go to Maine. But, how will we survive without your salary? How will we buy groceries and coal?"

"We have a little bit of money put away. After that's gone, maybe I can find a job with . . ."

The glass in our front door exploded with a deafening crash as a fist-sized rock smashed through it and bounced across our hallway floor, coming to rest underneath the settee. I stood frozen in the center of the hallway as Edith screamed and cowered behind me.

Matilda came running in from the kitchen. "What happened?"

Upstairs, both children began to cry loudly.

I rushed out the door in time to see two poorly dressed men run around the corner onto Governor Street. Realizing I couldn't catch them, I went back inside, my shoes crunching on shards of broken glass.

Matilda handed me a gray cobblestone upon which one red word had been painted: "Murderer!"

Ruthie and Raymond's hysterical cries continued from the nursery.

"Please go see to the children," I said to Matilda.

She hurried up the stairs as Edith steadied herself against the hallway wall, her face pale, her clasped hands shaking. Reading the word on the rock, she pretended to laugh. "Well, I guess that settles that. The children and I are leaving for Maine. Today."

I couldn't argue with her; we had to protect the children. So, I walked to the telephone on the wall, turned the crank several times, picked up the receiver, and instructed the operator to connect me with the local carriage rental company.

Edith spent the next hour packing. At nine o'clock, I rode with Edith, Ruthie, Raymond, Matilda, and their luggage to Union Station. At ten o'clock, I waved as their long, black train pulled away, heading north in a cloud of black smoke.

My family was now split asunder and I wondered if we'd ever be together again.

*   *   *

Alone in the house, I heard tolling bells calling people to the eleven o'clock service at St. Stephen's Episcopal Church, which was two blocks away on George Street. Edith and I had attended services there nearly every week since we'd moved to Providence. Why shouldn't I go today, as well? The pastor, George Fiske, was a personal friend of mine and had an uncanny knack for saying just what I needed to hear, when I needed to hear it. A good rousing sermon might do me a world of good today, I reasoned. I hurried up the stairs to my bedroom to change, foregoing my usual captain's uniform in favor of a plain suit. I saw no need to call extra attention to myself.

Arriving at the church, I stepped through its ornately carved wooden doors and paused to inhale the spicy aroma of incense which clung to the walls and ceiling. Then I strolled down the center aisle and slipped into our family's customary pew, ignoring the stares and whispers of others seated nearby. I knew that most of those present were probably aware of my involvement in the *Larchmont* accident, but I doubted anyone would say anything to me about it in church.

Removing my hat, scarf, and overcoat, I placed them on the pew next to me.

We stood and sang the entrance hymn as Father Fiske followed the four robed altar boys into the church and began the service. The familiar words and phrases calmed me and gave me a peace that I hadn't felt in over a week. For a few minutes, I let my mind drift to thoughts of Edith and the children, but I refocused my attention on the pulpit as the congregation sat in preparation for the delivery of the sermon.

"My brothers and sisters in Christ," my friend began, the sunlight glinting off his balding pate, "I stand before you today to tell you a story about cowardice."

For the second time that morning, I felt as if someone had punched me in the stomach. Everywhere I'd gone that week, I'd heard strangers ranting on and on in extreme ignorance about the accident, but I hadn't expected it from my own friend, not here in church. He hadn't named my steamship, yet, but I knew it was going to be the subject of his sermon.

He continued, "As you've heard me say before, I believe we are put here on this earth to help one another. That's God's plan. And those of us in positions of authority are doubly entrusted with this directive. God gives us the privilege of leading others, but with this privilege comes the added responsibility to assist our fellow man as much as is humanly possible. But, as I mentioned, my sermon today is about cowardice, about men in positions of authority who did not help their fellow man as much as they could. Who, in fact, did nothing more than look out for their own selfish well-being, leaving poor, innocent women and children to die."

I heard many whispers and saw some fingers pointed in my direction. Obviously, they too had suspected the pastor's topic.

And then he named it: "I am speaking, of course, about the *Larchmont* accident. Last Monday night, as you've no doubt heard by now, two ships collided in the Block Island Sound. One ship, the *Harry Knowlton*, was able to make its way to shore and, by the Grace of God, all hands were saved. But the other ship, the *Larchmont*, sank within a few minutes, taking nearly four hundred of her passengers with her to the bottom of the sea. May they rest in peace."

"May they rest in peace," the assemblage intoned.

Four hundred! Where had Fiske gotten his information?

"Now, this disaster would have been bad enough: the weather was dreadful, the ship sank quickly, and so many people died. But what made it even worse was that some of the senior crew members, who could have helped save at least a few of the terrified passengers, exhibited a display of cowardice, the likes of which have rarely been seen before."

My face burned and my heart pounded. Cowardice? What was he talking about?

"In fact, the captain of the *Larchmont* was in the first lifeboat to leave the sinking steamship. The *first* boat!"

Unable to listen to any more of Fiske's slander, I sprang to my feet and interrupted his homily with a ferocious glare. I picked up my overcoat, stepped out of the pew, and stalked down the center aisle, not stopping until the heavy wooden church doors swung shut behind me.

Standing outside on the church steps, I draped my overcoat over my shoulders and stared up at the sky, gray and heavy and threatening snow. I looked around me. From that vantage point, the East Side neighborhood was laid out before me like a giant map. Looking south, I could see John Street, where my house stood cold and empty, no one there to welcome my return. A block to the north, I spied Joe's Place, a tavern owned by a former ship's captain. When he'd gone into business a year ago, Captain Joe had invited me to stop in for free drinks anytime. Maybe this would be a good time to take him up on his offer. I closed my eyes and tucked my chin to my chest, taking a few deep breaths. When I opened my eyes again a moment later, I saw that the snow had begun to fall in great clumps and realized I'd forgotten my hat and scarf in the pew. Not knowing where I would end up, I stuffed my arms into my overcoat sleeves, pulled up the collar, and plodded down the granite stairs toward the street.

Chapter 26: The Tale of the *Elsie*

Sadie Golub

"Sadie!" my brother called up the stairs. "You have a visitor. May we come up?"

Trying to move my pain-filled arms and legs as little as possible, I propped myself up in the soft feather bed and smoothed down my hair. "Yes, Solomon. Please come." Since arriving at the Millikens' home six days ago, I'd had a steady stream of visitors, mostly well-wishing Block Island natives. And then, yesterday, my brother had arrived to accompany me back to Boston.

Back to Boston, I thought, a thump of disappointment hitting me in my chest. But just temporarily, I promised myself.

Millard was dead. The thought instantly brought tears to my eyes and a painful ache to my heart. Katerina's son had died, too, the one I'd been on my way to New York City to help nurse. Now I was the one who would need nursing, just until I could get back on my feet again. Nearly a week after the disaster, Dr. Larabee had finally agreed to allow me to travel home but had insisted that I have someone to accompany me. Hence, Solomon's presence here today. This would be my last day on Block Island and then it was back to Boston to live with Solomon and Bessie. Just until I was better. Then, I *would* open up my own dress shop, somehow, somewhere.

My handsome brother appeared in the bedroom doorway, his shirt and trousers free of paint splatters, for a change. He was accompanied by a tall, stocky, middle-aged man with brown hair, streaked blonde by the sun, and a face with that leathery look of someone who worked outside in all kinds of weather. Solomon ushered him into my room. "Sadie, this is Mr. Edgar Littlefield, one of the fishermen aboard the *Elsie* who rescued you and the others from that piece of wreckage. Mr. Littlefield, this is my sister, Miss Sadie Golub."

The man nodded. "I heard from Doc Larabee that you were leaving the island tomorrow, so I wanted to stop by and wish you the best. The last time I saw you, you weren't doing so well. You look much better now."

"Not my hands and feet." I held up my arms, which were wrapped in white gauze from elbow to fingertip.

Mr. Littlefield held out his hands, which were likewise bandaged, and gave me a knowing smile.

"Oh! From saving us?"

He chuckled. "Don't worry, Miss Golub. This isn't the first time I've had frostbite. Being a fisherman in New England, I've gotten used to it."

"But I sorry you were hurt."

Solomon said, "Mr. Littlefield told us the story of how they found your raft and how they rescued you. It's very interesting."

Turning to the fisherman, I said, "Would you tell me story too, please?"

He nodded and Solomon brought in two wooden chairs from the hallway. Once they were settled, Mr. Littlefield began. "Tuesday morning—that would be February twelfth—me and the rest of the crew met at the *Elsie* at four o'clock, as usual, but John Smith, our captain, decided that it was too cold and stormy to fish. A few hours later, when the call went out for boats to help look for survivors from the *Larchmont*, Captain Smith gathered us all together again and we all volunteered."

I said, "That was brave."

He shrugged. "That's what we do, miss. If someone's in trouble at sea, every able-bodied seaman tries to help. So we set out from Old Harbor in the *Elsie* at around eight thirty using a little bit of sail but mostly the gasoline engine. Because of the winds and the high seas, we stayed close to shore so the land would shelter us. Even then it was awfully cold. The spray from the waves kept freezing to the deck, sails, lines, and everything else." He chuckled. "I even had icicles hanging from my cap. Anyhow, at around ten thirty, Captain Smith spotted something in the water, which was a miracle considering how high the seas were. When we motored closer, we discovered that we'd found part of the *Larchmont* with people huddled on the roof coated in ice."

"It was so cold," I said, shivering with the memory.

Mr. Littlefield nodded. "By then the wreckage was sitting so low in the water, we were afraid that if we tried to tie the *Elsie* up to you, you'd capsize. So the Captain came up with the idea of motoring upwind, putting two dories in the water, and then letting them drift down to you."

"Dories?" I asked.

"Begging your pardon, miss. Dories are flat-bottomed skiffs—like rowboats."

I nodded.

"The Captain's plan worked like a charm and four of us in the two boats drifted right up to the wreckage. We took off eight of you, four in each boat. All the others were dead—God rest their souls—so we left them, planning to get their bodies later. By the time we got you all into the dories, Captain Smith had moved the *Elsie* downwind from the wreckage so we were able to let the wind drift us to the ship, nice and easy. Since you were all in such bad shape, so stiff and cold, transferring each of you to the ship took a long time. We had to use a rope and tackle to heave you aboard."

I shivered again.

"We got you on the *Elsie* and hoisted as much canvas as we dared to get you back to the island as soon as we could. Even then, one of your shipmates died before we could get you on-island."

"I told Mr. Littlefield," Solomon said, "that when I got here yesterday, I heard someone say that the mayor is going to recommend that the crew of the *Elsie* get medals for what they did."

"You *are* heroes."

Mr. Littlefield shook his head and looked down at his bandaged hands. "Most of the other Block Island fishermen went out looking for *Larchmont* survivors, too. We were just lucky to find you." He coughed deeply as he rose to leave.

"Oh!" I said. "That is bad cough."

"Probably just a cold. Anyhow, miss, I'm glad that you're feeling better. I wish you a safe trip home and a speedy recovery."

"And you get better, too." I smiled.

"I'll show you out," Solomon said, rising and gesturing toward the doorway.

The big man nodded to me and then followed my brother down the stairs.

I closed my eyes, succumbing to the exhaustion that had become a constant part of my life since the accident.

Chapter 27: The Inquest

George McVay

March 20, 1907, dawned bright and clear and unseasonably warm for that time of year in New England. This was the day that the Department of Commerce and Labor's Steamboat Inspection Service was beginning its hearings into the *Larchmont* accident at its office in New London, Connecticut. In order to reach the building by my appointed interview time of nine o'clock in the morning, Mr. Dow, the attorney for the Joy Steamship Line, and I departed by carriage from Providence, Rhode Island, in the pre-dawn hours.

As the carriage pulled away from the curb in front of my house, no one was there to say goodbye to me or to wish me well. Nearly three weeks had passed since Edith had taken Matilda and the children and had boarded a train to Brooksville, Maine, for an extended visit with her parents.

I'd been so lonely without them. On leave from my job, I'd spent the past several weeks bumbling around our house alone, trying to read or nap, but mostly just staring out our windows, wondering when this ordeal would be over. A few of the surviving crew members from the ship had stopped by to discuss the pending investigation. Like me, they desperately wanted their lives to return to the way they'd been before February 11. Such an awful day.

During the entire coach ride to Connecticut, Luther Dow, Esquire, dressed in an ugly gray suit that was several sizes too small for his fat body, coached me on my responses to various questions the Commission might ask. "Don't forget," he said repeatedly, "the Joy Steamship Line cannot be found financially liable for the accident. It would destroy the company." He was obviously expecting me to "fall on my sword" and take the blame for the disaster.

"Mr. Dow," I said, "I have no intention of being held accountable for something that was so obviously not my fault."

Dow regarded me with an air of pity. "I'm not sure that fact will be so obvious to others."

We arrived at the Steamboat Inspection Service's headquarters, a boxy white building, perched twelve granite steps up from the corner of Huntington and Federal Streets in downtown New London. In the large hearing room on the second floor, I was sworn in at precisely nine o'clock, wearing my best captain's uniform, perfectly pressed by my own hand. Dow and I sat at a long table in front of a paneled desk that stretched from one side of the room to the other. At the desk sat the Steamship Commission's panel of experts: a group of retired ship's officers from various steamship lines in the northeast. The chief examiner, a retired steamboater named Captain Withey, was a short, bald man whose white uniform was already stained yellow with sweat marks despite the early morning hour. He began by reading aloud the formal statement I had written regarding the accident.

After finishing, Captain Withey held up my letter, with a small, unpleasant smile playing across his lips. "Captain McVay, is this honestly the testimony you wish to give before this Commission?"

"Yes, that is my sworn statement." What was he insinuating?

"So you seriously expect us to believe that yours was the *last* lifeboat to leave the *Larchmont?*"

"Yes." I glanced at Dow, seated next to me, but he stared intently at his notes, refusing to meet my gaze.

Captain Withey picked up a packet of papers. Waving them in his left hand, he asked, "And what would you say if I told you that here I hold sworn testimony from several eyewitnesses who say that they saw your lifeboat being lowered into the water *first*, not *last*."

"We were the first in the water, but last to leave the ship."

"Excuse me?" The man's grin disappeared.

"I said, "It's true that Lifeboat No. 1 was the first to be lowered into the water, but we were the last to *leave* the *Larchmont* after she sank."

Captain Withey blinked rapidly for a moment, obviously flummoxed. "So, you admit to being in the first boat to depart the sinking ship? You, the master of the stricken vessel?"

"Yes. I had to be."

"And why was that?"

"Because my boat was attached to the same davits that needed to be used to lower one of the life rafts. In order for it to be launched, my boat must first be lowered and then cut loose."

"Rather a dangerous arrangement of life-saving equipment was it not, Captain?"

"It's the standard arrangement on most ships." Did he intend to hold me accountable for the architecture of my ship?

"Humph," he said. "Let's just leave that for the moment and concentrate on what you did after you launched your lifeboat, shall we?" A hint of his previous grin reappeared. "If, as you state, the *Larchmont* had a heavy list to starboard, why did you attempt to maneuver the boat around the bow to the port side, or high side, in the expectation of saving lives?"

"I believed that most of the passengers were located on the leeward or high side of the ship."

"Surely you must have realized that with the rough seas and a thirty-knot gale you'd have a difficult time rowing around the ship?"

"I did not, no, sir. I believed that one of those boats could be handled there easily."

"The result proved otherwise, did it not?"

"Yes, sir."

*   *   *

And so the questioning continued for hour after hour, with me answering questions as truthfully as possible while, at the same time, trying not to incriminate myself in any wrongdoing. As the sun was setting in New London, Captain Withey finally said he was "done with this witness" and ready to begin questioning someone else the following morning. I thanked God I would not have to return for more of that sort of torture the next day.

Based upon the day's proceedings, though, I couldn't begin to fathom what the results of the hearing would be. Would I be exonerated, as I hoped, or would the Commission select me as the guilty party, offering me up to the public as the scapegoat for the catastrophe, regardless of my innocence?

As Mr. Dow and I gathered our coats, hats, and papers, a pimply-faced court officer informed us that we would be notified of the Commission's decision within a year.

"A year!" I exclaimed.

"Yes, sir. That's the customary length of time for a decision to be reached."

"But I'd hoped with an incident as public as this one, that the Commission might try to expedite their proceedings."

The court officer shrugged with obvious disinterest.

"And what am I supposed to do for a living until they reach their decision?"

The young man shrugged again and walked away.

I turned to Dow, my heart pounding. "A year?"

He nodded while ushering me down the long hallway toward the front door of the building.

"But I was counting on a quick judgment declaring my innocence!" I felt my future vanishing before my eyes, like some sort of awful magic trick.

Dow shook his head as we continued to walk. "Unfortunately, it often takes a long time for the Commission to reach a decision and, by that time, the public has lost interest in the whole affair. Even if you are eventually exonerated, it's very likely that no one will ever know about it—or care." He held out his hand. "Best of luck to you, Captain."

I shook his clammy hand and followed him out into the crisp nighttime air.

At first, I didn't recognize the small group of people waiting on the top step in front of the building. Then, I asked, "What? How?"

Edith, looking beautiful in a stylish spring overcoat, smiled tightly and dropped Ruthie and Raymond's hands. I crouched down, and the children rushed to me and covered my cheeks with wet, sloppy kisses. I couldn't remember ever feeling such pure joy. When I stood up, Edith nodded stiffly at me and said, "Come on, George. Let's go home."

EPILOGUE

Millard Franklin

When the *Larchmont* did not arrive at its pier on the morning of February 12, 1907, members of the Joy Steamship Line management had no idea what had happened to her. The lifeboats began to wash up on Block Island, Rhode Island, at around six-thirty that morning, but communication with the mainland was difficult because of the high seas. After several attempts, the Block Island rescuers were finally able to broadcast some information about the collision, but the full extent of the disaster was not initially realized. As evidence of this, the Joy Line management instructed Captain Gray of the *SS Kentucky* to gather medical supplies, doctors, and nurses and to hurry to the site of the accident, hoping to rescue survivors, even though it was now a full thirteen hours after the ship had sunk. Finding nothing there, Captain Gray continued on to Block Island.

As the *Kentucky* anchored off the island near the Sandy Point Life-Saving Station, crew members noticed what they thought were large blocks of ice laid out in rows along the beach. What they were actually seeing were the frozen bodies of nearly thirty former passengers and crewmembers from the *Larchmont*. Captain Gray later said, "It was the most horrible thing I ever saw."

Bodies, some of them encased in as much as seven inches of ice, continued to wash ashore on Block Island for several days following the disaster. Eventually, all were transported to Providence, Rhode Island, where they were claimed by family members for private burial.

*   *   *

One of the ice-encased bodies that washed ashore was that of Millard Franklin, the Boy Houdini. When the famous magician, Harry Houdini, heard about Millard's death, he contacted Millard's mother and offered to pay for the boy's funeral and to assist her financially in the future since, as Houdini wrote, Millard had at one time been an employee of his.

*   *   *

Author's Notes: In real life, Millard Franklin was the son of a house painter from North Attleboro, Massachusetts. When his father died, Millard became a magician, known as the Boy Houdini, to help support his family. On the night of his death, Millard was traveling aboard the *Larchmont* on his way to perform magic shows in New Jersey. All of that is true. At some point in his young life, Millard did meet the real Harry Houdini, as evidenced by Houdini's letter to Millard's family following his death. However, they did not meet during Houdini's escape performance at the Charles River, since that event did not actually take place until 1908, a year after the ship sank. The reception at the Parker House Hotel, the Providence Lock Shop, and Uncle Henry were all fictitious elements, as well. For the purpose of crafting this novel, I imagined these things in order to more fully understand the person that Millard Franklin might have been.

Sadie Golub

On the morning of February 12, 1907, the crews of three Block Island fishing boats, the *Elsie*, the *Clara E.*, and the *Theresa*, risked their lives in an attempt to rescue Sadie Golub and other survivors of the *Larchmont* disaster. The weather conditions were horrendous: the wind was blowing at more than twenty-six knots, the seas were running fifteen to twenty feet, and the temperature was recorded as being three degrees below zero. The eight men on the *Elsie* were the only fishermen to find anyone still alive. They rescued six men and two women (one man died while the *Elsie* was returning to Block Island), more than a third of the seventeen people who survived the *Larchmont* disaster.

All eight of the crew members of the *Elsie* suffered some ill effects from their endeavors that day, ranging from minor frostbite to chronic respiratory conditions. Edgar Littlefield was one of the men who manned the dories used to transport the survivors from the wreckage of the *Larchmont*'s hurricane deck to the *Elsie*. Both of his hands were severely frostbitten during the rescue and his lungs were adversely affected, so much so that he had to spend an extended time in a sanatorium on the mainland. When he returned to Block Island, he was unable to go back to fishing but instead took up a life of farming.

For their effort, the crew of the *Elsie* did receive some recognition: Gold Medals from the Carnegie Hero Fund, which had been established specifically to reward civilians who performed incredible acts of heroism. The Hero Fund also distributed cash awards to the eight fishermen to provide college educations for all of their children, male and female.

For the rest of their lives, Captain Smith and his crew repeatedly said they never regretted risking their lives and health to rescue Sadie and her fellow passengers from the *Larchmont* and said that, given the chance, they would do it again.

*   *   *

Because of the night Sadie Golub spent stranded on the wreckage of the *Larchmont* in sub-freezing temperatures, she sustained severe frostbite to both legs from her toes to above her knees and to her right arm all the way up to her shoulder. After a week's recuperation on Block Island, she returned with her brother, Solomon, to his home in Boston so that he and his wife could care for her. Sadie continued to live with them and their children for several years after the accident. The United States Census of 1910 showed her as a resident of Solomon's household, which also included their younger sister, Esther, newly arrived from Russia.

Eventually, Sadie Golub made a full recovery from her injuries. In 1913, she married George Davis and the couple moved to New Bedford, Massachusetts. In 1918, George succumbed to the Great Flu Epidemic. Two years later, Sadie married Nathan Simon. Throughout their marriage and after Nathan's death, Sadie continued to live in New Bedford, where she was active in the Red Cross and Haddassah, an American Jewish volunteer women's organization. She died in 1971 at the age of 82.

*   *   *

Author's notes: At the Steamship Commission inquest, Sadie gave her occupation as "dressmaker," which became the basis for the fictitious sub-plots in this novel concerning her working for Mr. Miller, doing alterations for Mrs. Houdini, and starting her own business. Her relationship with Millard Franklin was also invented; Sadie and Millard were both teenagers traveling alone on the *Larchmont*, so I thought it plausible that they might become acquainted with one another, despite their religious differences. In February 1907, Sadie Golub was, in fact, moving to New York City to help her sister care for a sick child, but opening her own sewing shop and pursuing a relationship with Millard may or may not have been part of her motivation for leaving Boston.

George McVay

On January 10, 1908, William E. Withey and the other inspectors for the Steamboat-Inspection Service of the Department of Commerce and Labor issued their final findings into the investigation of the collision between the steamer *Larchmont* and the schooner *Harry Knowlton*. After interviewing the entire crew of the *Harry Knowlton* and all but one survivor of the *Larchmont*, they determined the following:

> *While it is true that Larchmont was equipped with boats and rafts in excess of lawful requirements, only a sufficient proportion of her boats to cover the boatage prescribed for passenger steamers of her tonnage was efficiently davited. It was therefore necessary that the surplus boats be handled by davits provided to raise, swing out, and lower her prescribed complement of lifeboats; and this in our opinion accounts for the fact that only 5 of the Larchmont's 8 boats reached Block Island.*

In other words, the Commission felt the reason so many people died was that the lifeboats were not readily available for launching. Considering that many of the steamer's crewmembers were trapped and drowned in the crew's quarters below deck and considering that the *Larchmont* sank so quickly, the availability of more davits probably would not have significantly increased the survival rate.

The Commission's report went on to discuss Captain McVay's role in the disaster:

> *Misfortune, the worst we hope that may befall him, came to George W. McVay, master of steamer Larchmont, in large measure. While we cannot commend or mention with approbation the judgment displayed by him in his efforts to save the lives of his passengers and crew, evidence is wanting in so far as to warrant our charging him with incompetency or misconduct.*

According to this report, although Captain George McVay was not technically at fault for the accident, his behavior after the collision was not exemplary, either. In short, the Commission felt he could and should have done more to try to save a greater number of the passengers.

*   *   *

George McVay was probably very disappointed with the Steamboat Inspection Service's findings, since, according to his testimony at the inquest, he felt himself to be blameless for the disaster. Because he was not fully exonerated, he seemed to feel that his prospects as a steamboat captain would be limited and so considered switching careers. Shortly after the accident, he told a reporter for *The New York Times* that he was contemplating becoming an undertaker for the town of New Haven, Connecticut. Instead, he, Edith, and the children moved to Norfolk, Virginia, where he captained a steamboat carrying freight up and down the Chesapeake Bay. In 1914, the family moved back to Providence, where George was master of a small steam freighter for thirty years until he retired.

Although his career may not have achieved the heights to which he once aspired, George seemed to have found peace and enjoyment in his later years with his family. He and Edith had five children together and were married for forty-five years, until Edith's death in 1947. At that time, George went to live with Ruthie, his eldest daughter, and her family in Boston, where he died in 1951, at the age of seventy-one.

*   *   *

Author's notes: Although much was written about George McVay's professional life, little was known about his personal/emotional life, so this was where I applied my literary license in his story. He was the son of a fisherman. He went to work on steamships at a young age, where he worked his way up from bow watchman to captain. He was in charge of the *Tremont* when it burned in New York Harbor and he did marry Edith Stevens, the daughter of another steamboat captain. His reasons for doing all these things and his justifications for his actions the night the *Larchmont* sank, as presented in this novel, were my inventions.

Anna and Louise Jensen

The Steamship Commission inquest into the *Larchmont* disaster estimated that, because of the speed with which the ship sank, at least half of the passengers and crew members never escaped the sinking vessel. Some were trapped in the mangled ship and drowned, some were roasted alive by the clouds of scalding steam that roiled down passageways and seeped into staterooms, and some died of hypothermia, succumbing to the frigid air and water temperatures.

*   *   *

Anna and Louise Jensen were among those who never boarded a lifeboat. Anna's frozen body washed ashore on Block Island a few days after the accident and was claimed and buried by her husband, John. Louise's body and the bodies of approximately fifty-eight other passengers from the *Larchmont* were never recovered.

*   *   *

Author's notes: In some instances, the actual facts of a historical novel are more difficult to make believable than the fictitious details the author invents. I found this to be true with the Jensens' story. John and Anna Jensen's daughter, Louise, really did marry John's greenhouse manager, Hans DeThestrup, while Louise was a music student in Boston. John and Anna found out about the marriage and the fact that Louise was pregnant and brought her back to live with them in their home in Providence, Rhode Island. After Louise's baby was born prematurely and died, John and Anna suddenly sold their greenhouse business and made plans to move back to Sweden. Anna and Louise were on board the *Larchmont* on their way to New York City, where they were to meet John and board a larger, trans-Atlantic steamer. All of this information is true. But why would Hans allow the Jensens to take away his wife? Why would Louise agree to go? And why would the Jensens abruptly sell their business and make plans to return to Sweden? Hans DeThestrup's feigned death, the pay-off by John and Anna, and the New Year's Eve party were story elements invented by me to explain the known facts about their lives.

The *Harry Knowlton* and the *Larchmont*

When the *Harry Knowlton* collided with the steamer *Larchmont* at ten-forty p.m., February 11, 1907, about three miles north of Block Island, the two ships separated so quickly that the crew aboard the *Knowlton* had no idea of the extent of damage to the *Larchmont*. To the men on the sailing ship, the steamboat seemed to continue on her way as if nothing had happened. And the *Knowlton* crew members had their own problems to worry about. The collision tore off their ship's bowsprit and jib boom and ripped a huge hole in her hull. The schooner began taking on water immediately, and it quickly became apparent that she was going to founder. Her crew abandoned ship into a lifeboat at around one a.m., and the *Knowlton* grounded herself on a sandbar off the coast of Rhode Island at around two a.m., where she was subsequently pounded to splinters by the fierce winds and monstrous waves.

The crew of the schooner was fortunate enough to row ashore in a lifeboat very near the Quonochontaug Life-Saving Station on Rhode Island's mainland, where they received treatment overnight for their hypothermia. All hands from the *Knowlton* survived the collision with no more than minor frostbite.

In the morning, the captain of the *Harry Knowlton* called a wreckage company to see if any part of the ship or her cargo could possibly be salvaged. This telephone call was the first anyone on the mainland knew about the disaster.

*　　*　　*

In the final paragraph of their report, the Steamboat-Inspection Service of the Department of Commerce and Labor placed blame for the *Larchmont* disaster:

> *We find, from the time that schooner Harry Knowlton and steamer Larchmont approached each other in such way as to*

*involve risk of collision, that schooner Harry Knowlton was
navigated in full compliance with the provisions of article
21, steering and Sailing Rules for Atlantic and Pacific Coast
Inland Waters; that the movements of steamer Larchmont
were in direct violation of articles 20 and 22 of the said
steering and sailing rules, and we therefore attribute the loss of
steamer Larchmont and schooner Harry Knowlton to careless
and unskillful navigation on the part of the first pilot of the
Larchmont, John L. Anson.*

This judgment was based upon the fact that a sailing vessel
automatically had right-of-way over a powered ship in public
waters, so by virtue of it being a steamship, the *Larchmont* was
responsible for getting out of the way of the *Harry Knowlton*.
Therefore, when the two ships collided, the fault was attributed
to the person in charge of the *Larchmont* at the time, First Pilot
John Anson.

*   *   *

During their interviews with the Steamboat Commission, the
crew of the *Harry Knowlton* testified that they maintained a steady
course throughout the incident. This testimony was in direct
conflict with that given by the surviving *Larchmont* officers, who
stated that the other boat had altered course at least twice, and
that it was, in fact, these alterations that caused the collision.
Although the truth will probably never be fully determined, several months after the accident, a rumor concerning the disaster
circulated among members of the New England shipping community. According to this rumor, at the time of the accident, no
one was at the helm of the *Knowlton*. In an attempt to escape the
bitter cold and ferocious winds, the crew had lashed the ship's
wheel and had all gone below deck to keep warm, allowing the
ship to go wherever the strong wind pushed it. This theory will
certainly never be verified, but it would explain the ship's erratic
change of direction noted by the *Larchmont*'s officers.

Acknowledgments

Many people contributed to the creation and publication of this novel and I thank them all with heart-felt gratitude:

- *Richard Hoffman and all the other members of the 2015 Fairfield Book Prize committee. Thanks for making my life-long dream of publication come true.*
- *Al Davis, Nayt Rundquist, Meghan Feir, Kyle Courteau, Sarah Dyke, Christy Smith, and all of the other wonderful folks at New Rivers Press. Your hard work and dedication made my thoughts and ideas into a reality that can be touched, read, and experienced.*
- *Hollis Seamon, Karen Osborn, and Richard Hoffman. Thanks for the great blurbs for my book cover, which were so incredibly complimentary and lent true credibility to this freshman effort.*
- *All of the faculty, staff, and fellow students of Fairfield University's MFA Program. You taught me nearly everything I know about writing and provided me with much-appreciated encouragement.*
- *The members of my various writers' groups (NK, FUMFA, Hi-Fi, etc.). Thanks for sharing your creativity, advice, and fellowship.*
- *All my dear friends and family members. Thank you for supporting my crazy dream of becoming a published author.*
- *And, most especially, my immediate family. Mom, Chris, Julia, and Laura. Your love, support, and forgiveness (for all my long hours at the computer) made this novel possible. I love you!*

About the Author

Lynne Heinzmann lives with her handsome husband, a cheerful beagle, and a grumpy cat in North Kingstown, Rhode Island. She is an architect by day and a writer by night (and on weekends), currently at work on her next novel. When not designing buildings or penning stories, Lynne enjoys teaching/taking English classes, making stained glass windows, and travelling the world, always in search of her next story idea. For more about Lynne and **Frozen Voices***, please visit her website: www.LynneHeinzmann.com.*

About New Rivers Press

New Rivers Press emerged from a drafty Massachusetts barn in winter 1968. Intent on publishing work by new and emerging poets, founder C. W. "Bill" Truesdale labored for weeks over an old Chandler & Price letterpress to publish three hundred fifty copies of Margaret Randall's collection, **So Many Rooms Has a House But One Roof.**

Nearly four hundred titles later, New Rivers, a non-profit and now teaching press based since 2001 at Minnesota State University Moorhead, has remained true to Bill's goal of publishing the best new literature—poetry and prose— from new, emerging, and established writers.

New Rivers Press authors range in age from twenty to eighty-nine. They include a silversmith, a carpenter, a geneticist, a monk, a tree-trimmer, and a rock musician. They hail from cities such as Christchurch, Honolulu, New Orleans, New York City, Northfield (Minnesota), and Prague.

Charles Baxter, one of the first authors with New Rivers, calls the press "the hidden backbone of the American literary tradition." Continuing this tradition, in 1981 New Rivers began to sponsor the Minnesota Voices Project (now called Many Voices Project) competition. It is one of the oldest literary competitions in the United States, bringing recognition and attention to emerging writers. Other New Rivers publications include the American Fiction Series, the American Poetry Series, New Rivers Abroad, and the Electronic Book Series.

Please visit our website **newriverspress.com** *for more information.*